Show Me Your Face

Goldie Gendler Silverman

Other books by Goldie Gendler Silverman:
Backpacking with Babies and Small Children
Camping with Kids

Show Me Your Face
Copyright © 2015 Goldie Gendler Silverman
ISBN: 1502453622
ISBN-13: 978-1502453624
Library of Congress Control Number: 2014917070
CreateSpace Independent Publishing Platform
North Charleston, South Carolina

O my dove, hidden in the cleft of the rock, in the secret places of the cliff,
Why are you concealing yourself from me?
Show me your *true* face, let me hear your *real* voice;
For your voice *seems* sweet, and your face *seems* lovely.

Song of Songs, 2:14 — as interpreted by a resident of SCAWF
(Seattle Center for Abused Women and their Famillies)

ONE

AUGUST

Molly wiped her eyes once more and then studied the linen cloth in her hand. She picked at the corner where the blue letters were coming loose, trying to push the threads back into the worn cloth. Ted's handkerchief. She would have to start using tissues soon instead of his old wonderfully soft handkerchiefs. She blew her nose and wiped her eyes again.

That bastard, that awful man in the white car. Why had she let him drive her to tears? She was so stupid. Dumb, dumb, dumb. After she had come this far, why was she crying now? She smoothed Ted's initials with her thumb. What would Ted say? No, she wasn't going to do that anymore. She was not a teen-ager or a young bride, she was an independent, fifty-two-year old woman, making her own decisions. She didn't have to ask a husband or a father. Besides, she knew what he would say: "*Non carborundum illegitimati.* Don't let the bastards grind you down." And that man in the white car. He was a bastard! Making such a big issue over his parking space! As if she was taking it over forever. He could see she was driving a rental truck. He must have known that there was only one ramp in the parking lot. That creep. That nasty, good-looking hunk in a great old car. That's why she was crying. Because he looked so—so sexy, yes, and she hadn't thought that about a man for a long, long time. Before he spoke, she had even thought, oh, dear, that he was looking at her with something, approval, maybe, some positive response. And she had thought, one of my new neighbors, maybe we'll be friends, and he looked, he looked like the fantasy a grown woman, a mature widow like herself, might have.

She had been unlocking the doors at the back of the truck when he had driven up in a white convertible, top down, black upholstery. His upper arms bulged under his white shirt. The sun had glinted off his red gold hair and the fine hairs on his arms. Gorgeous broad shoulders. She had smiled at him and worried about her hair. But in fact he didn't care about her smile or her hair. He was probably married and hated his wife. He probably hated all women. He had glowered at her, eyebrows drawn down over the bluest eyes, and asked in a cold voice, "Can you read?"

"I—I'm just moving in," Molly had stammered. It should have been obvious to him. "There aren't any spaces close to my unit, and there's a ramp…"

He sat unmoving. "This parking space is reserved for me. It's plainly marked."

"But I'll only be a short time…" Her throat had contracted and she had felt tears welling up in her eyes. It was clear he wasn't listening, and she wasn't going to let him see her cry. She had stomped around the truck and climbed into the cab once more. Tears blurred her view as she scanned the parking lot looking for an empty space. Not for him! She wasn't going to cry over him! She felt around on the seat beside her. Where was Ted's handkerchief? She had come so far, all the way from Nebraska to Seattle, by herself, driving this truck, found an apartment that was almost within her budget, and had a job waiting. None of her friends thought she could do it. She started the engine and drove across the lot. Ted's handkerchief had fallen to the floor. She picked it up and sat in the cab for a few moments, pulling herself together, fingering the monogram. Maybe she shouldn't use Ted's handkerchiefs anymore. Save them. She had only two left, the others lost or torn. She had so little left of him. She dabbed at her eyes again, folded the linen square and tucked it into the pocket over her heart. Back to the unloading. She climbed down from the cab of the truck.

The white convertible was now parked in the reserved space. She saw the sign, "Reserved Kevin Corwin," but the god of arrogance was nowhere to be seen. A young man in white jeans and a white tee shirt was standing behind her truck leaning on a handcart.

"Are you a Millionair?" she asked.

"No," he laughed, "I'm a working man. Ben Griffen." He extended his hand. "You can use some help."

2

"Molly Bennet. Yes, I guess. I—I'm supposed to have some helpers, my friend said she would call the Millionairs Club for me."

"Millionairs are usually pretty reliable. Did you call them?"

"They don't answer on Sundays."

"What about your friend? Is he reliable?"

"She. Yes, of course. She'd be here herself but she had some kind of conference. She's giving me a job here in Seattle." Molly tried not to think of those other times, the excuses of the old days.

"Well, we can get started with the small stuff while you wait for them," he suggested.

"Yes, of course." She unlocked the padlock and swung the doors open.

"What's this?" Ben peered into the truck with raised eyebrows.

"It's a jade plant. It's very old." She picked a withered leaf from a branch and pulled the big pot forward.

"And big, too. And you brought it all the way from, where? Kansas? Did you think we don't have plants out here?" He was pulling boxes closer to the edge of the truck.

"Nebraska. It's a very special plant. I've had it a long time." She thought of that Mothers Day, so many years ago, the pleased looks on the faces of Ted and young Joey, and felt tears welling up again. "My son gave it to me."

He shook his head. "I'm surprised it's still alive. How many days did you have it in the truck?"

"Six, I think. I didn't drive very fast, and then I had to look for a place when I got here. But I opened the doors every night so the plant could have light and air."

Molly had taken her own handcart out of the truck and loaded it with two boxes, one on top of the other. The cart teetered as she tried to hold it upright. "I guess I can't put the plant on top."

Ben shook his head once again. "Let me take that." He set the plant on the ground next to his handcart, turned some screws on the cart, and hit the handle. The carrier collapsed on itself, bent in the middle and was transformed into a small four-wheeled cart.

"That's great. Does my cart do that too? I didn't know I could do that."

"Not surprised," Ben said. "It's amazing that you got here, plant and all." He put the plant on the cart, added a few small boxes, and set off.

"I live in Building B," she called after him, trying to run while pushing her own handcart.

"I know," he called back.

It wasn't until he had to stop at her front door that she could talk to him. "Do you live in my building?" she asked.

"No." He lifted the boxes from his cart. "Just tell me where you want these," and was out of the apartment.

With the handcart unloaded, Ben was even faster than before. Molly was out of breath when she caught up with him in the parking lot, but before she could say anything, he was loaded and off again. When she reached her apartment, he was leaving. She thought of all sorts of questions to ask, but never had the chance. When all the small boxes had been removed, he waited for her at the truck.

"It doesn't look like the Millionairs are going to arrive," he said. "Do you think we can unload your stuff by ourselves? I mean, I'm willing to carry my end, but can you carry half a sofa?"

"I guess I can," Molly said. "I don't have a choice, do I? I mean, I can't afford to pay an extra day if the truck isn't back by six. Is there anyone else who could help?" She thought of the muscular man in the white car. "There was a man out here, in a convertible…"

Ben shook his head. "He can't help."

"Do you know him?"

Ben shook his head again. "Was he a really good-looking guy? I've seen him. He lives here too, but we can't ask him. And it's Sunday, not many people around."

"He wasn't so good-looking," she lied. No sense sharing her ridiculous feelings with Ben. "If you don't mind, and if we rest often, we can do it ourselves. I did all the yard work at my house so I'm pretty strong." Molly thought of the moving in and out that she and Ted had done in their early years, when all the neighbors had come out to help each other. Maybe her friends were right. Maybe Seattle was different.

While they worked together, she had a chance to ask Ben the questions she had been saving. Which building did he live in? He didn't, he told her. He was a houseman. He worked for an architect who lived at the top of one of the higher buildings. He liked his job. It was like being an ordinary housekeeper, he said, except that he did more work than a housekeeper would do, like washing the car or doing minor repairs around the house. Once Ben got started, Molly could hardly get a comment in. He had opinions about everything of hers—not only the jade plant, but also her sofa (too many cushions), her choice in art (too abstract), her mis-matched pots and pans that were losing their Teflon and should be replaced.

But on certain subjects, Ben was evasive. When Molly said, "Tell me about the other people who live in these apartments," he shrugged. They were friendly, outgoing. All kinds. Old people, little kids. Everything in-between.

When she persisted, "Tell me about your employer," he shrugged again.

"When you meet him, you can form your own opinion."

Was it her imagination, or was Ben deliberately looking away from her? They had stopped for a moment, the sofa on the ground between them.

"That man out here earlier, the one you said wouldn't help us, is that what he's always like? Just arrogant and selfish?"

"I don't know a lot about him." Now she was certain Ben was avoiding her eyes.

"Surely you must have an opinion."

He didn't speak again until they were shoving the sofa into place in her living room. "Now you tell me something. What would you have done if I hadn't shown up in the parking lot?"

Molly bit her lip. "I don't know. You're a godsend."

He laughed. "That's not who sent me."

In the taxi on the way back from the truck rental office, Molly found herself humming. She had a friend in Ben. Seattle couldn't be that much different from Omaha. That clod in the white car? Just a freak living among good people. In her head she tried to list as many disparaging words to describe him as she could—lout, jerk, boor, oaf, churl, cad, jackass, heel. Although why did she care? Why waste so much energy on him? Just because he was so good-looking. This reaction of hers toward him—that was something she would have to control. She needed to meet more people. More men. Maybe not as spectacular looking as Kevin whatever-his-name, but better than the tired parade of aging bachelors that her friends had steered her way.

Forget him! She was going to be just fine by herself, her things unloaded in her own apartment and her job waiting for her day after tomorrow. She had earned a reward.

She found a big towel in the box labeled "First Night" that Ben had thoughtfully left in the middle of the living room. Her swimsuit and sunglasses were in the bag she had packed for the road. She picked up her keys and set out for the pool. The path meandered between the buildings, past well-kept lawns and shrubs. What beautiful blue hydrangeas, she thought, such showy big clusters. Was it alum or lime that you added to the soil to get blue? She once knew, but she had never grown hydrangeas; her garden wasn't shady enough. The path sloped down a slight hill to the pool. These buildings had a much nicer view, she noticed, the pool and the city and mountains beyond,. Probably much more expensive than her view of the parking lots.

She could see the pool enclosure now, the fence and the gate. *He* was there, the swine with the golden hair.

He lay with his back to her, stretched out full length on the wide tiled edge of the pool, leaning back on his elbows. She recognized his hair first, shining through the chain link fencing, then those wonderful arms and shoulders.

Well, it's a big pool, she thought. I will walk past him without speaking. Closer, Molly saw that the concrete deck, except for the lounge area at the far, shallow end, was narrow. She had to walk around a stack of umbrellas, baby strollers and other stuff, even a wheelchair, to reach the gate. Then she would have to pass much closer to the reclining man than she would have chosen. As she stepped into the enclosure, the familiar smell, chlorine mixed with tanning lotions, brought back a rush of memories—lounging at the pool with teen-aged friends, swim dates with Ted when they furtively examined each other's bodies, supervising her son Joey's swimming lessons. Her eyes filled with tears. This was her day for weeping! She wasn't usually like this. She tried to blink them back but felt them gathering behind her sunglasses. She held her head up, looking away so that the man lying on the tiled edge was barely in her vision. Just as she walked by, he twisted his shoulders and rolled his whole body into the pool, sending up a great sheet of water. It drenched her hair and soaked her only large towel.

"Oh, oh, oh!" She wanted to scream at him, all those words that she had thought of in the taxi, but nothing came out. She couldn't remember the words. She clenched her fists and sputtered at him. "You stupid…you…you…"

He looked up from the pool, hair flat and blackened, water running down his face. "Did I do that to you? I'm sorry. I had no idea you were behind me."

Molly didn't stop to listen. She stomped off to the end of the pool, wiping the drops from her face with a corner of the towel. No crying. No tears. She'd had enough of that today. Not for that creep. She didn't believe him. That was no accident! He had rolled off the edge deliberately to splash her, because she had parked in his stupid parking space. She spread her towel over a chair to dry and lay back on a lounge. If he were really sorry, he would come after her to apologize, but he was still there in the pool looking at her. In fact, he was just where she had left him, at the far end, hanging on to the side of the pool where he had rolled in. Well, let him have the pool, she thought. I'm not joining him.

Someone came through the gate, a young woman in a wide-brimmed hat, and Molly saw him call to her. They spoke for a few minutes, and she turned back toward the gate.

Molly pushed her damp hair back from her face and adjusted her sunglasses. She watched him grab onto the edge of the pool and pull himself up out of the water, onto the tiled ledge. He spun around and sat on the edge of the pool, his legs dangling into the water. Macho show-off! Why didn't he climb up the ladder like anyone else?

Then the young woman, who had gone back to the pile of umbrellas near the gate, turned around and started back toward him. Now she was pushing a wheelchair. Was she someone's nurse? Molly hadn't noticed any older people in the pool enclosure. But the young woman was stopping, right next to the awful man with the great shoulders. She lined the wheel up next to the tiled edge, leaned over, and pushed a lever on the side. Then she walked away. She left it next to him. Why? It couldn't be *his* wheelchair! Molly watched him place his hands flat on the tiles behind him. The muscles on his arms bulged; she could see those wonderfully muscular arms even from where she sat. She saw him flip himself over on his stomach. He paused for a few seconds, and then he did a push-up. He held his shoulders up high, with his body sloping down toward the ground, his knees and lower legs resting on the tile. Then he flexed his arms, pushed himself a little higher, and his hands came up off the ground. Molly leaned forward, staring. This wasn't showing off! In a split second, when his hands were off the ground, he reached out, grabbed hold of the wheelchair and began to pull himself upwards, one hand at a time, almost like climbing

7

up the front of the chair. His legs trailed over the tiles, perfectly relaxed, limp, and not muscular at all, she saw, but really rather thin. When his hands reached the arm rests, he flipped his whole body once again and ended up sitting in the wheelchair. As she sat open-mouthed watching him, he began to roll toward her.

TWO

It was not the man in the wheelchair who opened the door when she rang.

"Ben!"

He laughed at her confusion.

"You said you didn't know him!"

He shrugged. "I lied."

"You said you worked for an architect," she sputtered. "You—you're the attendant."

"I'm not," he said, closing the door behind her and taking her shawl. "I'm the houseman."

"Words," Molly whispered. "You still take care of him." She had been thinking, as she dressed for dinner, about the young woman who had pushed the empty chair next to the pool, and about all the other chores that someone must be doing for her host this evening.

"Kevin takes care of himself," Ben insisted. "Who cleans your house?" he asked.

"I do."

"Do you enjoy it?"

She shook her head.

"Why don't you hire someone to do all the things you don't like to do?"

"I can't afford someone."

"Well, there you are. Kevin can afford me."

Quickly, Molly tried to reassess everything she had concluded about Kevin Corwin, who was rolling up behind Ben.

"How nice to see you again, in friendlier circumstances," he said. The look—admiration, interest, whatever she'd thought she'd seen in his eyes in the parking lot, before the shouting about his parking space—that look was there again.

Stalling for time, she walked across the living room to the windows. "What a marvelous view you have!" she said.

All of Seattle—all of Western Washington, it seemed—was spread before her, from beyond the Space Needle to Mt. Rainier. Windows in tall buildings glowed red with the reflection of the setting sun. Even Mt. Rainier shone pink in the early evening light. It was magnificent, and she was glad to have something to look at while she sorted things out.

She had been so dense in the parking lot. Now she understood why the parking space next to the ramp was reserved for Kevin, why he rolled into the pool with such a great splash. Ben worked for him, so he must be an architect. He must have sent Ben out to help her. That made him less selfish than she had thought he was, and from the way Ben talked, not as helpless, either.

"Yes, it is spectacular," Kevin agreed, his voice coming from somewhere near her elbow. "The highest point in the city is in West Seattle, and my hilltop is almost as high."

She willed herself to look down, to meet his eyes, but he was not looking at her. Is this going to be a long, uncomfortable evening? she thought, as her cheeks started to burn all over again remembering the events that brought her to this apartment.

When Kevin had rolled up to her at the pool, Molly had felt seven years old with ice cream in her lap. She had wanted to run away and never see him again, but she couldn't think of an excuse for leaving. She'd heard herself accepting his insistent invitation to dinner, as his way of making amends for splashing her.

He'd said she could come in her travel clothes, but she had one good dress in the bag she had packed for the road, just in case. She had not worn it at all on the long drive, too tired at the end of each day to do more than eat supper in her room, curled up in her pajamas. The dress was wrinkled when she took it out, but it was meant to look crinkly, a fine rose pink cotton gauze that fell from her shoulders in soft folds. It was her best color, reflecting a glow to her cheeks. "Although why do I care?" she'd asked herself as she tried to check her hem in front of the bathroom mirror.

"And I'm high enough," she heard Kevin say, "to have a western view too. Come and see."

She heard the wheels moving, a whispering noise, not a squeak, and she turned and followed the chair into a room that was probably meant to be a dining room, but was furnished with drawing tables, computers, and other efficient looking machines. Their dining room had served as Ted's office too, but nothing like this. She thought of the papers spread over their table, gathered up for the weekend every Friday afternoon, and the computer, when they finally got one, tucked away in the corner. But Kevin had rolled through the glass doors and was out on the deck.

"This is fantastic," she said, following him. Directly below them she could see the buildings of the apartment complex, the pool and parking lots. His was the tallest building of them all. Evergreen trees formed a barrier to the rest of the neighborhood, and beyond them she saw water glittering brilliant in the golden light, crisscrossed by boats, all kinds of boats, big freighters, ferries, sailboats, and tugboats towing strings of barges. Far beyond the water she saw a low mass of dark green, and above that, towering jagged mountain peaks outlined by the glowing light.

"That point of land, Alki Point," he said, showing her where to look in the green mass below them, "is where the first white settlers, the Denny party, landed in 1851."

Molly squinted into the setting sun. Like me, she thought. She was a pioneer too, coming to a strange new place, ready to tackle unknown problems.

"Then they moved into Elliott Bay," he went on, "and their little settlement spread out all over the hills."

Or not like me. They were a group of friends, they had each other. How many people did she know in Seattle? Louise, and now Kevin and Ben.

"I have my office on this side," Kevin was saying. "When I'm supposed to be thinking, I spend hours watching the traffic on Puget Sound."

"Yes, with a view like this, I guess no one would mind staying home all day just looking out the window," she responded, and then blushed again at what he might think. "I didn't mean…" she began, but then could not continue. Did he think she meant that a person in a wheelchair would be housebound and forced to spend lots of time looking out the windows? That was not what she intended, but if she tried to tell him that, wouldn't he think just the opposite? Talking to this man could be very difficult.

"I worked at home, too," she blurted. "Nothing like your office, of course…" Why would he be interested in their makeshift office? One computer. He had machines that she couldn't even name.

"What would you like to drink?" he asked, and she was grateful that he was ignoring her embarrassment. She saw a table nearby with bottles, glasses and ice.

"Maybe…just a glass of wine."

"White?"

"That's fine."

He nodded, lifted a bottle of Ste. Michelle Chardonnay from an ice bucket, and deftly removed the cork. When he handed her the glass, he motioned her to a chair at an umbrella table and rolled up opposite to her, directing his chair with one hand while he held his glass in the other.

It was better when she was sitting down. She could look across the table and see a very handsome man sitting opposite her. Relax, she told herself. Start over. She smiled at him. "This is very nice of you. This is the first meal I've had with company for more than a week."

Ben came out with a tray of hors d'oeuvres. All of the food was local, Kevin said, smoked oysters, cheeses, crispy cold vegetables, and wonderful breads, all from the Pike Place Market.

As he handed her an oyster on a toothpick, he asked, "Have you visited the Market yet?"

Sightseeing! She'd had no time for that. "I'm afraid I haven't looked at anything in Seattle but vacant apartments," she answered.

"Oh, of course," he apologized. "You haven't had a chance to be a tourist yet. Has it been a hard week?"

She began to tell him about looking for an apartment, and he leaned forward and asked questions, drawing her out. She found herself describing the drive from Nebraska, finding motels and restaurants that would accommodate the rental truck, some of her ordeals in parking and backing, and she realized that she was enjoying the conversation. This evening may turn out to be all right, she thought, settling back into her chair. It's a beginning. She would have one acquaintance among the neighbors.

Ben came out with more bread and refilled their glasses.

"I've talked enough," she said. "Tell me about the Market. It's definitely on my list of places to see."

He told her how the Market was started in 1907 so farmers could sell directly to consumers, avoiding the huge commissions that had been added by middlemen. He described the way it had grown in the 1930s and then declined after the war. He told her about the architect, one of his teachers, who had organized the fight to save the market from urban renewal.

"I could take you there tomorrow," he said. "I have the day free, and I love to show off my city."

"Oh, no, I couldn't do that," she said. "I have too much to do."

"Haven't you earned a day off?" he asked.

She shook her head. "I have to unpack, hang pictures. All the settling-in jobs. And I have to buy a car. It will be the first time I have ever bought a car by myself! And then I start work day after tomorrow."

"Ben can hang your pictures. He doesn't have anything to do tomorrow," he persisted. "I have a good friend who sells cars. We can shop for a car in the morning, and tour in the afternoon."

She was tempted. She liked him. He was good company, knowledgeable and kind, and she knew that if they were to be friends, she would have to get over the feeling of being attracted to a man in a wheelchair. It was ridiculous—she felt like a schoolgirl.

Ben came out to tell them dinner was served inside.

"Ben tells me you like plants," Kevin said, rolling back from the table.

Ben tells you lots more than he tells me, she said to herself. It's plain where his loyalties lie.

"We could arrange for you to have a little garden here on the grounds."

"I'd love to have a garden, but I can imagine how the management would react if I started gardening here…" she said, thinking of the beautifully land-scaped grounds she had walked through.

"It's a big place, and there's plenty of room. We'll choose a quiet spot with lots of sun for you."

"We can't do that," she said, and the men both laughed.

"We'll have dinner first."

This man would arrange my whole life for me if I let him, she thought, as she followed him inside. Ben had set a table next to the other view. The lights of the city reflected in Elliott Bay mingled with the lights of the boats in the busy port.

Ben appeared again and announced that, if there was nothing more that Kevin needed, he was leaving for the evening. Kevin served from the covered dishes that Ben had left—cold poached salmon, tiny new potatoes in a spicy sauce, and a salad of greens she had never tasted before, with flowers mixed in.

"Am I supposed to eat the flowers?" she asked. "Or are they decorations?"

"Those are violas, miniature pansies, and yes, they are edible," he assured her. "These greens used to be considered weeds," he went on, pointing, "rocket, shepherd's purse, vetch, mizuna, and chickweed." He showed her how to eat the salad with chopsticks, so she could savor the different flavors. The violas had a faint, perfumery flavor, she thought, but some of the greens were sharp and bitter.

"Do you like them?" Kevin asked. He seemed to want to please her, and she couldn't hurt his feelings. She nodded, and sipped her water to wash away the taste.

"These wild greens are the latest eighties trend in food," he said, lifting a solitary leaf from his plate. "They grow them now especially for the table." Then he told her how the earliest explorers to sail into Puget Sound had gone ashore and picked the same native plants to eat, and how their logbooks showed they made beer seasoned with spruce from the evergreens growing along the banks.

They sat at the table talking long after they had finished eating. In the dim light she hardly saw the wheelchair, except that he had a strange habit of pushing his body up every few minutes, laying both arms flat against the armrests and lifting himself out of the chair.

He talked about buildings, what designing buildings meant to him. "The most important thing about a structure," he said, "is not how it looks, but the way the people inside will use it, the way it will influence their lives, for better or for worse."

Later, he said, "My buildings aren't created in a vacuum. I see them as part of a continuum, the continuation of ideas of all the design that has gone before me. That's why I like to use elements from the past in my buildings. Not to try to replicate by-gone times but to pay homage to them."

She wanted to ask what it was like, working from a wheelchair, what he did about visiting building sites and inspecting buildings under construction, but she stumbled over the questions. He reached across the table, took hold of her hand, and said, "Molly, we can't have this. You turn all shades of red and purple whenever you need to say 'chair.' It's all right to talk about my chair. I know that I'm a paraplegic. It's okay to say walk or run when we know I'm really going to roll."

Then he told her about the network of assistants that he had, young graduates in architecture who worked with him for up to three years as a prerequisite for their architects' licenses. "You'll meet them," he promised. "They are my legs. They go out into the field with cameras and paper and pencil, and bring back the information I need. But there's one assistant I've done away with. I don't need messengers to take drawings to clients anymore. I can call a client and send a drawing to him over the telephone. We can discuss a project with the drawings in front of us without ever meeting face-to-face."

Then, "Enough about me," he said. "I heard you say you had an office at home too. What business were you in?"

"I helped my husband in his mail order book store," she said. "He had the business in our home. Our garage was the warehouse. We located rare books, or found discounted lots for classes or book clubs, and shipped books all over the country. We had a fantasy," she laughed, "that some day all books would be sold that way

He shook his head. "Don't sell yourself short. I'll bet you were a partner."

Most strangers assumed that she worked for Ted. Yes, she knew she really had been a partner, an important asset to the business, but even Ted implied that she worked for him. She'd never made an issue of it. Ted needed to feel successful, and she didn't, so that was that. But this man recognized her contribution. He asked how they—not Ted, but the two of them—had started in business together. She found herself telling him things about herself that she had not said to anyone for a long, long time. How she had grown up struggling for independence from very protective parents. How she fought to take drivers' education in high school, but still was rarely allowed to take the family car. How she lost the battle to attend an out-of-state college. How she met Ted in a botany class at the University of Omaha, and married without ever having the opportunity to be independent.

Kevin said, "You should really be proud of yourself for moving across the country all alone. That's not easy for anyone, and it must have been especially difficult for someone like you, with a family that tried to stifle your independence."

"Yes," she said, "yes. I guess now, in 1983, it's not so unusual for a young woman to move across the country all by herself, but for me and my friends…" She sat back, basking in the warmth that filled her body, traveling all the way to the tips of her fingers and toes. Strange, this wonderful feeling she had, not really her own emotion, but a passive sensation, something coming from him. As if he knew what drove her, and approved. For so many months she had been getting negative comments, resistance to all her ideas and plans. Except for Louise, who had arranged the job for her, none of her friends or family had given her any encouragement about moving or any credit for determining what her life should be. But from Kevin, she felt admiration, approval, and appreciation.

The problem with trying to become independent, she told Kevin, was that it was so much easier to be protected. Ted was the voice of their company, calling resources all over the country, and she handled all the paper work. He tried to shield her from the unpleasant parts of the business—dealing with late shipments, unsatisfactory stock, irate customers—while she made a conscious effort to handle problems herself. Whenever she had a question, she would say to herself, "What would Ted do? I can do that myself."

Kevin sat quietly while she talked, watching her face but not saying anything. She realized that this was the first time she had talked about Ted to someone who hadn't known him. She asked, "Do you really want to hear all this?"

He nodded.

She took a deep breath. "When Ted first found out he had cancer, he waited almost four weeks to tell me. Then our roles began to change. As he became weaker and weaker, I took over more and more. I managed the business and cared for him. He needed more and more help, but he wouldn't allow me to bring in a nurse or any outsider. He hated the fact that he was not in control, and so, everything I did for him, I tried to make it seem to be his request, his decision. Even when I helped him make arrangements for after his death, he was in charge."

She paused for a few minutes. Why am I telling him these things, she thought. I hardly know him. "I'm sorry, I don't know how I got so morbid. Shall we change the subject?"

"No, if you feel like talking about your husband, I want to listen."

So she told him how she learned to puree Ted's food in a blender and pass a tube down into his stomach to feed him. Ted wanted to die at home, and he did, although at the end he could not have known where he was. She could not believe how strong she had been in those days.

For a moment, Molly stopped talking, remembering. After Ted had died, she had been surrounded by caring friends who thought they knew what was best for her. And at first they did know: the phone calls and casseroles and quiet visits, with lots of tears. Some of Ted's old friends, and some husbands of her close friends, also came around to tell her that they were ready to supply what she needed. Not tonight, she thought, but maybe some other time she would tell Kevin how she had tried that too, for a night or a discreet weekend, and found out that what they had to offer was not helping her.

She skipped all that, and instead told him how she still tried to rule her life by asking herself, "What would Ted want me to do?" But as time passed, she saw that what her friends thought she should do, even what Ted may have wanted her to do, was not necessarily what she wanted for herself. She had sold the business. When her friend told her there was a job for her in a battered women's shelter in Seattle, she had packed up and driven west.

In the dim light, sitting across the table from Kevin, Molly did not see the wheelchair. She saw only a man who was listening to her intently, a man very easy to talk to. She tried to understand, to explain to herself what was happening. When her husband was alive, before he got sick, they had talked and talked and talked. Now she couldn't recall what they had talked about, but she remembered the special feeling she had talking to him, that nothing could be as absorbing or as important as the things they had to say to each other.

Talking to Kevin was almost like—no, it was the same, it really was the same special feeling. In all the time since Ted first became sick, she had never talked to anyone else in that way.

But the mood changed when they finally left the table. She started to clear the dishes, but Kevin insisted that she should leave them, that he would do them later. Maybe she tried too hard. Maybe she made him feel helpless. He turned up the lights and she had to watch him do all the work from his chair. It was fascinating to see how skillful he was. He put the dishes on a cart and pushed it into the kitchen. Then he rinsed the dishes, opened the dishwasher and loaded it. She saw that his kitchen sink was lowered and open underneath, and the pipes were set back so that he could pull right up to the edge. He didn't need her help, but seeing him in the chair again, capable as he was, changed her feelings about him. He was no longer the gorgeous man who had sat opposite her at dinner; he was a cripple in a wheelchair.

She turned away from the kitchen and walked over to the windows again. Thank heavens for the view! When there was nothing else to say, she could talk about the view.

"I recognize the Space Needle," she said, "but tell me about the rest of the city. Where's Wallingford Avenue? Near 35th? Can you see it from here?"

"Maybe," he answered from the kitchen. "At this hour it's just another set of street lights. But why Wallingford? What's so special about that?"

"It's special because I'm going there day after tomorrow. That's where the battered women's shelter is, the one I'm going to work in."

He rolled in from the kitchen, scowling, looking as angry again as he had been in the parking lot. "Do you know what you just did? You should never—ever—tell anyone where a battered women's shelter is located. Didn't your friend tell you about confidentiality? Do you know anything about battered women in shelters? There are men—there are angry men—who would kill their women, or anyone who helps them, if they could find them."

"Well, I don't think telling you is going to—" she began, but he would not let her finish.

"You don't know me. Think about it. You just revealed a confidential location. That was a stupid thing to do. You have a dangerous job—"

She interrupted him. "Don't tell me about my job! You don't know anything about it. You can't tell me about my job, and you can't call me stupid!"

"You're not stupid, that's why you shouldn't do such a dumb thing as telling the location of a shelter. An abusive husband shot a lawyer here a few years ago. A therapist was killed. People who work in shelters don't like to be known in the community. Why do you think your friend brought you in from Omaha? Do you think there's no one in Seattle who can handle your job?"

She would not answer him. He had no right to attack her—but he was right! Louise had told her when she offered her the job that the location of the shelter was confidential. When she asked him about Wallingford Avenue, it had just slipped out! The wine, the food, the relaxed evening had put her off guard. Kevin would not tell anyone, she was sure. It was a good lesson for her, and she was glad it happened with someone she could trust. But she wouldn't tell him so.

The evening was over. She found her purse and shawl, thanked him for dinner and started for the door. He offered to walk her back to her apartment. She said she could manage by herself. He insisted on coming with her. Riding down in the elevator, he apologized. He said he should not have used the word "stupid." He said that Seattle was a big city, bigger than Omaha, and that he would not want to see any harm come to her. Outside the building, there was no view; they talked about the landscaping and the weather. As he rolled along by her side, she smiled to herself to think that a man in a wheelchair should be so concerned about her well-being, that he would imagine that he could protect her from an evil world.

THREE

Her doorbell rang at eight-thirty the next morning. It was Ben, carrying a ladder, a large red thermos, and a carpenter's box of assorted tools.

"You again," Molly said. "Do you enjoy turning up in unexpected places?"

"Your apartment is my assignment for today," he said, sounding surprised himself. "Did you forget?"

"Forget? I never agreed—" Molly protested as he walked past her and leaned the ladder carefully against the living room wall. "Where are you going?"

"I thought I'd leave the ladder here while we make plans."

"It's too early for this, Ben, I have a lot to do today."

"Right," he agreed. "Kevin wants you to meet him at his car at ten, so we'd better get started."

She followed him into the kitchen, where he was unwrapping china mugs from the open box on the counter.

"Now just a minute," she said, but he had turned on the water to rinse the cups. When he was drying them with a paper towel, she tried again. "Ben, I don't need you to come in here and take over. I can settle myself into my own apartment."

He filled the cups with steaming coffee from the thermos and handed one to her. "Of course you can. I am ordinarily a take-charge kind of guy, but I will let you make every decision about the arrangement of your apartment."

The coffee smelled so good. Molly's coffee-maker was still hidden somewhere in one of the boxes stacked on the counter, and she had been fretting about starting her morning with instant coffee. The rich, hot liquid soothed her feelings as it warmed her body.

"I do appreciate the intentions, Ben," she said, "but I can't accept all this assistance from you and Kevin."

"Why not?" he asked. "Don't people in Nebraska help new neighbors move in?"

She thought of her old friends. "Of course we help, but we don't send our…our housemen over to do the work."

"Ah, but Kevin would be here himself if he could," he answered quietly.

She buried her burning face in her mug. *O sole mio.* Damn them! Damn the two of them! When they weren't trying to run her life, they were embarrassing her.

"Well, let's get started, then," he said. "You tell me where you want the art to go, and I'll put them up while you're gone. Do you have picture hooks?"

She showed him the nails she had brought, and he rolled his eyes in dismay. "Those things! You'll have walls like Swiss cheese. See, Kevin is protecting his investment, sending me down here."

"Kevin's investment? What do you mean?"

But he was back in the living room, sorting through her pictures. "You'll have to tell me which way is up on these, I might hang them upside down. Oops! Just kidding!"

They toured the small apartment, listing the jobs that needed doing. She told him where the pictures and mirrors should be hung, which plants should be lined up under the windows and which could tolerate low light. She asked for a hook behind the bathroom door, showed him where the paper towel holder should be mounted, and made him promise that if he washed her dishes and cooking utensils, he would leave their arrangement in the kitchen cupboards to her.

At nine-thirty, she was standing in front of the bathroom mirror, applying eye make-up. It wasn't easy. It had been months since she had used eye shadow or mascara. She frowned at the tiny brush in her hand, at her reflection, at the wrinkles near her eyes, at the gray in her hair. Maybe I should color my hair, she thought. Maybe just some light streaks to disguise the gray. She snapped the brush back into its box. Why am I doing this? she asked herself. It's not as if I'm interested in him.

When she walked out to meet Kevin at ten, she found him already sitting in the open car, talking to one of the gardeners. His chair was tucked into the back seat behind the passenger side. Strange. Shouldn't it by on the driver's side?

Kevin turned toward her. "We've just been talking about you," he said. Then, turning back to the gardener, "This is Mrs. Bennet, the new tenant who needs a garden plot."

The gardener nodded and looked at her appraisingly. "Yes, sir, we'll find a nice, level spot in the sun. A cutting garden, was that what you wanted, Ma'am?"

"Vegetables, too," Molly murmured, stunned.

"We'll take care of it."

Kevin backed the white convertible out of its space.

"I think I was a few steps behind everyone else in that conversation," Molly said. "Will you explain to me how you managed that?"

The car moved forward through the parking lot. "I thought you might have figured it out," he said. "I'm the owner of this apartment complex."

"The whole thing?" She tried to add up what that meant: eight units in her low building, his high-rise, and other buildings, too. He must be a wealthy man.

"Now I do," he said. "Own the whole thing." They had started down the hill and picked up speed. The wind blew through her hair, and she tried to hold it in place with both hands. "There's a scarf in the glove box," he said.

She chose a sheer pink scarf from several in his collection and tied it over her hair. So I'm not the first woman you've taken for a ride, she thought to herself.

After a moment, Kevin continued. "I built the apartment complex with three partners. My investment wasn't as great as theirs because I supplied the design. Later, they wanted to expand, I wanted to keep the green space, so I bought them out."

At the bottom of the hill, they turned onto a busy highway. It was a perfect day for a drive in an open car. Kevin was wearing a floppy white hat and sunglasses. Molly took out her own glasses and watched him through the dark lenses, the arrogant way he sat at the wheel, even in that floppy tennis hat. She had never seen anyone use hand controls before. There was a lever near the steering wheel connected to the pedals by a series of rods. His left hand stayed on the lever as he drove. His feet rested limply on the floor of the car.

Kevin was fiddling with the radio dial. "What kind of music do you like?"

23

"My husband always kept the car radios tuned to the classical music station."

"I didn't ask what your husband liked. What kind of music do you like?"

She hesitated. "Well, to tell you the truth, I'm kind of low-brow. I like the music I grew up with. Swing. Big band. Tunes you can hum."

"Jazz?" He didn't wait for her answer. "There are two good jazz stations here, and I have lots of tapes." The music came up louder. "Duke Ellington. 'String of Pearls.' Do you like that?"

"Oh, yes. Doesn't it make you feel like getting up and dancing?" Instantly her face blazed hot.

He grinned. "Yes, it really does start the fingers snapping and the shoulders shaking." The car wove from side to side. "Of course, I have to drive."

Thank heavens, he isn't angry, she thought. Change the subject. "I love this car," she said. "This is like one of my junior high fantasies, driving fast through the sunlight in a slick white convertible. How old is it?"

"Fifteen years."

"Is it? It looks newer than that." She ran her fingers over the leather dashboard.

"It's been well-cared for," he said. "I keep it in the garage in the winter, so it doesn't stay out in the rain."

Molly wondered why he parked the convertible outdoors. The garage under his building would be much more convenient for him. She could not afford the extra cost of the covered parking space, but he was the owner, he could have anything that he wanted.

"I always wanted a convertible, but my husband said they weren't designed for Nebraska weather. Maybe I should buy a car like yours, if I can afford it."

They were on a bridge now, darting back and forth between the lanes, scooting around slower vehicles. She caught her breath at his daring, but he seemed to enjoy the game. He said, "A convertible is fun, but not very practical. With your new job, will they expect you to be driving people around, picking up donations?"

"I don't know. Louise didn't say that." But that was no guarantee. Louise had often neglected to pass along important information in high school, but she was a social worker now, she had an important job. Surely she would have said something.

"A station wagon will hold a lot if you're going to be moving stuff around," he said.

Hauling stuff or people, that had been Molly's job. She'd always driven a station wagon. Ted drove a sporty-looking car, two doors and a cramped back seat, but when it came time to deliver books to the post office or take Joey and his friends somewhere…Would she be expected to be a hauler at the shelter? Then she should probably buy a station wagon again. But a low, sleek, speedy little car, maybe a red one, with a sun roof…

Kevin was still talking. "For me, there's no question. I have to drive either a van or a two-door. I can't roll a chair into the back seat of a four-door."

I could please myself, she thought, and have a car that Kevin could ride in, too. The shelter will have to accept me as I am. I'll take smaller loads. If I buy a car that Kevin can't get into…. How did he get into this car? He must have some system for getting into his own car. I wonder if he'd even want to ride with me. He's probably like Ted that way, wanting to be the driver all the time.

" Molly? What do you think?"

"Hmm? I'm sorry."

"I said a hatchback is a good compromise. What were you concentrating on so intently?"

"I was thinking about cars."

Kevin took over the task of choosing her car with his old friend Art, who came out and leaned on the convertible as soon as they drove onto the lot. After Kevin had introduced her and the two men had covered all their news since the last time they had seen each other, they began the car selection process. She listened to them talk about her needs without consulting her, and about "Blue Book" prices and *Motor Trend* Car of the Year and *Consumers' Report* and handling and mileage and guarantees and recalls. She could have stayed home. She kept telling herself she was lucky to have found someone to help her buy a car, but it was her car, not Kevin's, and she wanted to choose it. She knew a lot about cars. Ted and Joey had been sports car buffs and she had gone along with them to lots of car shows. Kevin was taking over what she wanted to do herself.

When the two of them finally settled on a model and a year and a price, she followed Art out onto the lot to find it. Surprisingly, Kevin did not offer to come along. He started to instruct her on the road test, but she cut him off. "I've been driving for thirty years, Kevin. I know what to look for."

The car they had chosen for her was clean and quiet and much less expensive than she had feared she would have to pay. The red hatchback turned out to be lots easier to drive than the old station wagons she had owned in Omaha. Nevertheless, she purposely stayed out with Art testing it longer than she needed, just to show Kevin that the final decision was hers.

Kevin was inside the building when they returned. He had made arrangements with a young man working in the shop to deliver the car to her apartment. When they finished all the paper work, Art joined them for a long lunch at the little restaurant next door.

Afterwards, as she walked along beside Kevin's chair, returning to the white convertible, she realized that they were headed for the passenger side of the car. She did not want—did not need—to have the car door opened for her. Did he feel obligated to act the part of an old-fashioned gentleman, just because it would not be expected of him?

He reached out and opened the door. Molly said, "This isn't necessary—" but his stern look stopped her.

"I get in first."

Molly stepped back as he maneuvered the wheelchair around so that the left side of the chair was close to the car seat. She gasped when he jerked the left arm of the chair and pulled it loose, but he murmured, "It's okay," and tossed it on to the floor behind the seat. Then, reaching into the car with his left arm, he pulled himself out of the chair and pivoted onto the car seat. She couldn't believe how fast he had moved.

Sitting in the opened doorway with his legs hanging between the car and chair, he grinned up at Molly. "That's called transferring," he said. One at a time, he lifted his thighs with both hands and swung his legs into the car. Then he moved across the seat toward the driver's side.

Molly started forward, her hand out toward the wheelchair. "Not yet," he cautioned, pushing the back of the passenger's seat forward and leaning across to grab the wheelchair. He yanked on the chair, making it fold together, and rolled it into the back seat. Molly couldn't move. The chair was stowed so quickly! He must do that every time he gets in or out of his car. No wonder he has such great shoulders.

"Molly?" he called. "You can get in now."

They spent the afternoon on the tour of Seattle he had promised. Kevin was a terrific guide. He knew architecture, of course, and also the kind of off-beat history that doesn't get into schoolbooks. In Pioneer Square, he told her how one of the city's founders sold the city a defective water system that failed during the Great Fire. In Ravenna Park, he told her how a park commissioner, entrusted to preserve the giant trees, had harvested them for lumber, one by one.

When they drove through the Market in the open car, with the sun reflecting off the shining white metal and the breeze mussing Kevin's red-gold hair, he talked about farmers and vegetables. She saw people turn to look at them, envy and admiration on their faces.

His tour of the city included all the sites of his growing up, the houses he had lived in, his schools, the grounds of the University of Washington. "This is a beautiful campus," she said. "I guess these buildings bring back lots of great memories."

"Not really," he answered. "I remember lots of days of sitting at the bottom of a flight of stairs, waiting for people to drag me up."

On the way home, Molly asked Kevin to stop at her bank so she could check on the funds she had transferred. The parking lot was half empty, but a car was parked near the doors in the space marked with the blue and white wheelchair sign. Kevin stopped and examined the car. A gray-haired man sat in the driver's seat, reading a newspaper. Kevin leaned past her. "Hey!" he shouted. "That's a disabled space."

The man looked up. "I'm waiting for someone."

"It's okay, Kevin," Molly said. "If you park over there, I can just run in. It will only take a minute."

"No," he said, with the set and angry look she remembered from yesterday. "Hey, you!" he shouted again. "You see that sign? Are you waiting for someone disabled? Are you disabled?"

The man looked up from his paper, scowling. "There are plenty of spaces, buddy. Help yourself."

Kevin's face grew redder.

"It's not important, Kevin. Let's go," Molly whispered, putting her hand on his arm. "I can take care of this by phone."

"You don't understand," he muttered, shaking her hand off. "Hey!" he shouted once more. "That sign isn't just for decoration. You move your car now, or I'm going to block you for the rest of the afternoon." The white convertible rolled forward a bit, narrowing the driveway behind the parked car.

The other driver grumbled something, glanced at the front of Kevin's car and started his engine. Kevin backed up a few feet to make room, and the other car pulled out of the space. A woman carrying a large shopping bag came out of the bank just as Kevin's white convertible turned into the vacated slot. She took a few steps toward it and stopped. Behind them, a horn honked. The woman hurried off.

Molly had never seen such a display of temper in a grown man. "Don't come in with me," she said. "I won't be long."

Kevin didn't answer, and he didn't say anything when she came out a few minutes later. They drove home without speaking.

As she started to open the car door to get out, he took hold of her arm. "I know what's bothering you, Molly. Let's talk about it."

Molly shook her head. "I've only known you for two days," she said. "I have no right."

"Two days," he agreed. "But we're going to be friends for a long time. Aren't we?"

Molly took a deep breath. "I've known you for two days," she repeated, "and both days I have seen you get unreasonably angry over a parking place."

Kevin held on to her arm for a moment without speaking. Then he put both hands on the steering wheel. "You have no idea," he said, "what it's like to be trapped in a body like mine. I have no control below my waist. I can't move my legs or feel whether they're hot or cold or bent or straight."

Molly started to protest, but he went on. "I used to think, I'll get used to it, but that never happened. The only time I feel like a whole man is when I'm driving my car." He thought for a moment before he continued. "Then I have to get out of the car, and I'm right back in a chair again."

"Kevin," she said, "you don't have to tell me this."

"No," he said, "I have to tell you about special parking places. Did you ever stop to think about where those blue signs came from? Do you think the city just gives away parking spaces? That banks and stores are nice, friendly, caring places?" His hands tightened on the steering wheel and his voice grew angrier as he spoke.

"We had to fight for those spaces. Special license plates. Curb cuts. And that's not the end. If we don't protect what we've won…people like that jerk at the bank...people don't give a damn when it becomes inconvenient." He pounded his fist against the wheel.

Molly raised her hand to restrain him, but he would not stop talking.

"Do you have any idea how hard it is to go public, to roll yourself out in front of the city council and say, 'Hey, look at me, I'm a gimp, and I can't get off the curb, or I can't get out of my car, or I can't get into the men's room, unless you guys pass a law?' And then see the laws ignored?"

He paused for a moment. Molly said, "Kevin, I'm sorry—" but he interrupted her.

"Don't be sorry. I don't want sorry. Not from you or anybody." He pushed himself up from the seat for a moment, and then put his hands back on the wheel.

"You know what I want from you?" he asked. "The look on your face yesterday when you first saw me here in the parking lot. In this car. You know why I keep this big, old, flashy car, no good for a gimp? For the look on your face."

Molly felt a rush of blood to her face. She knew what her face must have shown, seeing that gorgeous man for the first time.

"Hey, it's okay. I'm crippled, but I'm not blind. I know what I look like. Hell, I go out of my way to look good to women. It's a package, me in my car. You said it, junior high fantasy. Until I transfer. I put that off as long as I can."

There was nothing more to say. Molly stepped out of the car and waited for him to slide across the seat, transfer to his chair, and close the car door. This time she knew enough not to try to help.

When Molly reached her apartment and closed the door behind her, she felt cold all over. It was a warm August day, but she was shaking; her hands and feet were ice. She filled the tub, took off her clothes, lay back and let the warm water rise around her body. What exactly had Kevin said? No control below his waist. No movement. No feeling.

She tried to imagine being Kevin. She wanted to feel it for herself. She lay perfectly still and let her legs float half out of the water. When the water stopped lapping against her legs, she could still tell where the water ended and the air began. She could feel the prickly sensation of water drying on her exposed skin.

She closed her eyes and willed herself to ignore the water, to stop sensing her legs, but still she felt warmth, presence. Her buttocks pressed on the hard, flat surface of the tub. She could tell where the abrasive strips on the bottom began and ended. She could tell, she knew even with her eyes closed, the exact point where the contact, skin against tub, ended, and skin and water began. A little muscle spasm trilled through her knee from the effort of holding it still. She knew her legs were there.

She opened her eyes. The washcloth lay on the edge at the far end of the tub. Without thinking, she lifted her leg, caught the cloth in her toes and knocked it into the tub. She kicked it up toward her hand. Kevin couldn't do that. How did Kevin bathe? How would he get into the tub? How would he catch the soap that was floating out of his reach?

Questions raced through her head as she scrubbed her body. She had always loved the rough feeling of a soapy cloth on her skin. She imagined old cells sloughing off, blood tingling near the surface. Kevin couldn't feel that, not below the waist. Did his skin get a rosy glow even if he didn't feel the tingle? Could he scrub so hard that he'd hurt himself and not even know it?

The soapy cloth moved up and down her thighs, between her legs. Soap bubbles caught in her pubic hair. Could Kevin have sex? She had been trying to push that question out of her mind, but it wouldn't go away. She felt such a strong attraction to him, the first man in a long time who interested her that way. And he felt something toward her, a sexual interest, she was sure of it. Or was that only her imagination? And what could he do about it? He said he had no control below his waist. Did that mean he couldn't have erections? Maybe he meant that he couldn't feel whether he was erect or not. Molly was out of the tub now, drying herself with the big towel. She liked Kevin, and he liked her. He had said, "We're going to be friends for a long time." Friends. But was that all it was going to be?

FOUR

Molly stood on the sidewalk in front of the big white house. This must be it, a shabby house on a street of similar homes. She climbed sagging stairs to the porch and pushed the button on the intercom box. Nothing. She tried again. Silence from the small speaker, but sounds of movement inside.

"Hello? Hello?" she called. No answer. She tapped on the door, waited, then knocked more forcefully. "Hello?

A voice from behind the door. "Who is it?"

"Molly Bennet. I'm going to be working here."

"Who do you want?" the voice asked.

"I'm the new employee, Molly Bennet."

"No one named Molly here."

"No, no, I'm going to work here. Molly Bennet." She took a deep breath. "Is Louise Joiner there?"

"You want Louise? Just a minute." Sounds of footsteps moving away.

While Molly waited, she studied the house. The doorway had once been grand, with windows on either side and a fanlight above. Now unpainted plywood filled the window spaces. Paint curled from the roof over her head. A cheap replacement light fixture hung there, out of character with the fine wood trim under the peeling paint.

In a few days, she told herself to still the panicky feeling in her chest, this will all be familiar. It didn't help. She looked out at the quiet street, the green tunnel of trees. What was she doing here? The doubts that had kept her awake most of the night ran through her head again.

How could a fifty-two-year old widow who had not worked since high school try to take a real job? And in a shelter for battered women? Everything she knew about battered women she had learned from television. How could she have left her home, pulled up her roots and come to a strange place just because an old friend said, "I think I can help you?"

It had seemed so simple five weeks ago. An opening at our shelter this summer, Louise had said. The job didn't pay well, but between it and what Ted had left, Molly would be able to support herself in Seattle.

"What kind of job?" Molly had asked.

Louise had smiled. "The simplest. Office work, mostly paper moving. And generally helping out where you're needed. Sometimes the counselors, the day-care worker, get overloaded. You used a computer when you worked with Ted, didn't you?"

Molly nodded, thinking back to their dining room.

"Well, then, you can handle this."

"I don't know," Molly hesitated. "A shelter...I don't know anything about abused women. What if I don't like it?"

Louise had laughed. "You won't like it. And you won't stay. Nobody does. But it's a first step. And then, when you've had a little experience, you'll go on to a better job."

The door opened, jarring Molly back to the shabby front porch. Louise, red-faced, panting, apologizing, let Molly in and locked the door behind them, saying, "We didn't expect you until nine."

"I didn't know how long it would take to get here," Molly explained. "I tried to allow plenty of time."

"I'll have to find a key for you," Louise said, "but I'm so glad to see you. Everything is just wild this morning." She turned away from Molly toward a long hallway.

Little wisps of hair had escaped from the green rubber band holding Louise's hair in a limp ponytail. Gray wisps, now. I guess I'm supposed to follow her, Molly thought. She heard the slap of Louise's bare feet against her sandals, saw an edge of white showing at the bottom of her dark skirt. Same old Louise. Probably still isn't shaving her legs either..

"...tried to call you this morning," Louise was saying, "...come in early. But you had already left."

From the end of the hall, Molly heard a hum of voices and the clink of silver and dishes, but Louise turned through a doorway, still talking. Molly followed, straining to hear.

"Just wild this morning," Louise repeated. "This will be your desk." Two desks nearly filled the small room. At least the computer looked familiar. "Most of our counselors are on vacation, and the one for this shift called in sick. I'm still trying to find a relief worker. But we'll manage. I know I can depend on you. You're so reliable."

Louise stopped for a moment. "Reliable," she repeated. "That's you. And that's what we need here. No surprises. We get enough of those from our clients."

She waved toward an open door. "My office is in there. I'll be right back. Urgent phone call." Louise started out and then turned back. "Read this while you wait. As a staff person, you'll need it."

Molly nodded. Her stomach tightened and growled. Had she understood Louise correctly? No counselors, just she and Louise? Did that mean that Louise expected her to take the role of counselor, on her first day? Talk about reliable! Louise certainly hadn't changed. She should have known when Louise's Millionairs didn't show up to help unload the truck.

Molly opened the worn looseleaf notebook that Louise had handed her. The Manual for Staff and Volunteers at the Seattle Center for Abused Women and Families. SCAWF. She leafed through it. Mission statement. Procedures. Rules.

The section on rules began with a box, printed in capital letters: CONFIDENTIALITY. NEVER, NEVER TELL ANYONE THE LOCATION OF THE SHELTER. She blushed, remembering how she had blurted out the neighborhood to Kevin.

She read on. Only staff could unlock the door. That explained her long wait this morning. She turned the page. No drugs, no alcohol. No violence. No racist remarks. No problems there, not for her. A section on language and profanity. Some of the residents used strong language, but staff and volunteers should try to avoid profanity in front of them. That would be difficult for her. She liked salty language. She found it liberating. Her son Joey had been so embarrassed when she said "shit" in front of his friends. Shit was an acceptable word coming from a young teenager, but not from one of their mothers.

She and Joey had made a pact: he would not say "shit" in her presence, and she would try to avoid saying it in his. Instead, they agreed to use substitute phrases. She had chosen, "*O sole mio.*"

Louise came back. "Something's come up," she said. She moved around the room and sat at the second desk. "There's always something," she sighed. "Anyone who gives us the littlest bit of money expects us to jump through their special little hoops. This morning it's Frank Alexander." Molly waited while Louise frowned at the desk. "Actually it's not such a little bit. Frank is the trustee for one of our biggest donor organizations. Rebecca Ryan was released from prison, and Frank wants to pull his money out. Give it to the eye bank or Easter Seals."

Molly stared at Louise. What was she talking about?

"Rebecca Ryan? You don't know who she is?"

Molly shook her head.

Louise told her about the badly abused woman who had killed her husband a few years ago, after several attempts to leave him. She had been convicted and imprisoned, but recently the governor had commuted her sentence. As she talked, Louise opened and shut the drawers in the desk, leaving them not quite closed.

"SCAWF was one of the groups that lobbied on Rebecca's behalf," Louise continued. "Now Frank claims she took the law into her own hands. He says his foundation isn't going to support us anymore. So I'm going to have to spend the morning downtown, putting out the fire."

Louise? Putting out a fire? When they were girls, Louise had been the one who always needed rescuing.

As if she had read Molly's mind, Louise wrinkled her nose. "Can you believe it? Me, charming a wealthy contributor? It's part of my job. Keep the money rolling in." She took a large key ring from a drawer and unlocked the padlock on a door behind Molly's desk.

Molly saw a closet, shelves stacked with jars, bottles, boxes on top of boxes, and bundles of disposable diapers.

"Don't we have anymore of those panty hose?" Louise asked. "We used to keep panty hose in here. I'm going to have to look like a lady when I meet the reluctant donor."

She emerged from the closet, a flat packet in her hand. "Oh, Molly, you know what this means? I'm not going to be able to spend the morning with you. I'm sorry." From a place deep in her memory, Molly heard the echo of other excuses. Lost books. Forgotten appointments. Term papers that were supposed to be co-authored. Louise was still talking. "But Naomi is down the hall, with the children. You can begin working with her. There are two really experienced volunteers, Helen and Tiny, upstairs with the residents. You don't have to worry about anything. And I'll be back after lunch to get you started here."

Molly stood up and placed the volunteer's manual back on the shelf. What she would like to tackle first was the messy closet, but she should probably look for Naomi. Louise had started to retreat to her own office, but she turned back. "Molly, I'm sorry I couldn't help you move. Are you settled in your apartment?"

"More or less. One of the men in the complex helped me."

"One of the men?" Louise asked, looking surprised. "What about...Did I forget...?" She paused for a moment, frowning. "Oh, Molly, I'm sorry." Her face changed again, questioning. "A special man?"

"Yes, special. I mean, not him, the man who helped me, but the man he works for." Molly felt her face grow warm, and Louise made it worse by giving Molly her full attention. Molly blundered on. "We had dinner together the first night, and then he took me shopping for my car."

There, it was out. After two days of wanting to talk to someone about meeting Kevin—she'd had no one, no sister, no best friend, to tell—what a relief. If only she didn't redden so, every time she felt any kind of emotion. Molly knew Louise would misinterpret her blushing face, and perhaps scold her about not rushing into an involvement so soon after arriving. If only she could tell Louise about her confused feelings, the attraction she felt when Kevin sat opposite her, the fears when she was reminded of the limiting wheelchair. But Louise had never been that intimate a friend, not even in high school. She waited for Louise to comment about her face or about Kevin.

Louise tapped the package in her hand with one finger, her head tilted to the side, watching Molly. While Molly was speaking, Louise had changed somehow; her back seemed straighter, her eyes intent, her whole bearing less that of the careless school girl. For the first time, Molly could see Louise as a working professional.

"You know, Molly," Louise said in a voice that Molly had not heard before, "women in your situation...that is, women who are coming into the singles scene after having had a partner for many years, needn't feel that they are all alone. There are support groups available. Here at SCAWF, we frequently get announcements of group meetings for women in transitional life stages. Some of the sessions are about meeting new friends, forming new relationships. Red flags to watch for. You'll be opening the mail. You should watch for them. You might plan to attend."

———

In the hallway, Molly turned away from the front door with its boarded up windows. The sounds of voices and clinking dishes were gone. Now the hall smelled of soap and bleach. If they would replace the glass, she thought, the room would be much less gloomy, and I could find Naomi.

She stepped into a room at the end of the hall. Sunlight poured through tall, narrow windows, blinding her.

"You're too late. Breakfast is over."

Molly turned toward the voice, but she could not see anyone.

"Past nine o'clock. What d'you expect? Breakfast is over at eight-thirty."

Molly put her hand over her eyes. Through her fingers, she saw the shape of a woman, standing behind a long table. "Naomi? Are you Naomi?" she asked.

"I'm Tammy. Naomi's in the playroom."

As Molly's eyes adjusted to the light, the woman and the room became clearer. Tammy's blond hair, almost waist-length, hung in wispy, thin clumps. Between the clumps, her scalp glowed bare and pink.

"Tammy, I'm Molly. I'm going to be working here." She studied the top of the dirty table carefully to avoid staring at the bizarre haircut.

"You don't want breakfast? Might be there's some coffee left." Tammy wiped her sponge back and forth across the blue and white checked plastic.

"No, I just want to find Naomi and get to work."

"I thought you were a new one. I thought you wanted breakfast. It's not fair, people come down and want breakfast after nine o'clock," she said, attacking a second table.

"No, of course not. People should come to meals on time," Molly said, finally looking directly at Tammy.

"It's not fair. I've had breakfast clean-up three days in a row. When I finished yesterday, I stopped to make one phone call, just one, on my way to get the counselor. But before she came down to check me off, someone came in and messed up the counter and the sink, and I had to do them all over again." She stopped wiping and looked up at Molly. "So I said, I don't want breakfast clean-up again. But when I went in this morning, everything else was taken."

"Well, I don't know how jobs are assigned," Molly said, "but I'll try to find out if anything was done that wasn't right."

"You can't do anything. The counselor just told me, get up earlier if I want a different job." Tammy swept the crumbs into her cupped hand and dumped them into the wastebasket. "That's all they do here, they say you can do this for yourself, or you can do that for yourself. You can get a haircut, you can see a lawyer. There's no one here to help you."

"Oh, surely they will help you," Molly said. How could they not help?

"No," Tammy shook her head emphatically, the blond clumps swinging. "They don't do anything for you. You have to do it yourself."

Tammy picked up a broom that was leaning against the wall and began to sweep under the tables. Her strokes were careless and uneven. Molly could see that she was missing much of the mess from breakfast.

"So, I tried to do something for myself. I wanted to get my clothes. When I came here, I could only bring one little bag, that's all CSO would let me take. So I called…"

"I'm sorry," Molly said. "What's CSO?"

"CSO? Those special police, don't you know?"

Molly shook her head.

"The police that come to take you to a shelter or something."

She would have to ask Louise.

"CSO will come for you, but they won't go after your things," Tammy was saying. "So I called my neighbor for her to go over and get me some clothes, and you know what she told me? What that bastard is doing?"

Molly shook her head again.

"She said he's having a garage sale! A fucking garage sale! He's selling everything my kids and I left at home, clothes and toys, stuff that was my mom's. And I can't do anything about it, because he's still my husband and I haven't been able to get any papers served on him."

I don't belong here, Molly thought. What can I say to this woman to comfort her? Tammy and her children, here, in this shelter, separated from the people and rooms and objects that were familiar, unable to go back. What would become of them? Molly had chosen to leave the familiar behind, but not her clothes, not any of the treasures that connected her to her past. How could she have felt sorry for herself? What could she do for Tammy?

She must have been staring. The younger woman interrupted her thoughts. "You think I look strange, don't you?" Tammy had stopped sweeping and was glaring at Molly. "Some kind of weirdo, right?"

"No, no, it's your privilege…" Molly began, but Tammy was still talking.

"You think I like to look like this. You think I did it on purpose." She shook her head. The clumps flew around her face. "Ricky did it. My husband. I had beautiful hair. I had beautiful clothes." She started to cry. "He said I was showing off for other men. He said, 'Bitch! I'll give them something to look…'" Tammy continued, talking, crying and gulping for air, but Molly could understand only a few words: "…want…clipper…hacked…"

Molly moved around the table and took the sobbing girl in her arms. She held Tammy's head against her shoulder and stroked the remnants of her long hair. In the patches of pink, fine soft new hairs were growing. The bare scalp against her cheek felt like Joey's little hairless head.

"Beautiful hair," Tammy was sobbing. "Beautiful clothes."

They stood together, the young woman clinging to Molly. If this is my job, Molly thought, I can do this.

"It's okay," Molly said. "You're going to be all right. Your hair will grow back and you'll get some new clothes." There must be clothes somewhere, maybe in the messy closet. Tammy was quieter now. "And you can get a haircut," Molly went on, "so your hair…"

"No!" Tammy shouted, pushing herself away from Molly. "I'm not going to cut my hair! Nobody can make me cut my hair."

"I just thought…" Molly tried to say, but Tammy wasn't listening. She turned her back and ran out of the room, her long hair bouncing behind her.

Knees shaking, Molly reached with both hands to the back of a nearby chair and clung to it. Not a good start, she told herself. I really messed that up.

"Molly?" A young Asian woman stood in the doorway. "I'm Naomi. I'm the daycare teacher. Louise said you're supposed to work with me this morning."

Should she go with Naomi or follow Tammy? Maybe Tammy wanted to be alone. Maybe later, after Molly had time to think of something to say, she could try to find Tammy.

"I thought you were lost," Naomi said, leading Molly through the hallway to a door on the opposite side of the house.

"I was," Molly answered. "I still don't know where I am."

"You were in the dining room. This is where the children are, those who don't go to school," Naomi said, pushing the door open.

There were lots more children in the room than the sounds from outside had led Molly to expect. Most of the noise was coming from two boys who were building a wall almost as tall as themselves from tattered, brick-stenciled cardboard blocks. They shouted instructions back and forth, ignoring the two women.

Molly tried smiling at a red-haired boy with bright blue eyes and freckles who reminded her of her son Joey. He had stopped pushing a wheel-less toy truck across the floor to stare at her, but he ducked his head down and wouldn't return her smile. Then she smiled at a girl with shining ebony skin whose head was covered with tiny braids, each one fastened with a bright-colored barrette. The child looked down at the doll in her lap and twisted its head around and around.

"Very good cooperating, children, that was very good," Naomi said. "Thank you for waiting for me."

The children turned back to their play, each one absorbed in what he or she was doing. They were so quiet! Molly thought back to the preschools that Joey had attended. How noisy they had been, with children chattering back and forth, curious about each other's games. But here, except for the boys at the wall, the children played alone. And when Molly looked more closely, she saw that the children weren't all preschoolers. Some of them looked big enough for first or second grade; a few looked even older.

"Those boys playing with blocks," Molly said to Naomi. "Aren't they a little old to be here? Shouldn't they be in school?"

Naomi was arranging small chairs in a ring. She sighed deeply, as if Molly's question required great effort to answer. "It takes time to get kids into a new school, you know." She moved two chairs back a small distance and frowned at her arrangement. "We try to send them back to their regular schools, if the moms can get transportation and it's safe. When those boys—they're brothers—came here with their mother, her husband threatened to kill them all. If we send them to school, we risk his finding them. And her." She opened a cupboard under the windows and pulled out a stack of pillows. "I'm afraid we don't have enough chairs for everyone. We have a lot of kids today. Your circle will have to sit on the floor."

On the floor? Molly thought. I can get down there, but I'm not sure I can get up again. She frowned at the pillows. They were not very big. Naomi was watching her.

"You know, circle?" Naomi said. "When the children sit around and share? Talk? When there are two of us here, I like to divide the children, so we can have smaller circles."

Molly tried to remember visiting Joey's schools, sharing in a circle. "Do you mean show and tell?" she asked.

"No show. Tell. Start a game or a song. Get the kids talking, and make sure that everyone has a chance to speak up." Naomi turned away from her and clapped her hands together. "Circle time! Circle time. Everybody come into a circle. We have a new teacher today. This is Molly. Big kids come into circle with me. Little kids go with Molly." She walked around the room clapping her hands. "Anyone who has ever gone to school before, come with me. Everyone else go with Molly. Daniel, you go with Molly. Lance, David. That's right. Stephanie, come with me." She moved around the room, sorting the kids until they were seated in two somewhat equal groups.

Molly moved to the circle on the floor and sank on to the remaining pillow, conscious of her tight slacks and creaking knees. She squirmed into a cross-legged position, trying to get comfortable. The girl with the braids and the red-haired boy were both in her circle, looking up at her expectantly. What were the songs and finger games Joey had learned in school? Molly couldn't think of a single one. Louise had told her there would always be a teacher in charge when she helped with the children. Share, Naomi said. Was that the extent of her supervision?

Six little faces, twelve solemn eyes studied her. "Good morning, children." No answer. "My name is…my name is Molly." She could have been using a foreign language. Well, maybe she looked like a foreigner to them. Once she had taken training to work with refugees who couldn't speak English. She still remembered the first day's lesson. "My name is Molly," she said, pointing at herself. "What is your name?" She pointed at the red-haired boy, sitting on her right.

"David," he answered shyly.

She shook her head. It isn't working. Exaggerate. "My," pointing at herself, "name is Molly. What is your," winding up and pointing with a flourish, "name?" She waggled her fingers at him in a beckoning motion. Come on, come on.

David giggled. "My name is David," he said. "What is your name?" He jabbed her in the right breast.

Tears sprung to her eyes. She wrapped her arms across her chest, rubbing her hurt breast. "Not quite. Try again." She took his hand and touched it to his chest. "Say with me. My name is David. Now," patting his hand against the arm of the child to his right, "what is your name?" The children looked confused. She repeated the whole process, moving David's hand, then beckoning to Daniel. "My name is David. What is your name?"

"Daniel." The second little boy laughed out loud. "My name is Daniel. What is your name?" He turned and punched the child on his right.

"No hitting." Molly reached across David to catch Daniel's arm. "Let's go around the circle now without touching."

The children loved the name game. They went around the circle twice, and when they finished Molly knew all their names: red-haired David, Daniel, Samantha with the braids, Erin, Kuntah and Lance. Now what?

Numbers. "Let's play with numbers. How many—how many—" she looked around for something to count. The wall of blocks stood just a few feet away. "Daniel, can you go over to that wall and bring me two blocks, and David, can you bring me three blocks?"

The little boys scrambled to their feet, hands reaching for the blocks.

"Don't touch that! That's our wall!" A young body flew out from the other circle and crunched against the boys. Small fists pounded them.

"Hold on there, stop that," Molly yelled, jumping up and reaching for the older boy. "We're not going to hurt your wall," she panted, trying to pull the big boy off the two smaller ones. "Stop that."

Naomi joined her. "Tommy, no," she said firmly. "No hitting. There is no hitting here. You can't stay here if you're going to hit."

Tommy rolled off the little boys and stood up, fists clenched. "That's my wall," he said.

David cowered on the floor, legs curled under his body, face hidden behind his hands, but Daniel lunged forward and plowed into Tommy, butting his head into the bigger boy's stomach.

"Daniel, no," Molly yelled, grabbing the little boy. He whimpered in her arms, wriggling and kicking. Metallic smell of sweaty little boy. How strong he was! She grew hot and sweaty herself, struggling to hold him. Was she hurting him?

"It's all right," Naomi said. "They're just borrowing the blocks for circle. You can build the wall back after circle. Let's go back." She put her hand on Tommy's shoulder and directed him back to his chair.

Molly released Daniel when she saw that Naomi had Tommy under control. He glared at her, wiped his sleeve across his face. Breathing hard, her hair sticky against her scalp, she helped David up from where he still cringed on the floor. His eyes were wide, the freckles dark against his pale skin, but he was not crying. "It's all right, it's all right," she kept repeating, patting the little boys on the shoulders. Should she take the blocks now or not? She didn't want to set Tommy off again, but it was important for him to learn that other people had rights too.

"Let's get the blocks," she said, but David shook his head. He went back to his pillow and sat down, staring at the floor. Molly led Daniel to the wall and handed him two blocks. Tommy glowered at her but stayed in his seat. She picked up two blocks herself and returned to her circle. Her knees creaked as she lowered herself to the floor.

"How many blocks in my hand?" she asked, lifting one of them.

"You were scared," Daniel said, pointing a dirty finger at David.

David shook his head, not answering, but the girl with the braids, Samantha, piped up, "I wasn't scared."

"Not me." "Me neither." "I wasn't scared." All the children except David asserted their fearlessness. What could she do for him?

" Molly!" Naomi hissed. Naomi was gesturing at her, scooping both hands toward Molly. "Scared. Pick up on scared."

"So, you weren't scared. Well, it's all right to be scared," Molly said. Poor David. He wouldn't look up. I was scared myself, David, she thought, does that help? "Everyone's scared sometimes," she went on.

"Like on Hallowe'en? I was scared on Hallowe'en," Samantha offered.

On Hallowe'en, it turned out, all of them had been scared. And in the dark, many of them were scared.

"I was scared when the police came to get my daddy," Lance said.

Yes, that had been scary. They had seen the police come to get their daddy, or "John," or "Uncle Steve," and there had been yelling and red lights and broken glass. The little voices spilled out, one over the other, eager to share the details of noise and struggle. Is this what Naomi wanted?

Suddenly there was a loud banging in the hall. Someone was pounding on the front door.

FIVE

Bam! Bam! Bam! Was someone knocking, or trying to break in? Whoever it was didn't believe in doorbells. The six children shrank into their cushions, frozen, watching her. Molly looked at Naomi, whose hands were pressed up against her mouth, palms together, as if she were praying.

"You go," Naomi said. "I'll stay with the children."

"Me?" Molly's heart was racing. "I can't go. I don't know anything about this place."

Naomi shook her head. "I can't leave my children. They don't know you, and you're not a teacher."

The banging at the front door continued. Sweat prickled on Molly's upper lip and gathered in her armpits. "What about the volunteers? Can't they go?" she asked, but as soon as the words were out she remembered the instructions in the manual.

"Staff," Naomi said. "You and I are staff. And I have to stay with my children."

And Louise is downtown putting out fires, Molly thought, as she pushed herself up on shaking legs and started toward the hall.

The pounding went on, and now, between barrages, she heard a man yelling. "Brenda? Brenda, I know you're in there."

Molly felt her way along the wall with icy hands. "*O sole mio,*" she said to herself. Oh, shit. Less than two hours ago, she had been standing outside this same door, waiting for someone to let her in. What did the voice on the inside ask her then?

She opened her mouth, but no sound came out. She swallowed and tried again. "Hello? Hello," she called. "Can I help you?"

"Yeah, sure, you can help me," a man's voice snarled. "Open the fucking door, that'll help me."

"Well, uh, who did you wish to see?" Molly asked. She tried to make her voice sound authoritative, but she couldn't stop its quavering.

"My wife. My wife, who you got locked up in there, that's who I wish to see," he mimicked. "Open the fucking door." More pounding. The plywood in the window spaces shook with each blow. No wonder the old glass was gone.

"Well, uh, if you'll tell me who you are," Molly said, trying to remember the instructions in the manual, "and who you want to see, I'll see if I can help you."

"I don't need help from you. You lesbian cunts, I know what you're trying to do. Just send down my wife and stop interfering in my life," he shouted.

Behind her, Molly sensed another person. She turned. A young black woman, scarcely as tall as Molly's shoulder but with a huge puff of curly black hair, beckoned her back toward the office. Thank heavens! She didn't want to stay in that dark hallway.

Three women huddled in the space between the desks, filling the small room. The woman who had beckoned Molly and a tall, red-haired, freckled woman had to be Tiny and Helen, the volunteers. They were bent protectively over a woman who must be Brenda. She glanced up at Molly for just a moment. A thin, delicate face, the black eye and split lower lip starkly contrasted with the pale skin. Black and red bruises showed above the collar of her round-necked sweater, and on her arms below the elbow length sleeves.

Tiny looked up at Molly. "Don't stay out in the hall," she whispered. "He might have a gun."

A gun! That ugly voice on the other side of the door, with all the pounding—Molly thought an enormous man might force the door in and knock her down on his way to get at his wife. But if he had a gun! Molly saw a shot breaking through the wooden panel, splinters flying, the bullet smashing into her body just inside the door. Her knees started to buckle. She clutched the edge of the desk and inched her way around to the only empty chair. The child David had cringed on the floor in front of the bigger boy, making himself as small as possible. She wanted to hide like that. "What am I supposed to do?" she asked herself. "I am the staff person," she said out loud.

The tall woman nodded. "We know who you are." She pointed at herself and at the other women. "Helen, Tiny, Brenda." Molly gasped. Had she spoken her thoughts out loud? But the other women ignored her. Brenda was crying, twisting a tissue to shreds that fell into a pile in the hollow of her dark skirt.

"It's your decision," Helen was saying. "You gave him a lot of years, and you know how he treated you. You don't have to go back if you don't want to."

"Brenda? Brenda, I know you're in there," the man yelled. "Brenda? I've come to take you home. It's going to be different this time. I'm going to change. Go to counseling. Whatever you say. I need you."

"Remember the last time you went back to him?" Tiny asked. The mass of black curls shook as she spoke. "Remember his promises? He didn't keep them then, did he? He didn't change. They don't ever change."

More banging on the door. "Brenda, you know you can't get along on your own. You're too stupid. Come out here. You need me. Brenda? You bitch. Cunt. Whore. Get out here."

From far away, Molly heard the sound of a siren. She looked at Helen. "We called as soon as the banging started," Helen whispered. "We have an understanding with a sergeant in our precinct."

The pounding continued for a few seconds more, and then stopped with the sound of the police car's arrival. Noises of scuffling came from the other side of the door, followed by silence and then a knock, a polite rap.

"It's Sergeant Martin." Helen nodded to Molly. "Let him in."

"Are you sure?" Molly asked, her mouth still dry and tight. "I'm the only staff person…"

A derisive sound exploded from Tiny. "Girl, do what she says."

What if the shouting man was still there, huge-fisted, crazy-eyed? What if he broke away? Molly opened the door a few inches. She saw a shiny badge on a blue uniform. Beyond, at the street, another officer with a man spread out against the hood of the police car. Skinny, pale, unkempt. He couldn't be the source of the ugly shouting.

"You're not the wife," the sergeant said. It was a statement.

"Come in," Molly said, pulling the door open. She'd never been so glad to see a police officer. There was a comforting smell of sweat and a clink of metal as she closed the door behind him. Leading him to the office, she resisted the impulse to reach out and touch his sleeve, to gather into herself the confidence, the safety, radiating from the uniform.

He walked directly toward Brenda and stood over her. "We have him in custody now," he said, with no emotion at all. "You're safe for a while."

Brenda looked up at him and tried to smile with her ruined mouth. She winced.

Sergeant Martin studied her face. "When did this happen? Have you had medical attention?"

Brenda nodded yes and bent her head to hide her face.

"Was this the first time you were beaten?" He was writing in a little notebook he had taken from his pocket.

She shook her head no, her brown hair falling forward like a veil over her face.

"Did you report this incident to the police? Do you have an incident number?" His voice scarcely rose at the end of each question.

Brenda shook her head again and mumbled something.

"Pardon?" the officer asked.

"I don't want to send him to jail."

Sergeant Martin took out a card and began writing on it. "You don't have to talk to me now. This is my name and number. You can call me as soon as you're ready, and I'll take a report from you then. I'll give you the incident number of the report I'll file today." A trace of warmth came into his voice. "Will you call me?"

She shook her head no. He snapped the notebook shut.

Helen squatted on the floor in front of Brenda. "You know," she said, "Washington and Minnesota are the only two states in the country where battering is a crime. You don't have to file charges against him. The police will do that." She looked up at the officer.

"That's right," he said.

"But they can't convict a man unless they have witnesses. Your kids. A neighbor." She looked up at the officer again. "Right?"

He nodded. "We can take him in for trying to break down your door," he glanced around at the other women, and then turned back to Brenda, "but we can't hold him for very long. Were there any witnesses when you were beaten? Did you call the police before?"

Brenda shook her head again. She did not look up at him. "He'll kill me if I send him to jail," she mumbled.

"We understand how you feel," Helen said to Brenda. "But it won't be you sending him to jail. When those reports start to pile up, the police will go after him. Not you. Them. Will you call them?"

Brenda nodded yes, but Molly didn't think she meant it. She glanced at the others. No one in the room believed Brenda would call.

"One more thing," Helen said, standing. "We want you to write down everything you remember about the events and the way you felt during the beatings and afterwards. Don't you agree, sergeant?"

"Yes, good idea," the officer confirmed. "Sure."

"Write it down and put it away in a safe place," Helen went on. "It will make you feel better and maybe it will be useful some day."

"What will happen to her?" Molly whispered to Tiny.

Helen heard her. "She can't stay here any more," she answered. "We'll arrange to send her to another shelter." She put her arm around Brenda and helped her to her feet. "Tiny, I'll take Brenda upstairs to pack, and you get on the phone, see who has space. It's okay," she said to Molly. "We've done it before. We know what to do." Someone needed to be in charge, and Helen seemed to have taken over.

Molly and Tiny walked Sergeant Martin to the door. He touched his hat to them, "Ladies," he said, and left. They locked the door behind him.

The two women started back down the hallway. "I guess I should thank you for calling the police. I didn't know I should..." Molly began.

"Not just any police," Tiny interrupted. "Just some police. And even he doesn't get it."

"He doesn't? I thought he ..."

Tiny interrupted again. "He did his little thing, but that was it. He could have, should have, done lots more."

Molly's head was spinning with questions. "I don't understand. Then why call him?"

Tiny snorted. "We know him. He knows us. We know he can keep us secret."

"But the police..." Molly persisted. "They should all know..."

"Yeah, right," Tiny laughed a derisive laugh. "And where will their wives go when their husbands beat them up?"

A door opened at the far end of the hall, and Tammy stuck her head out. "Tiny? Is he gone?"

The other woman nodded. "It's okay, Tammy. You can come out."

Tammy's arms were wrapped across her chest, hugging herself. "I was afraid he was after me."

"How did he find her?" Molly asked. "I thought no one was supposed to tell where the shelter is located."

Tiny sighed. "No one is supposed to tell, and none of the women do, just to their mothers or their best friends. People they know are completely trustworthy."

Molly saw a look of alarm flicker cross Tammy's face and knew that she had revealed the location to someone outside.

"Except," Tiny went on, "those other people think they know better what's good for the women, or they have some notion of where their duty lies, and so the men find them."

"Did she really go back to him?" Molly asked. "Leave, and then go back? I mean, how could she stay in the first place?"

Tiny turned on her. "Why did she go back? How could she stay?" Her voice became high and strident. "Shee-it. You're asking the wrong questions. You're talking shit. You're making the victim responsible. Shit." Tiny's face reminded her of her son Joey's defiant looks when he tried to shock her with street language. "What are you doing here? Did you ever live in a shelter? Ever been beat up?"

Molly tried to answer, but Tiny wasn't finished. "When I came here, I knew what questions to ask. You should be asking, 'What's wrong with that mother-fucker? Why did he beat her?'" Tiny continued, glaring at Molly. "Shit. If you're here to work with battered women, you better start seeing that they are the victims. It's not their fault."

Molly pulled her shoulders back and lifted her head to stand up as tall as she could. Did Tiny think her fake street slang would intimidate her? Did this little woman think that Molly was some kind of naive, uncaring princess? Maybe Molly didn't know the shelter routines yet, maybe she wasn't a battered woman herself. That didn't mean she couldn't learn. It didn't mean she didn't care about Brenda, or Tammy, or yes, even Tiny. If Tiny thought that she could shock Molly with foul language, well, Molly knew a few words herself. She'd raised a son and been around awhile. There were spray-painted walls in Omaha. What was it that she had been seeing on bumper stickers all the way across the country when she drove out this summer? Molly looked down at Tiny, stared her right in the eyes and shrugged. "Shit happens," she said, and pushed through the door into the playroom.

SIX

At noon, the mothers returned from their job searches and from their agency appointments to take their children to lunch. "We're through as soon as we tidy up the room," Naomi announced. She pointed to the broom and dustpan in the corner, and then turned away.

Molly waited for Naomi to comment on the morning, the man at the door or the children, but she worked silently, putting the toys in the cupboards, capping the jars of paint and setting the brushes in a can of water to soak.

Now that it was over, "what ifs" crowded into Molly's mind. What if the police hadn't come? What if that man had had a gun? Her stomach knotted into a hard lump, and she couldn't stop shaking. Grabbing the broom, Molly attacked the floor, reaching back into dark crevices behind the radiators and under the bookshelves that looked as if they hadn't been cleaned for a long, long time. She threw her whole body into the sweeping, reaching and pulling with all the energy she would have spent on fighting off the man at the door.

Naomi sat down at a table where Molly had already swept and opened a big red notebook. "We keep a log of what happens every day," Naomi told her. "You should read it. Then we'll talk if you still have questions." Molly nodded. She was full of questions, but she understood that Naomi didn't want them right now. She swept the dust and bits of play dough into a pile, picked them up in the dustpan and dumped them into the wastebasket.

Naomi looked up at her and smiled. "Tomorrow will be easier," she said, closing the notebook. She opened the door of the playroom and stood waiting for Molly.

I guess I'm supposed to leave, Molly thought. What next? Naomi didn't want to stay and chat, that was clear, she couldn't wait to lock the door to the daycare room and march to the front door. Behind the dining room door, Molly could hear the mothers and children at lunch. Lunch! She remembered putting her own lunch out on the kitchen counter at home, while she looked for her keys. It must still be there. Anyway, she couldn't eat. Her stomach was still knotted from the morning. She wandered down the hall, looking at closed doors, until she arrived at the office. Someone was seated at the second desk, talking on the phone. A round-faced woman, plump, freckled, with curly light brown hair. She waved at Molly and pointed to the phone.

Molly sat down at her desk and looked around. What to do? She turned on the computer and punched up the directory for the hard disk. Lots of familiar names. At least she wouldn't have to learn new programs. She tapped a few keys and brought up accounts payable. No bills paid yet this month. None paid last month, either. Well, at least she knew where to begin.

The plump woman said into the phone, "You don't deserve that kind of treatment. No one deserves that kind of treatment." She was quiet for a while, and then she said, "It's up to you. You're the only person who can decide that."

Molly tried to concentrate on the screen, but it was hard to shut out the conversation at the other desk. "When you decide it's too much, that's when it's too much. Not your mother, not your minister. You."

A breeze through the hallway. The front door slamming shut. Louise appeared, high-heeled pumps in her hand. "Oh, boy, that was a pain."

"Your feet?"

"That too," Louise agreed. "Frank Alexander. This closet should be kept locked," she added, as she threw her shoes into the open door behind Molly's desk. "How did your morning go?" she asked, reaching up under her skirt and pulling her panty hose down.

Molly looked away. How could she tell Louise about the morning's events while Louise was busy rolling her panty hose past her knees?

At the other desk, the woman was ending the phone conversation. "Call us when you're ready. There's always someone here." She smiled at them. "You must be Molly. I'm Patty, the relief counselor. I guess you were with the children when I arrived."

"Oh, I'm sorry. I thought you two had met." Louise balanced on one foot and then the other to pull her feet free. She held the bundle of nylon in her hand, looked around, then dumped it in the wastebasket. "There." She disappeared into the closet and stepped out wearing her old sandals. "Much better. So, how did it go this morning?"

What should Molly say? The fighting children, the man at the door, Tiny's arrogance, Naomi's coldness? "Lively," she answered.

"Well, I'm back now. We'll have the whole afternoon to get you settled. Have you had lunch?"

Molly shook her head. "I forgot it at home."

"That's no excuse. Come on, no one ever goes hungry here."

Later, they sat at a clean corner of one of the blue-and-white-checked tables in the dining room, eating bologna sandwiches on white bread. Crumbs and spilled milk still decorated the tables and the floor, but the room was quiet. In between explaining Molly's duties, Louise continued to apologize. Just like old times.

"It's okay, Louise. Plunging right in is just another way of getting started."

Louise nodded, chewing her sandwich. "I knew you could handle it, but I could have helped, shown you around, introduced you. Like with Tiny, a very competent volunteer. She used to be a client here, and she's very proud of that. And Naomi, she's very shy, did you notice? She's wonderful with the children, but some people think she's unfriendly. It would have helped her if had introduced you."

Helped her? What about me? "I'm sure we'll get along," Molly said. "She showed me where to find the broom and the log."

"The children's log. Good. There's another log on the counselor's desk. You should write up an incident report for the police visit. You'll pick up little things like that."

The way Helen had known what to do this morning. Will I ever be that competent? "Louise? Is it common for women to go back to the men who hurt them?"

"You're thinking about Brenda." Louise sighed, and put down her sandwich. "Some women go back and forth, from the shelter to their abusers, over and over, until they finally wake up. All we can do is help them make a safety plan and hope that their abusers don't find out where we are."

"Is that what you always call them? Abusers?"

"What else should we say? Husband? Boyfriend? Partner? Until we know who we're talking about..."

"It sounds so...so clinical."

Louise shrugged. "You'll get used to it. I know everything must seem strange to you, but it will begin to make sense with time. Don't be afraid to ask questions—the counselors, me, the volunteers. Don't hide your feelings. You were very frightened this morning, weren't you?"

Molly paused for a moment, one finger tracing a pattern of crisscrossed lines on the blue and white table. "I felt so afraid for Brenda. For myself, too, but for her...that awful man...and now she's going off to a strange place where she doesn't know anyone." Like me, she thought. I'm in a strange place where I don't know anyone either, except Louise, one person, no three, I know Kevin and Ben. Am I like Brenda?

"What are the women here like?"

"There's no typical profile. They're not all poor. They're not uneducated. They are...stuck in a bad place. What they have in common, besides being abused, is that somewhere in their past they made a bad decision. And then some of them never had, or they've somehow lost, the ability to fend for themselves. I sometimes think that the psychological or emotional abuse does more lasting damage than the physical abuse." Louise laughed. "You're getting my begging routine, for potential donors." She sat up straighter and continued in a mock-serious tone, "At SCAWF, we give a woman a few days grace, the time to help her find the knack, the adequacy, to be her own person."

Do I have that? Molly thought. Now I do...but before Ted died.... "Some of us never get that ability until we're forced to take care of ourselves."

"That's not true." Louise dropped her head-of-the-agency manner. "You would never have stayed several weeks in a shelter like this. I mean, if you had had to run away from your husband, you might have come here for a night or two, but then you would have gone to a friend's house or taken your credit card and checked into a hotel. But our residents..." Louise turned her head toward noises from the hall.

Angry shouting., then a quick, sharp sound that could have been a slap. A child crying. More shouts, louder now. Louise jumped up and ran out. Molly followed her.

At the bottom of the stairway, two women, their mouths distorted with yelling, confronted each other. Like mirror images, each leaned forward into the face of the other, one arm protectively around a child, the other arm thrust out in front of her, fist clenched. Molly heard, "Keep your hands off my kid, you bitch!" and "You're so high and mighty, you think your shit don't stink?" She couldn't tell who was screaming which words.

Then Patty came from somewhere, stepped between them, hands up and open, motioning them apart. "Stop this," she yelled. "Stop this right now. I want to know what's going on!" Red blotches streaked across Patty's cheeks and down her neck. The women ignored her. She tried again to shout them down. "Stop it. Now. We're going to get to the bottom of this."

The words changed. Now the women began yelling "she" instead of "you." Patty shouted again. "Hold it! You'll get your turn! Quiet!"

Louise put her hand on Patty's shoulder and pulled her back from between the two women.

"You!" Louise said, pointing to the woman on her right. "You go sit on the stairs and stop yelling. And you," she turned to the other woman, "you go stand over there. Now, we'll all take a two-minute time-out."

The women retreated, breathing heavily. Patty, too, panting hard, stepped back. For a moment, there was no other sound in the hall. Molly could hear the whoosh of her own breath, feel the effort to inhale, exhale. Her heart pounded in her chest. Smell of dust and sweat. She looked around the group. Mother and child, mother and child. The women glaring, jaws set, the children alert and bright-eyed. Patty's red streaks beginning to fade. Louise in control.

"Okay," Louise said, "do you want to settle this now, or shall we wait until after dinner?"

Now, the women both agreed. Louise nodded. "You first. One sentence. Tell me what happened."

"Her brat wouldn't let my Devon go past him up the stairs, and when I told him to move, he called me a bitch."

"Your turn," she pointed to the woman on the stairs.

"My son was just playing a game, and that little bastard kicked him in his privates."

"Wasn't no game!"

"In his private parts, he could have been mutilated."

"One sentence," Louise asserted. "You've each had your say. Now, where were you when your kids were on the stairs?" She didn't wait for an answer. "You are responsible for your children. Kids stay on the same floor as their moms unless they're in bed or in daycare. If your kids can't get along, keep them apart. That's it. No further discussion."

The women grumbled, but went off in opposite directions with their kids, one pair up the stairs, the other toward the front door.

Louise turned to Patty. "Are you all right?" Patty nodded. "Don't ever step between two women who are having an argument. You have to protect yourself. You know that, Patty." She turned back toward the dining room.

"But they were getting violent," Patty objected. "I thought I should stop it."

Louise said, over her shoulder, "Not when it means you might get hurt yourself."

"But, shouldn't you…we…"

Louise stopped, the dining room door half open. "Violence is the only way to solve problems that some of our women have ever known," she said. "We can try to change them, in group sessions, house meetings, but in a confrontation—that's just not a safe time."

"So you just let them say their piece? And that's it?" Molly asked.

"There's no place for violence in the shelter. The women who come here know that. If they can't live by the rules, they have to leave." Louise shrugged. "Those two never did get along, and they both have had recent setbacks. Deanna learned yesterday that she didn't get the job she had hoped for. Maggie is supposed to leave day after tomorrow but her rental has fallen through. They can avoid each other until then."

"Where will she go?"

Louise shrugged. "She has two days. She had other choices." She stepped into the dining room.

Their sandwiches were gone from the table.

"Weren't you done in here?" A tall blond woman looked in from the kitchen. Dark circles around her eyes. Circles? Or fading bruises? "I had to start after-lunch clean up."

Louise looked at Molly. "I think we need some coffee." She filled two mugs and started back toward the hallway. "I hope you aren't getting a wrong impression, Molly. This has been an unusual day."

Molly wrapped her arms across her chest to stop shivering. "Lots of excitement."

"It's very unusual," Louise emphasized. "Most days here are extremely quiet. Nothing more will happen today."

Molly nodded, speechless.

"So, where would you like to begin?"

"I'd like some time with you at the computer."

"That will be the easiest part of your job. You know, I've been thinking, Molly, about an orientation to the shelter, and it occurred to me that if you took the training course for volunteers…." Louise was walking down the hall as she spoke, sandals flapping, and Molly didn't catch every word. "…basic information…cycle of violence…new group…Tuesday and Thursday evenings…downtown YWCA… on your way home…can't give you time off…meeting people…new in town…"

They sat down in front of the computer. Louise spent much too much time, Molly thought, going over programs in the computer that she already knew, but at last she was gone. Just as Molly was finally left alone with the bills, Patty came in with a new client she had just picked up. "This is Sandra," she said. "Would you help me with her please, while I do her intake?" Sandra was a mass of scratches. Molly found plastic gloves in the closet and went to work with calamine lotion. As soon as Patty had taken her up to her room, Molly turned back to her work, but it was hard to concentrate. She couldn't help mulling over Sandra's story. The afternoon was flying by, and she was accomplishing nothing. Helen and Tiny came to the door. "Quitting time. We're going out for pizza and a movie. Want to join us?" Helen announced.

"We're seeing *E.T. The Extra Terrestrial*," Tiny added, with no trace of hostility. "We thought, you being new in town, and all…" Molly sensed it was meant as an apology.

"That is so thoughtful of you," she answered. "I'd love to do that, some other time, but there's still so much unpacking at home to do, and I'm not finished here." She hoped they understood. Some other time she really would like to go out with them.

They left, she had another half-hour of work, and she was just shutting down the computer when Louise returned.

"Oh, one other thing, Molly, before you go. You'll be responsible for picking up the mail. We have a post office box downtown. I'll give you the key."

"Downtown?" Molly echoed.

"Well, we can't have one out here, the zip code might give away our location. Downtown is safer, but still, you should look around when you pick up the mail to be sure that no one is watching the box. No one is following you."

"Following me."

"It's just a precaution, Molly. Don't get upset about it."

SEVEN

Molly didn't see the box until she almost tripped over it, right in front of her door. It was another close call. She'd had a couple of those driving home. It was amazing that she had arrived without an accident, her head so full of the events of her first day, playing the scenes over and over again in her mind like a movie gone berserk. Who needed E.T.? There was the man at the door. The children. Brenda leaving for another shelter, all she owned in two paper shopping bags.

Louise saying, "Lots of abused women go back to their abusers, and more than once." That was information that Molly would have to work on accepting, it seemed so hard to believe.

And then the woman with all the scratches—Molly's fingers felt sticky with calamine lotion again, just thinking about tending to her.

Home at last, what was this box on her doorstep? A leftover from unpacking, dropped on the way to the trash bin? Well, tomorrow she would carry it out, she thought, kicking it aside. But when her foot hit it, she realized the box wasn't empty. She carried it inside and set it on the kitchen counter, pushing aside the brown bag containing her forgotten lunch. She washed her hands and shook them dry—she hadn't yet filled the paper towel holder—and then opened the box. Cold chicken, a container of fruit salad, some little sandwiches of alfalfa sprouts and sliced tomatoes on whole wheat bread. Kevin's note said, "I'm sure you don't feel like cooking. Do you feel like talking?"

Suddenly she was very hungry. She kicked off her shoes and stood at the counter, eating the chicken with both hands. It was tender and succulent, flavored with honey and soy sauce, with a few sesame seeds scattered over the skin. The juices ran down her chin. She leaned over the counter so that the dribbles would not fall on her shirt. Then she licked most of the sauce from her fingers, and finished cleaning her hands and face with a large paper napkin she found in the box. She carried the other packages to the table and sat down to finish the salad and sandwiches.

She didn't feel like talking, at least not to Kevin; she wanted to talk to Ted. If Ted were alive, they would snuggle up together on the sofa, he would stroke her hair and she would tell him all her impressions of her first day of work, about the women she'd met, the exhaustion of trying to learn too much in too little time. On the other hand, if Ted were alive, she wouldn't be here, going out to work in a strange place, in an unfamiliar city. It was Ted's fault that she was so tired and discouraged. If he hadn't died…

She tossed the remnants of the supper into the garbage can, threw off her clothes on her way to the bathroom, and soaked in a hot tub for half an hour, all the while missing Ted and feeling sorry for herself. But when she was out of the bath and rubbing herself dry, she began to think differently. It was early, only seven-thirty. Seattle's sun was still high in the late summer sky. Facing a long and lonely evening, maybe she wanted company after all.

A best friend would be wonderful, but she didn't have one. Who else did she know here? As she pulled a light summer dress over her head, she thought about what she would say if she called Kevin. When she grew up, girls—nice girls, that is—didn't telephone boys. What did women in the 1980s say when they called men? Thank him for the food, of course. Maybe he had expected her to invite him to join her.

Could she say, "Thank you for your dinner, which I've already eaten without you. Now I've decided I'm lonely and need someone to talk to, so I'd like to see you?"

Should she invite him to her apartment? It was her turn, if the old rules had not changed. He should be able to get his wheelchair into her house with no problems. Or should she invite herself into his home? His apartment was more lovely and spacious than hers, and it had that great view. But if she called him, shouldn't she invite him to her home, and not the other way around?

Even as she was dialing his number, she wasn't sure of what she would say. "Kevin? Hi. It's Molly." She tried to think of something to say next. "That was a great dinner." Now what? All the things she had practiced saying had disappeared from her head.

There was a long silence. What was he thinking? They both started to talk at once. She said, "Would you like to visit?" He said something about talking. Neither of them heard the other clearly. After another too-long silence, he said, "Would you like me to come down?"

———

Molly's living room sofa had five huge, fat, striped pillows across the back and two little ones in each corner. She sat on the sofa, scrunching one of the small pillows under her elbow and indicated that he should roll his chair opposite her. She had placed a pitcher of iced tea on the table at her side. When they were settled with their glasses, he said, teasing, "Tell me about your dangerous job. Only what you're allowed to say, of course."

Could she tell him about the real danger of that morning? No, he might get upset again and fret about her safety. "Well," she began, "It's going to take me a long time to learn the ropes. It's not at all what I expected."

"And is your friend helping you, or are you left to figure things out on your own?" he asked.

"No, it's not like that," she lied. "SCAWF is a good place, a caring organization." That much was true. She owed some loyalty to Louise.

"Scoff?"

"That's what they call it. S-C-A-W-F. Seattle Center for Abused Women and Families."

He nodded and murmured, "An acronym. I hate acronyms."

"So do I. So does everyone I know." She shrugged, "So who goes around inventing them?"

"Right," he agreed, pushing himself up against the arms of his wheelchair. She couldn't help noticing the way his arms and shoulders moved beneath the blue velour running suit. "What's this SCAWF like?"

"It's a big house," she said slowly, "with room for thirty women or children. Now we have twenty-five. I thought it would be something like a dormitory, and I'd be the housemother. Do you remember housemothers?"

"Certainly," he nodded. "I was in college in the fifties. Not that I ever knew any housemothers myself. I never lived on campus." He paused for a few minutes. She sensed what he was thinking: people in wheelchairs didn't live in dorms in those days. Then he went on, "I understand that dorms have student supervisors nowadays."

"So I hear. Well, the SCAWF building used to belong to a Catholic board-ing school that closed a few years ago. Lots of rooms upstairs, cells, really, downstairs a sitting room for the residents and a play room for the kids."

"St. Claire's School. I remember it. We used to play on the swings in their playground. The nuns would come out and chase us away."

"Oh my goodness. *O sole mio.*" She clapped both hands over her face. "I've given it away. You know where the shelter is."

"No, you didn't give it away," he said. "I already knew where it is. I grew up in the neighborhood, and I keep track of what happens there. Besides, architects hear things. There was some remodeling when the shelter moved in. Meeting city codes, that kind of thing. You didn't realize, did you, when we were on our tour yesterday we were only a couple of blocks from your SCAWF?"

She shook her head. "I wasn't looking for it. I thought I was seeing your city, not mine." She thought for a few minutes, and then said, "So you already knew where the shelter was when you scolded me the other night."

"Yes." He waited for her reaction. "Are you angry?"

"No, I'm too tired to be angry." She turned to the pitcher at her side and refilled their glasses. "You really want to hear about my day?"

"Continue," he said, pushing himself up again in that funny way he had.

"Well, it's not a dormitory and I'm not a housemother. It's hard work. I'm not sure I can do it. The girls—the women—have had such hard lives. The children have seen unspeakable things. I didn't know what to say to them."

"You have a son," he said gently.

"Yes, but these children….This morning I was supposed to draw them out, get them to talk, and all I could think of was a stupid exercise for teaching refugees English."

"Tomorrow will be easier," he said, leaning forward in his chair. "I'll bet you already have plans for something better to do tomorrow."

"Oh, yes," she said. "After the kids left, I thought of a whole lot of things I could have done instead of that dumb game. But that's not all of my job." She sighed. "In the morning, I was with the kids, and I could manage. But in the afternoon, I'm in the office and I have to deal with the abused women, and I'm not sure I can handle that."

He nodded, waiting for her to go on. When she was silent, he asked, "What kinds of office work do you do?"

"It's not the work so much," she answered. "Bookkeeping. Letters. Checking residents in and out. The hard part is talking to people. The women in the house, or the women who call up to talk about abuse, but they don't want to leave their abusers," she said, rolling the pillow into a tight little bundle. "We keep a log of calls, and some women will call up dozens of times before they finally decide to get out."

"Do you encourage them to leave?"

She shook her head. "We're not supposed to. We encourage them to make their own decisions. Empower them, that's the word the counselors like to use."

"Why are you taking calls? Was that part of your job description when Louise hired you?"

She shook her head again. "There are at least two people all the time, a counselor and a volunteer, to handle crisis calls and make arrangements for women who need to come in. I'm the back-up when those two are busy."

"Who picks them up? You?"

"No," she shook her head more vehemently. "At least, I didn't do that today. It's risky. You always pick up a client at a neutral place, never at her home, but still…" She watched him for a moment, expecting another lecture on safety.

"If you don't like the job, if it's not what you expected it to be, I know a lot of people. I can help you find something else."

"No, no, I want to succeed at this job," she insisted.

After a silence, he said, "What are the women like?"

It was an echo of her own question. "Each one is different. All kinds, and yet they are so…so ordinary. Most of them, when they first come in, they're very subdued. The women who've been there a while are lively, but the ones who have just arrived—some of them just stayed in their rooms and didn't come down to meet me."

"I suppose they feel like failures," he said quietly.

"And that's a sad thing," she agreed. "They feel ashamed of what's been done to them, as if it's their fault."

For a moment, Molly hesitated. She wanted to tell Kevin about the woman who had come in that afternoon, but just thinking about her, remembering the poor bruised body, made Molly angry, and it took her a few seconds to get herself under control.

"We checked a woman in today who was covered all over with scratches. Her whole body had long, deep scratches everywhere. And can you guess how she got that way?"

"Tell me."

"This man picked her up and threw her—well, actually shoved her—into a clump of thorn bushes!" Molly's voice grew louder as her indignation increased. "She was sunning herself in her own backyard, and the man who lived with her, not her husband, thought she was displaying herself to some men who were working in a yard down the street." She paused to take a breath. "So he pulled her up and began shaking her and slapping her. When she tried to run away, he pushed her and she fell into the vacant lot between the houses."

"Blackberry vines," he said. "Every vacant lot in Seattle is full of blackberries—the most wicked, cruel thorns."

"And every time she struggled out," Molly went on, "he pushed her back in."

"How did she stop him?"

"The men down the street heard her screaming and made him stop. Now she's afraid to go home, and it's her house."

"She could go to the police, get a protection order," he suggested.

Molly shook her head. "He's not going to be put off by that." She thought back to the discussion between Sandra and Patty as they entered her story in the log. "He's the kind of man who thinks he can do anything he wants, because he's so big and strong. Look what he did to her, shoving her into the bushes so many times. A man who can throw people around doesn't pay attention to laws."

"That's not necessarily true, Molly. I'm not like that." He sat up straighter in his chair. The room was growing dark around them, but she could still see the muscles under the blue velour. "I could pick you up and throw you across the room, but I'd never do a thing like that."

"You!" She bit back the words she was about to say. Of course he had those great muscles, but to throw her across a room?

"Yes, me. I'm very strong. That doesn't make me a lawbreaker. You have to tell your girls—'scuse me, women—that they have the law on their side and they have to stand up for their rights. That's what your SCAWF is supposed to be teaching them, isn't it?"

"It's not that easy. The system doesn't work so perfectly." She was silent, then, thinking about the woman afraid to go back to her own home. The lights came on outside the building and shone in through the windows, gilding the leaves of the jade plant that Ben had set up on the sill.

After a few minutes, Kevin began to talk. "Your SCAWF is certainly different from the St. Claire's I remember."

"Tell me about your St. Claire's. I'll bet it was wholesome. All-American. Norman Rockwell."

"Forty years ago, it was the neighborhood hang-out. Their playground had better swings and bars than the public school." As he spoke he rubbed his hands across his blue velour thighs. "I remember that the kids wore uniforms. Boys wore white shirts with dark blue trousers. And the girls wore plaid skirts."

"Which they probably weren't supposed to get torn or dirty."

"Then during World War Two, it became the collecting station for grease and cans and foil."

"I remember that!" she said eagerly. "I remember saving bacon fat and cans to take to school. Why didn't you take your stuff to your own school?"

"I don't know. We just didn't. We took it to St. Claire's."

"My brothers took care of the grease and the newspapers," Molly said. "It was my job to get the cans ready. I rinsed them out and took off both lids and stomped them flat. Did you do that?"

"I remember the collecting, but I couldn't stomp on the cans."

Oh dear, she said to herself, *O sole mio*, I've done it again. Kevin couldn't have known the satisfying thunk of stomping a tin can flat, could he, if his legs didn't work? But he was still talking.

"I remember running at St. Claire's, running away from the nuns. I was very fast when I was a little kid, the fastest kid in the neighborhood. I won lots of races. My dad thought I would be a track star in high school and college, maybe even be an Olympic runner."

The only light in the room now came from the lamps outside the windows, big rectangles of brightness shining on the floor. Molly thought, I wonder if he would be telling me this in a brightly lighted room. She sat very still, afraid that if she moved, he would stop talking.

"Then my legs started to get weaker and weaker. Little things, like not being able to stomp a tin can. I began to fall. Often. My parents thought I had polio, but all the tests were negative. In those days, the fancy technology for looking inside the body didn't exist. I entered high school in a wheelchair."

"Did you ever find out what it was?" Molly whispered.

His voice came softly through the dark. "Years later, they discovered I had a tumor, a benign, slow-growing tumor, pressing on my spinal cord. As it grew, it crushed the nerves in the cord. Like slowly slicing through them. I had surgery to remove it, but it was too late to repair the damage." He paused for a long time. "These days they can find and remove that kind of growth before it does any harm. I guess I was born too soon."

She felt tears gathering in her eyes, a big lump in her throat. She tried to speak, but no sound came out. She swallowed and tried again. "I can understand why you're angry," the words came out softly, "over things like the parking spaces yesterday, and the things you can't do anymore."

He laughed shortly. "The parking spaces are something else. A political issue. And I may have frightened you yesterday, but I'm not angry all the time." It was too dark to see him, but she heard the rustle as he shifted in his chair. "No one can be angry all the time. And the things I can't do—I try not to think about those. I can remember how it felt to run, the wind blowing my hair back and my feet pounding the track. But, I get around. What's so great about pounding feet? I get the wind in my hair driving with the top down. It's the things I never had that I miss. I would have liked to have kids. I would have liked to be a father. To watch my kids run. That's what I miss. Funny, isn't it, missing things I never had."

Sitting in the darkness, Molly was overwhelmed with a feeling of great tenderness. She wanted to comfort him. If Ted were telling her his secrets, she would have reached out to him, touched his arm, made some physical contact to say, "I'm here." She put her hand out to touch Kevin's arm, and felt beneath her fingers the soft velour of his running suit. Through the cloth, her fingers made out a knobby bone. Not his arm… his knee! She had touched his knee! She jerked her hand back for an instant, and then returned it to where it had been. They sat in the darkness for a few moments, no sound in the room except their breathing and the noises of traffic far away, her fingers resting lightly on his knee. It was one of the most daring gestures she had ever made. He might misunderstand; he might reject her. Then, as Molly's scalp began to prickle and the hair on her neck rose, she realized what was happening between them. While she believed that she was making herself vulnerable, making an open and compassionate move toward Kevin, he, numb from the waist, was totally unaware of what she had done.

EIGHT

SEPTEMBER

What a beautiful day! Molly could smell dried leaves in the breeze blowing into the open window of her car, a hint of fall in the warm air. Red and gold vine maples decorated the open slopes next to the road, an unexpected contrast to the dark green evergreens on the landscaped grounds. The light was different, too, a golden glow on the buildings of the apartment complex. Could any place be more beautiful than Seattle on an afternoon in September? It was too beautiful to stay inside. She pulled her car into its place in the lot and stepped out. It was a day to run with the breeze, fly a kite, roll in the leaves. Maybe just take a walk with a friend—if you had a friend. Or sit outside with the only friend you had.

Well, why not? I can call him up, she thought. She was past the hesitancy she had felt after her first day at work. She had seen or talked to Kevin almost every day since then. He watched for her car coming up the hill on the nights she attended the volunteer training sessions. Then he called her and sometimes came down for a cup of tea when she came home. One evening, when she had gone out to a club with the other trainees, he had been very worried about her, and scolded her for being out, alone, so late at night. And how many afternoons had she stepped into her apartment to find a note under the door, or the phone ringing while she still had the key in her hand? Ben had been on a cooking binge, or someone had given them an enormous salmon, or they had some other excuse for feeding her and keeping her company when she was bone-weary, too tired to do anything for herself, but desperate for food and companionship.

This day, though, was different. The air, the light, or maybe getting used to her job. All the volunteers had come in today, on schedule, so she hadn't been needed to fill in on the phone. Not one single phone call all day! She felt like throwing her arms out, grabbing big armfuls of golden air and holding it tight. No, she wouldn't call Kevin. She would just drop in and see him.

It was all right to do this, she reminded herself as she rang Kevin's doorbell. They were friends now, this is the 1980s, and this is what friends did.

Ben's eyebrows shot up when he opened the door, but he recovered quickly. "I just made a fresh pot of coffee," he announced, waving his arm in a grand gesture and bowing her into the room.

Molly heard voices from Kevin's workroom, the former dining room. She didn't want to interrupt, but that's where Ben was headed, so she followed him. Three people stood at a slanted drawing table near the window. One of them, at first glance, appeared to be a delicate, slight young man. Then Molly realized it was a woman. She was dressed just like the young man next to her, trim slacks, striped shirt with sleeves rolled back, and a loosened necktie. "Oh, excuse me…" Molly began, and then stared at the three. One of them, the tallest person, was Kevin. Standing!

He recovered first. "Molly, what a nice surprise. I'm glad you're here. I want you to meet my associates. Molly Bennet, Leatrice Wood and John Jeffries."

The two young people nodded at her, murmuring greetings. The woman inspected Molly with open curiosity. Molly must have answered them, although later she couldn't remember what she'd said. She knew that she had managed to avoid blurting out the words she was thinking: "I didn't know you could stand!"

"John and Leatrice will be working with me this year," Kevin went on. "They are fresh out of the university, June graduates, eager to correct all that I've been doing wrong." Leatrice threw her head back and laughed, but John looked from her to Kevin, his eyes switching back and forth rapidly. A twitch ran across his cheek.

"We'll be done in just a few minutes." Kevin gestured toward the kitchen. "Would you like some coffee? Ben is about to come out and make the rounds."

"I'll find him," she said.

As she pushed through the swinging door, Ben handed her a bright blue steaming mug and then took the pot out to the workroom. She clutched the mug with both hands. In the weeks she had known him, except for the few minutes in the pool, she had always seen Kevin sitting down. She had learned—she had made an effort to learn—to accept the wheelchair, to see the man in the chair and not the chair itself. But seeing him standing, now, had affected her strongly. She didn't understand her own reaction.

Ben came back and returned the coffee pot to its warming stand. He grinned at her. "Took you by surprise, didn't he?"

Ben had that annoying habit of being dead right at guessing her thoughts, but never revealing anything about Kevin. Still, she had caught him off guard when she appeared at the door. Maybe she could catch him again. "Yes, I didn't expect to see Kevin standing." No questions. Let Ben lead.

After a short silence, Ben offered, "It's called a standing frame." She nodded, but didn't say anything. "It's a remarkable device," he went on. She murmured agreeably and waited.

"Kevin's own design. Made from standard hardware store parts. Really cheap and easy to put together. I think he should patent it and market it, but he's willing to let anyone copy it."

"That's very interesting," she said, and bit back the questions she wanted to ask.

"A doctor he knows has written an article about the frame," Ben informed her. "Turns out it's beneficial to use it for two or three hours a day—puts weight on the leg bones and keeps them solid."

"I'm glad you told me all that, Ben," she said, raising her mug to her lips and watching him over the blue rim. "Kevin hardly ever talks about himself."

He turned abruptly to the sink. "I have these vegetables to clean."

Ben hadn't revealed any confidential information, but she liked knowing that she had outwitted him. It added to the expansive feeling of her beautiful day.

Leaning back against the kitchen counter, she let the sunlight pouring through the western windows wash over her shoulders. She sipped her coffee and listened to bits of conversation from the other room. She heard "garden approach," "administrative wing," "second means of egress," "subdividable space option," ---a steady, comforting mingling of voices, even if it didn't all make sense. When the voices changed to sounds of leave-taking, she carried her coffee to the other room. John and Leatrice had moved to the door, but Kevin was still standing by the window.

He smiled at her and she walked over to stand next to him. It gave her the chance to study the device that held him up, a system of thick pads at his waist and hips and knees that were suspended from a metal framework. She exchanged proper pleasantries with the young people—they were all glad to have met each other—and they were gone.

"Well, this is a nice surprise," Kevin repeated, beaming down at her.

"It was such a beautiful day," she began. She turned away from his glance. Her face probably showed too much. What if he had not been glad to see her? "Tell me about your project," she said, focusing on the drawing table.

"And then let's go for a walk," he said, as if he had read her mind.

"We're doing a retirement complex," he told her, rolling out the big sheets of drawings, "on a wonderful site north of the city." He moved a bar on the table to hold the drawings flat. "Three centers for three life-styles. Here, on the top of the hill, retirement apartments and townhouses for what the client calls 'active retirees.' Attached garages, putting green, pool." As he spoke, he pointed to places on his drawing. He was so proud of it, like her son Joey coming home with his art projects. "Then tucked under the hill, so the residents of the two centers won't be so aware of each other, there's another building for less independent folks—central dining room, a supervisory staff..."

"Like an old-age home," Molly said.

"The developers don't like to call it that, but yes," he agreed. "And here, in the trees, is the infirmary, which you would probably call a nursing home."

"It all looks wonderful," she said. "Who is going to live there?"

"The client calls them 'the affluent elderly.' He expects the project to be very profitable."

Ben came out of the kitchen to pick up the dirty coffee cups. "Profit," he said, "is what we are losing by not selling standing frames."

Kevin laughed. "What do you think of my work station?" he asked, pulling himself up straighter. "You were startled, I could tell."

"I've never seen anything like it," she answered.

"And he's giving it away," Ben put in.

"I don't need to make money from spinal cord injuries," Kevin said. "I'll make enough on this retirement complex, if my new associates get the field work done by next week."

"But those are old people," Molly protested.

"Rich old people," Kevin admonished. "Now if someone will wheel my chair over here…"

"I'll do it," Molly offered. Ben raised his eyebrows again but didn't try to stop her. She found the chair at the side of the room, wheeled it up behind Kevin, and set the brake the way she had watched him do it. "There you go," she said. He turned toward her and nodded. She had to look up to meet his eyes. It doesn't matter, she told herself while she watched him release some catches at his knees, hold onto the frame with one hand, unfasten the strap at his waist and lower himself into the chair. It doesn't matter at all, but a part of me is glad that he is taller than I am.

Looking up was fine. Looking down and sideways gave her a crick in her neck. Walking with Kevin was harder than she had expected—walking and talking, that is. She had to bend forward past her elbow to see his face, and he was leaning sideways in his chair in a way that looked equally uncomfortable. But if they straightened up and looked ahead, half their words were lost, carried away by the same breeze that had brought the wonderful autumn smells into her car.

After repeating several times, "I'm sorry," or "Say that again, please," they stopped trying to talk. With gloved hands, Kevin pushed the hand rims just fast enough to keep his chair moving alongside Molly. They followed a wide path that circled the apartment buildings and ambled through the grounds, enjoying the fall colors. Kevin must have designed this path for himself, Molly thought. It's so lovely. She wished she knew what he was thinking. Does it matter to him that I'm here with him? Not that we have to talk all the time. When she had walked with Ted, holding hands, or with her hand tucked into his elbow, they didn't need to talk. But here alongside Kevin, she had no way of reading his feelings. Was their being together enough for him? Or was he bored with her company?

"This is a good place to stop," he said, turning his chair between two huge rhododendrons.

"Where are we? I never noticed this spot before." They had entered an outdoor room, red and gold leafy walls surrounding a concrete pad. The wind had died, or the trees behind them deflected the breeze. She sat down on an old-fashioned park bench, and he moved opposite her.

"It's a quiet place," he said. "Like the Japanese; they build a meditation garden outside their teahouses, so they can prepare themselves mentally before they enter." He pushed himself up in his chair. "I like to design some surprises into all my projects. It's the romantic in me."

The second time today, she thought. First the drawings, then this lovely space. He wants me to like his work. To like him. He isn't bored. He likes me.

"But by bringing me here you are giving away your secret," she teased.

"I think I can trust you with my secrets," he said.

"It's like the song," she said. "And the autumn weather turns the leaves to gold..."

"Flame."

"What?"

"To flame." He sang, "The autumn weather turns the leaves to flame, and we haven't the time for a waiting game."

"And the days dwindle down," her voice joined his, "to a precious few..." They finished the song and sat without speaking for a while, facing each other. Then she told him about her day with no phone calls, the good feeling she had driving home. The sunlight grew redder on the trees around them, and then was gone. She began to shiver. They started back.

"Let me take you to dinner," she said. "It will be a good way to finish my good day."

"I'll take you," he insisted.

"No, it's my day, let me do this. I saw a restaurant I'd like to try, Vietnamese, not fancy."

"Is it accessible?"

"Yes, I checked. It's in a little house. A long path up to the front door, then just a little sill to go over."

Half an hour later, they were settled in Kevin's white convertible. "Tell me about your new associates," she suggested.

"I think they'll work out well," Kevin said, looking over his shoulder to back out of his special parking place. "Good students, both of them. But you never can tell. I've made some poor choices before. Anyway, it's only for one year, and then we'll decide."

"One year?"

"To see how we get along. Architectural graduates have to spend three years working with a licensed architect before they can be licensed themselves, but all three years needn't be with the same architect."

Molly thought about that for a while. She had assumed that the young architects working in Kevin's office were his employees, to do the legwork that he couldn't do himself. It hadn't occurred to her that they might need him as much as he needed them.

"I never heard of a woman architect in Omaha," Molly remarked. "Is she unusual here?"

Kevin paused before he answered, watching the road in front of them. "Not so unusual. There are a number of women in the field now."

"I thought at first she was a man," Molly commented. "With that shirt and necktie. One of the boys."

Kevin nodded, eyes on the road. "Some women still believe they have to become like men in order to compete, even in the 1980s."

"Leatrice?"

"I don't know yet." They pulled into the oncoming lane to pass a slow-moving truck. "Architecture is a competitive field, and some women are very competitive."

"And how do they do?"

"The only limit to how far a woman can go is her own ability."

Cafe Vietienne, a small house on a quiet street, had no parking lot. Kevin parked the car on the street, then slid across the seat after Molly. While she waited for him to transfer to his chair, the street lights flickered, then steadied, although the western sky still held a rosy glow. They walked under small, dark-leafed trees, through the mottled shadows and dry leaves on the sidewalk. Through uncurtained windows she saw people moving, trays held high. An open gate invited them to come into the yard, stroll down the path and then turn to the left under a long blue awning.

"Smells marvelous, doesn't it?" Molly asked, breathing deeply, as she turned and stepped up under the awning.

"Molly."

She turned back. "Oh my gosh."

Something steely in Kevin's voice. "Did the restaurant claim to be accessible? Did you see a wheelchair symbol? Or did you just decide for yourself?"

"Oh, no, no, it wasn't the restaurant. My fault. I—I came and looked. I stood at the gate and looked straight ahead at the awning. I should have walked up to see this step at the door. Oh, Kevin, I don't know what to say. I am so dumb." She turned and stepped down beside him.

"It takes getting used to. It's okay."

"I'm so sorry." Should she offer to help him up the single step? She could do it. She had bumped her son Joey's stroller up onto the curb hundreds of times, when he was small. It couldn't be that different. No, Kevin wouldn't like that.

"Shall we just go home, Kevin? Or pick some place that you know. I'll still take you to dinner."

"Watch this." He leaned forward, then quickly thrust backwards, pulling up on the handrims. The chair tilted back onto its big wheels, back, back. Oh dear, Molly thought, he's going to tip over! But Kevin's hands had moved to the hand rims, turning them forward, backward, balancing the chair on the big wheels while the little wheels in front rose off the ground, higher, higher, until they topped the stair. Quickly he spun the hand rims forward and the big wheels rolled up onto the higher walk.

He turned to her, grinning. "I haven't popped a wheelie for I don't know how long."

"It's dangerous!"

"Could be. Come on, let's eat."

"How will you get down?"

"That will be even more dangerous."

Molly continued to apologize until they were settled at their table, when Kevin insisted, "It was a mistake. Forget it." He turned to the menu—she should have known he would be an expert on Vietnamese food—and proceeded to order.

The Vietnamese egg rolls arrived first, eight little fried pillows along with bowls of sauces and vegetables. Kevin reached across the table. "Give me your hand," he said. What now? Too much excitement for one evening. He laid a lettuce leaf on her open palm, filled it with vegetables, sauce and a pillow, and then showed her how to fold the whole thing into a tidy packet. Once she had bitten into it, she couldn't put it down. She knew it would fall apart if she let go. Three bites, and the roll was gone. She sipped her wine, then tried an egg roll of her own. Her packets weren't as neat as his. Juices ran down her hand. By the time their plates had been cleared away and fragrant seafood soup set in front of them, she had forgotten her blunder with the step.

They talked some more about his project, the retirement complex. He was trying to convince his client that a daycare center for the employees' children on the grounds would keep the staff happy and also brighten the lives of the elderly residents. Molly kept thinking about Leatrice, with her little necktie, shoulder to shoulder with the other architects.

"I can't get that young woman out of my mind," she said. "She's so professional."

"Let's hope so," Kevin murmured.

"Taking her place in a man's world. Young women today are so different from what my friends and I were like when we were that age."

"If they have it easy, professionally, it's because women like you paved the way for them."

"If my friends and I had had a tenth of her assurance," Molly mused. "No one I ever knew aspired to be an architect. A girl like that—we weren't women in those days—would have been a real trailblazer. We were secretaries and nurses, maybe even teachers, if we worked at all." She chased a shrimp around her bowl with her chopsticks. "Of course, none of us really expected to work. A profession was something to fall back on if some tragedy happened."

"Like losing your husband," he said quietly.

"Or a divorce." She thought for a moment. "That was disgrace as well as tragedy. Times have sure changed."

"But you didn't become a secretary or a nurse."

"No, I went from the protection of my family to the protection of my husband without pausing for any independence in between." They waited while the waiter removed their bowls, and set down an array of colorful dishes.

Kevin heaped a mound of rice on her plate, then helped her to portions of each dish. "You ran a business with your husband."

"I learned on the job. School of hard knocks. Not worth a lot on the job market."

"More than you think." He took her hand across the table again. No lettuce leaf this time. "I know lots of people, Molly. Let me help you find a better job."

"I couldn't do that to Louise. I promised her a year."

"But she has you doing work you never agreed to do. Crisis calls. Running to the post office. Wait until the weather changes. That decrepit, drafty old building. You could be in an elegant office with people who don't dump problems on you."

She laughed and pulled her hand back. "You want to rescue me. They tell us in training not to do that. When you rescue someone, you take away her initiative. Then you become responsible for her."

"I wouldn't mind that."

Molly caught her breath. She could hear her heart beat so loudly—surely Kevin could hear it too. She didn't know what to say. They liked each other; they had settled that this afternoon, without speaking. She was beginning to feel so comfortable with him. It seemed as if they could talk about almost anything, except the attraction between them. She wasn't ready yet—she didn't know how—to talk to him about that.

Kevin's voice took on a formal, lecturing tone. "I'm sure you know," he said, "that something sometimes occurs between two people that is popularly called chemistry. Even though it's not correct to label it a physical force, Molly, you can't deny that it's there between us, and I think we should do something about it."

Molly pushed the food around on her plate, not looking at him. Finally she said, "Can we postpone this conversation for a few weeks, until we know each other better?"

Kevin looked hurt. "I was only leading up to inviting you to a picnic this Sunday. I want you to meet some of my friends."

Meet my friends! Molly knew this would be no ordinary picnic. Meeting each other's friends was an important step in a courtship, when your crowd or his inspected the latest attachment, and gave or denied their blessing. But Louise had already invited Molly to a gathering of her friends on that day. "I promised Louise I'd go to a party with her on Sunday."

"Louise! You see her every day. Give yourself a break."

Would Louise understand? When they were teenagers, it was a given that you could break a date with girlfriends if a boy asked you out. Molly looked up at Kevin. He was six-years-old, waiting for approval. She said, "Kevin, I'd love to meet your friends."

NINE

So many wheelchairs! Had she ever seen so many wheelchairs assembled in one place before? Half the people gathered on the lawn were seated in shiny chromium. Her mother's voice in her head reminded her, "Don't stare! Act natural." But their mothers' voices weren't reminding them. They were all looking at her, appraising the woman Kevin had brought to the party. Well, Molly was prepared for their scrutiny. Kevin had told her the picnic was an annual reunion of all those who had shared the rehabilitation floor in the hospital many years ago. Molly had expected them to be curious about her.

Kevin introduced their hosts, "my old friends John and Faith Wheeler," and Molly murmured the proper responses. They were older than Kevin, by ten or fifteen years. John was tall, his full head of hair glistening silver. Kevin had said he was a sharp attorney, but he looked like a country storekeeper, stooped-shouldered, wearing old jeans. Could his shoulders look like that from decades of pushing Faith's wheelchair?

But Faith's wheelchair was electric. She directed it with a little switch on the arm, back, forward, back again until she and Kevin were close enough to exchange a kiss. The motor made a little whirring sound as she moved. She smiled up at Molly. Pale, thin face. Wispy gray halo. Brown eyes asking, who is this woman Kevin has chosen?

I can do that, too, Molly thought, returning the measuring look. There was an air of frailty about Faith, as if the setting she was placed in, the chair, the loose blue denim dress, were somehow too big, too rough for her. Stick-thin arms projecting from the oversized sleeves contrasted with the sturdiness of the fabric. One hand stayed on the switch, the other rested, palm up, in her lap, delicate skin covering fine bones.

"And how did you meet this lovely lady?" Faith demanded, after her inspection.

Kevin looked up at Molly and grinned. "I found her in a parking lot."

"Is that something for now or for later?" Faith asked, nodding at the bowl in Molly's hands.

"It's dessert, tiramisu," Molly answered.

"Then it goes to the refrigerator," Faith ordered. "Come with me. You can meet the others later."

Molly followed Faith in her whirring chair down a walk and across a broad patio. Brilliant blossoms in wooden planters marked the edges of the smooth concrete—nasturtiums, chrysanthemums, and petunias. Those little pansies, violas, that Ben had mixed into their salad. Pale purple chive blossoms. Dark purple leaves, were they basil? And was that parsley, in with the flowers?

"Do you like my borders? John built them for me," Faith said, brushing her hand against the foliage.

Molly saw that the planters were just the right height to be tended from a chair.

"I decided to be different this year. Everything I've planted here is edible," Faith continued. "All my flowers. Every one of them."

She opened a wide screen door—Molly jumped to catch it with her shoulder—and led the way down a long hallway, also unusually wide. No doors inside, just broad openings into a living room on one side, a dining room on the other. Beyond, another opening into the kitchen.

Faith turned her chair, backwards, forward, to face Molly. "I'm so glad you could come today. We're all so eager to meet Kevin's new girlfriend."

Molly felt her face grow pink and warm. Not again! Oh, damn. *O sole mio.* She had tried to program herself not to blush today. "I'm not exactly Kevin's girlfriend," she explained. "We're really just neighbors. New neighbors," she added, reflecting on Faith's 'new.' Was there an old girlfriend? She remembered the scarves in the glove box.

"Let's make some room for your dessert." Faith wheeled over to the refrigerator, opened it, and started moving platters and bowls around on the shelves, onto her lap—"Oh, that's cold!"—and back into the refrigerator. "Here," she said, "this can go in the oven now. It's Kevin's favorite."

Faith held out a large casserole, but Molly was still clutching her dessert. Kevin's favorite? In the last few weeks, Molly and Kevin had eaten together many times, but Molly couldn't name his favorite.

Faith placed the baking dish in her lap, took Molly's bowl and put it into the refrigerator. By the time Molly reacted, her "Can I help?" was too late. Faith had rolled away and placed the casserole on a counter. Which one of us is supposed to be helpless? Molly thought. Score two points for Faith, one for speed and one for Kevin's favorite. And one more for the tiramisu. Faith hadn't hesitated a minute over it, while Molly had never heard of the Italian version of trifle until yesterday, when she went to the library to find a recipe for an unusual, impressive dish to bring to the pot luck.

"Just some cheese for the top before it bakes," Faith said, removing the plastic wrap from the top of her casserole. "Can you do that?"

"Of course," Molly answered, taking the block of cheddar and the grater that Faith handed to her. Tortillas wrapped around some kind of black bean mix. Enchiladas? How did Faith know this was Kevin's favorite? He'd never told Molly that he liked Mexican food.

Faith moved around the kitchen in her chair, opening big drawers under the counters and pulling out napkins, plates, and bowls. "So you and Kevin are new neighbors," she said. "Are you new to Seattle, or just new to the neighborhood?"

"I moved from Nebraska," Molly answered. Good. That means Kevin hasn't told Faith much about me.

"I love your big kitchen," Molly commented, carefully pushing the cheese down against the metal grooves. "You have some wonderful touches. The knife slots here. The tile inlay."

"Oh, yes," Faith answered, leaning from her chair into one of the big drawers. "Isn't Kevin a marvelous cook? Or hasn't he cooked for you yet? But then his man Ben is a good cook, too."

One more point for Faith. She sticks to her subject. Aloud, Molly said, "Yes, some of the details in your kitchen are a lot like Kevin's."

"But didn't Kevin tell you?" Faith looked up from rummaging in the big drawer. "He designed this kitchen. This house was his first commission. There aren't many kitchens around like ours, not in Seattle."

"I didn't know that." Molly concentrated on scattering the shreds of cheese evenly over the tops of the tortillas. "I guess I just assumed that a lot of people…" three weeks ago she couldn't have said this…"I mean, people in wheelchairs—would have low counters. And knee holes under the sink."

"Oh, my dear, you can't imagine how difficult it was to convince an architect to lower the sink. Until Kevin."

A handful of cheese spilled over the side of the dish. "I thought he was a boy when you met. Not an architect," Molly said, brushing the cheese shreds into a little pile.

"He was a boy then. We were all very young, though we called ourselves adults. I was twenty-three when I had polio. And Kevin was thirteen, fourteen. He was special, the youngest among us, almost a pet. We've all kept in touch since. Kevin was ready for his first independent commission just at the time that we had reached a dead-end, trying to find someone to design a house for me. And here we are."

Faith rolled closer to Molly, peering at the black bean enchiladas. "Lovely. Now we'll just let them bake," she said, placing the casserole on her lap. She rolled up beside the oven, opened the door, pulled out the shelf and pushed the baking dish inside. "There. Now let's meet the other guests."

The day slid by. Molly moved in and out of the house, from the lawns to the indoor pool, sometimes with Kevin or Faith, sometimes on her own. She made a point of meeting everyone, learning their names, telling them, yes, she was almost settled and she loved Seattle.

How ordinary it seemed, most of the time. The flowers, the women in their lovely late summer dresses, all might have been lifted from the pages of a home and garden magazine. Some of the men joined in a raucous game of water polo, splashing the spectators. Only the lift swinging out over the water, the cluster of wheelchairs at one corner, conveyed the therapeutic purpose of the pool. John warned her, "You may not like to swim here. We keep the water a little on the warm side."

Kevin's friends reminded her of her Omaha circle. A bit older, perhaps. They greeted each other with hugs and kisses, the able-bodied bending down to reach the wheelchair-bound. Some of them had the same habit that Kevin had, of lifting themselves up in their wheelchairs every few minutes. Not all of them; Faith didn't do it. They talked about their children, their travels, friends who weren't present. The women traded recipes, and the men discussed cars.

"Henry has a new Dodge pop-up with an electric lift," Molly heard. Eavesdropping on the men was more interesting at the moment than grandchildren.

"Yes, I guess that helped. He was pretty depressed when he had to switch to the power chair."

"We're all getting older."

"I hate to think it. I'll do almost anything to keep pushing my own chair, but I know my arms aren't as strong as they were last year."

"We did it to ourselves. All those marathons."

"Basketball. Who ever thought we would wreck our shoulders?"

"But it was sure fun while it lasted."

"Yes, each time you think you can't live with the next step, but when it comes…"

They were quiet for a moment. Then, "Kevin, are you still driving that muscle car, the old convertible?" someone teased. "When are you going to switch to the van?"

"October first, probably. Whenever the rain begins."

In the late afternoon, another couple arrived, the man in a more massive wheelchair than any of the others. "Oh, there's Walter Seemons," Faith told her. "Come with me. You must meet him."

Molly followed along to the new arrival, hanging back from the chairs that crowded around him. She saw a handsome man sitting very straight in a chair that rose up behind his head. He was the only man there dressed in a coat and tie, and he wore some kind of hard plastic collar around his neck. She noticed that everyone greeted Walter by touching him. The women kissed him or brushed their hands across his cheek; the men reached out and tousled his hair.

"This is Molly Bennet," Faith was saying, as Walter turned his head to look at her. "Kevin's friend."

"So happy to meet you," he said.

Molly started to put her hand out, then pulled it back. Both of Walter's hands were wrapped with straps and metal, and lay unmoving on the armrests.

His eyes flickered. Had he seen her interrupted movement? Someone came up on his other side and touched his face. He blew into a tube coming up from his collar, and turned away.

Molly stared after him. Faith's voice at her elbow startled her. "Walter is the only quad among us." Faith's brown eyes were testing her. "Quadriplegic, that is."

"Is that why you all touch his face? Because he can't move?"

Faith shook her head. "Because he can't feel. He's starved for physical sensation."

"My God." A shiver ran down her spine as Molly watched Walter progress through the crowd, moving the enormous chair with little puffs of breath into the tube. "And where's his wife? I didn't meet her."

"His attendant. I imagine she took off for the rest of the day."

———

Just before supper, when the other guests were arranging their bowls and plates on the long buffet table, John took Molly's elbow and led her to a bench near the edible flowers. She saw a look pass between Faith and John as Faith rolled into the house; they had planned this tete-a-tete ahead of time.

"We think a lot of young Kevin, you know," John began.

"And he's very fond of you," Molly responded.

"We go back a long time," John continued slowly.

"You all met in the hospital," Molly prodded. "Kevin told me."

"But in those days," John went on, as if she hadn't spoken, "things were different. People stayed in hospitals months and months. And they became like family." He rubbed his big hands back and forth across his knees. "Like family," he repeated.

"When I first met Faith, she was living at the hospital. She was out on a pass at a Sunday afternoon concert. And when I came to pick her up for our first date, that's when I met Kevin." He smiled at her. "I'll tell you a funny story. I tell it to everyone. You're the only person here who hasn't heard it a hundred times. When I came up to the ward to get Faith, I was really nervous. I didn't know how to act with the chair. And I took the doc aside, and I said, 'What should I do if I want to put my arm around Faith? Do I put my arm around her, or around the chair?' And he said to me, 'I don't know about you, but I never get much of a thrill out of hugging a chair.'"

He's telling me this, Molly thought, because he sees how awkward I act with Kevin.

But John went on. "Kevin didn't really belong on that adult ward. Some of the patients had polio, like Faith, but more of them were accident cases. They put Kevin in there because the children's ward was full of polio, and there wasn't any other place for him. And he and Faith became special friends. Faith told me then she thought of Kevin as the younger brother she never had."

Now it's coming, Molly thought, whatever it is that Faith and John want. To reveal some secret? To warn me off? But John wasn't quite ready. "Kevin told me you are a widow, Molly. Tell me about your husband. Was he ill for a long time?"

Molly sucked in her breath and sat up straighter. That is no concern of yours, she thought. She stared at John, but saw in his eyes a clear compassion and concern. She stopped herself from saying the words that had first come into her mind. *How many years have you been with Faith? It must be at least forty.* Instead she said, "There were days when it seemed like forever, but in the course of a lifetime, no, Ted's illness didn't last a long time."

Just at that moment, there was a crash and a shout. John looked toward the house, jumped up and ran off.

"What happened?" Molly asked Kevin when they found each other, lining up for the buffet supper.

"It was nothing. John worries so. Faith dropped a casserole she was taking out of the oven and spilled some on her lap, but she didn't get burned. That was all."

Outside on the patio, Molly could see Faith moving around from table to table. She was wearing a different dress.

Molly's tiramisu was a great success, the first container on the dessert table that was emptied. She had to tell them over and over how she had assembled the layers of ladyfingers, coffee liqueur and mascarpone cheese, and that the Italian name meant "pull me up."

After the plates and food had been cleared away, the guests moved to the living room to watch the slides of Faith and John's vacation. It took a long time for everyone to settle down. Since there wasn't enough room for all the wheelchairs, some people transferred onto the sofas, and John moved their chairs away. Others rolled around to get the best views.

Kevin transferred to the sofa next to Molly, casually draping his arm over the fat cushions behind her. Someone moved to her other side, and she found herself pressed against Kevin, under his outstretched arm. When the lights went down, his arm fell lightly on her shoulders. It was hard to concentrate on the slides—some place in South America—with Kevin's hand touching the bare skin of her arm. Around them, other couples were holding hands or cuddling. Like the necking parties in high school, Molly thought, tingling with awareness of Kevin. Here, in this room, we are a couple. You're acting like a teenager, she scolded herself. Yes, but I feel like a teenager. Except this time around I'm enjoying it.

———

In the swirl of guests gathering casseroles and coats, transferring back to their chairs and hugging each other good-bye, Molly found herself sitting in a corner, no, trapped in a corner, opposite Walter Seemons.

"I'm sorry that I upset you," he said, looking directly into her eyes.

"You didn't upset me," she tried to assure him.

"Frightened you, then."

She decided to be completely honest. "I've never met a quadriplegic person before."

He nodded. "Horrible, isn't it?"

She didn't know how to respond.

"When I first found out, when I woke up after the accident, I was sorry I had survived." He watched her face as he talked. "Then I decided that if I had to be quadriplegic, I'd be the best damned quad in the world."

"And are you?"

"Best I know. People could envy me, after they're done praising the Lord they're not in my shoes, I mean, in my chair, of course." He smiled. "I'm a wealthy man. I buy the best equipment there is, hire the prettiest girls to cart me around. I don't look like a bum. Anybody feeding me drips on my clothes is fired."

The current pretty girl had arrived at his side. "Any time you're ready, Walter."

"Good-bye, Miss Molly. Next time I hope we have more time to talk."

"Good-bye, Walter. I hope so." She smiled at him, then reached out, as she had seen the others do, and stroked his cheek.

"Gimme a kiss," he said.

Well, why not. She stood up and leaned forward, her lips aimed for his cheek. He turned his head, and his mouth, wet and open, covered hers. She jumped back and glared at him. He laughed. The attendant was laughing too.

"You're all right, Molly," he said, as they moved away from her.

She rubbed her hand across her mouth, wiping away his kiss. What an awful thing to do. Why me? Had anyone seen it? Kevin? When she told him... Would he be angry? And yet, if Walter was so starved for physical sensation.... She looked around the room. No one was watching. She couldn't make a fuss. Maybe she'd just forget it. Not tell Kevin. Where was he?

She found him at the door, with Faith and John. "This will only take a few minutes," Kevin assured her, as the last of the other guests left the house.

"An architectural consultation," John added. "Faith wants to add a greenhouse."

"You can keep me company," Faith said, leading the way to the kitchen. "I'm just going to put a few things away."

"Don't you want to go along?" Molly asked. "I mean, it's your greenhouse."

Faith shook her head. "No, no. John knows what I want, they don't need me." The chair whirred forward. "But I'm glad we have this time to talk."

I'll bet you're glad, Molly thought.

Faith pulled the dishwasher open and waved away the cloud of steam. "There are some towels hanging under the sink behind you." She took the towel Molly handed her, folded it, and laid it in her lap. "If you will put the cups in that drawer," she said, pointing, "I'll take care of these." She lifted the silverware basket and set it on her lap.

"Can you hold that on your lap? Weren't you burned?"

"No, I'm fine," Faith said, moving away. "I guess I'm lucky, if having polio can be considered lucky. You know, Kevin would have burned himself badly if he had been in my seat."

"Yes, but Kevin is always very careful. He puts a thick pad on his lap before he sets anything hot down."

"As I should too. And I probably would if I couldn't feel the heat, like Kevin can't. Although maybe I wouldn't. Kevin thinks things out so carefully, and I just let things happen." Faith went on arranging the silverware in the drawer without speaking for a few minutes. Then she said, "That is, I let things happen to me. When it's my family or someone I care about, I plunge ahead and try to change things." She looked up at Molly. "I guess you think I'm a nosy, controlling old woman."

"Well, I don't know you well enough to judge," Molly laughed, patting the towel against the tops of the cups in the lower rack. "Ask me again later."

"If you're around later," Faith said, shoving the drawer closed and rolling back to face Molly. "Are you going to stick around? That's what I want to talk about."

"That's not entirely up to me..." Molly said, but Faith interrupted.

"It is entirely up to you. I know Kevin. I watched him grow up. I see the way he looks at you. I don't want to see him hurt again."

"Again?"

"You didn't know Kevin was married?"

Molly shook her head.

"Well, there I go, plunging in where it's none of my business. But Kevin's welfare is my business. And I'm sure he'll tell you, when he thinks it's time."

"Then maybe we should wait," Molly murmured.

"Not good enough," Faith insisted. "Not for me. I want to know if you intend to stay, or walk out."

Is that what happened? His wife walked out? Why, because he's disabled? She wouldn't ask Faith. "Kevin is such a private person," Molly said. "He wouldn't like this conversation, if he heard it."

Faith was unstoppable. "It took Kevin a long time to get over her. I want to know about you."

What a strong person you are, living in that frail body! Molly thought. "I know about loss," she said carefully, "but Kevin and I aren't exactly a couple yet." Although what had she been thinking, just a few minutes before? "So it's a little too soon to talk about either one of us leaving."

They heard the men returning. "I'll be watching," Faith promised.

I'm sure you will be, Molly thought, but she let Faith have the last word.

There was no reason why Kevin should have told her he was divorced, Molly assured herself as they drove away from John and Faith's home. Still, she would have liked to learn it from him, and not from a stranger. But he had no obligations to her. Probably he had intended to tell her himself, when he felt like it. After all, this was 1983. It wasn't as if divorce was the disgrace it had been in her parents' time, or even when she and Ted were young. Though it was certainly not as common then as now. In fact, few of their friends were divorced. Only Ron and Cathy, and that had been a relief to everyone. She remembered how they all had cringed at the way Ron belittled Cathy: "Oh, what do you know, you're so stupid," he would say, or something far worse. He was so humiliating to Cathy. Now she knew that humiliation was a form of abuse. Ron had actually been an abusive husband, a psychological batterer. She knew that now, from her training course, but she hadn't she known enough then to have been of some help to Cathy.

"Why so quiet?" Kevin asked. They were speeding along the freeway toward the lights of downtown Seattle. "Didn't you enjoy the party? Was it awful?"

"No, it was fun," Molly said. "I liked the people." She would definitely never tell him what Walter had done.

"Even Walter Seemons? Walter has a way with women he's just met. Did he catch you?" Kevin sounded amused.

"You knew what he might do, and you didn't warn me?"

"Well, I wasn't sure that he was coming, so I didn't think I needed to.... Besides, he's pretty harmless. He's a quad, after all."

"You could have told me and you didn't? I should be angry at you," she laughed. "Then I'm not going to tell you what I thought of your wonderful house!"

"Thank you. It has worn very well, and it still works for Faith and John."

"Why didn't you tell me you designed it?"

"I don't know. I guess I left it for Faith, because I knew how much she would enjoy telling."

"Oh, yes."

"One of Faith's pleasures is spreading news," he went on. "She likes to be the first to know and tell, and I try to indulge her in that."

"Well, she certainly had her chance tonight."

"What awful things did she reveal about me?"

Molly glanced over at Kevin. In the dim glow from the instrument panel, she saw that he was smiling. "She said the casserole that she dropped, the black bean enchiladas, are your favorite food. I didn't know you like to eat Mexican."

He laughed. "That! Forty years ago, when I first knew Faith and John, it was my favorite food. I don't eat like a teenager any more."

"She said they were your very first clients."

"And I am ever grateful for that. Taking a chance on me."

"But she also said that no other architect would design a house for her."

"They had a problem. Back then, it was hard to find someone to design for the disabled. Now there's more acceptance."

"So they should be grateful to you, too."

"No, Molly, it doesn't work that way. Do you know how hard it is for young architects to get started? No one, except a relative or very good friend, is going to entrust his or her project to an untried architect. I owe them. After the wheelchair crowd saw their house, I did some remodels and then some smaller homes, and then people started to call who weren't disabled at all. But someone had to believe in me enough to give me that first opportunity."

So that explains Faith, and why Kevin puts up with her, Molly thought.

"She also told me..." Molly began.

"What?"

"She told me you had been married."

"What?" The car lurched a little from side to side. "Faith told you? I can't believe she'd do that!"

"Believe it."

"Molly, it wasn't anything I was trying to keep from you. Don't think..."

"Of course not. Divorce isn't a nasty secret these days."

"That woman. She thinks she's my mother." She heard the exasperation in his voice.

"Your sister," she murmured, but Kevin wasn't listening.

"It was all over so long ago," he protested. "I hardly ever remember that I was once married."

"But you let me go on and on talking about Ted."

"That's different. Ted is important to you. My ex-wife—my marriage—just isn't a very important part of my life anymore. I don't even know where she is."

Molly couldn't resist asking, "Faith said she left you, but she didn't say why."

"Didn't Faith tell you? I'm surprised that she left something for me."

"I wouldn't let her tell me more."

"Well, there's not a lot to tell." They were approaching the exit to West Seattle. For a moment, driving took all of Kevin's attention. They swung off the freeway and headed over the bridge. Then he continued. "She was an architect. We met in college. And when we graduated, we both became associates, with different firms, so that we wouldn't compete."

Far off, on Puget Sound, Molly saw the winking lights of ferries passing on the dark waters.

"We each worked on our own projects, but we had architecture in common, and that was great for about ten years, until…I became successful first."

Architecture is a competitive field, she remembered Kevin saying, and some women are very competitive, but wasn't it—isn't it still? —hard for a woman to succeed in a man's world?

"It wasn't that I was the better architect. It was just that I had recognition, a reputation, before she did. I tried to advise her on ways to advance, changing firms, but she wouldn't listen to me. It became harder and harder for her to live with my success, and she wouldn't take my advice. Then she couldn't live with it, so she left."

She believed him. The other idea, that his wife—whatever her name had been, Molly didn't want to know—that his wife had left because of his disability, that was Molly's problem. She was the one who had a hard time accepting Kevin as he was. Caring, generous, loyal, successful, handsome—but still a man in a wheelchair. Not now, of course, not at this moment. Racing up the hill to their apartments, driving faster than she would but still in complete control, now he was whole. The way he talked to her, the concern in his voice. His disability wasn't a problem for him or that unnamed ex-wife, it was Molly's.

They reached the parking lot and pulled into Kevin's marked space, where she had parked the rental truck only six weeks ago. She opened the door on her side and swung her legs out of the car. She heard Kevin sliding across the seat behind her. He was talking about Faith again. How could she have violated his privacy like that? Old friends, even surrogate family, had to draw a line somewhere. What did she think she was doing?

Molly knew. Faith was trying to protect him. Maybe she was testing Molly. Maybe Faith sensed her ambivalence, but Molly didn't want to be the instrument of the end of that long and deep friendship.

"Don't be so hard on Faith," she said, turning back toward Kevin. He was right behind her, one arm on the back of the seat, the other stretched out to the dashboard. She had turned into the circle of his arms. He brought his left arm around her.

"Faith," she stammered, nose to nose. "She didn't mean to hurt you."

"I'm hurt," he said. "You can make it well." Their first kiss.

TEN

OCTOBER

Molly looked up from her computer when the phone rang. At the other desk, Patty, head bent sideways to hold the telephone receiver in place, lifted a pencil to point at Molly. You take it. Molly picked up the phone with one hand and with the other pulled a sheet marked "Telephone Screening" from the box at her side. How easy the routine had become.

"Hello, this is SCAWF." They had one bed left. She hoped the caller would be a single woman, and not someone with kids. She had already told three callers today that there wasn't enough room for a woman with children.

Man's voice, asking for Christine. She plunged into the incoming call routine. "We don't give information about residents at SCAWF." Never say "I'm sorry, but…"

A testy edge to his voice. "I need to talk to her."

"This is our policy. I can take a message, and if we have someone by that name here, I'll give her your message. If she's here and wants to talk to you, she'll call you."

"Let's not play games." Now he was angry. "I know she's there. I left my name last night, but she didn't call."

"Then either she doesn't want to talk to you, or she's not here." Molly glanced up at the board. No Christine in residence.

"So what am I supposed to do? Call every damn shelter in town and leave my name? Is that what you expect me to do?"

Molly sighed. "I don't expect you to do anything, but if you're trying to get a message to Christine, then that's what you'll have to do."

"And what if she doesn't call back?"

95

"Then I guess she's sent you a very clear message, hasn't she?" She held the phone away from her ear, waiting for the crash. *Bastard! I hope you broke your phone!* She turned back to her computer. If no one else interrupted, September would be balanced out by the end of the day.

The buzzer sounded. Patty's head still bent to the phone. Molly walked around her desk to the intercom. Front door. "Hello?"

"Louise here."

She pressed the button for the electric door opener. A gust of wind swept down the hallway. Louise followed shortly, her hair in wispy strands escaping from her ponytail.

"I'm sorry, I've got my key here somewhere but I couldn't wait to find it. It's really blowing hard."

"It's okay." Molly's mind was back on the computer.

Louise opened the desk drawer and took out the big key ring. "Oh, my goodness, what a nice surprise. You cleaned the closet."

"Well, I had the volunteers do it." Molly had half-expected Louise to hang up her coat without even noticing the new order in the closet. In place of the old jumble of stacked containers, the shelves were now lined with open white boxes, labeled "Baby Care," "Dental," "Hair products," "Medications."

"It's something I've been wanting to do since my first day here," Molly added.

"It looks so nice."

"Yes, well, it will be much easier to find things if we keep it in order. See, we put the items we reach for most often, like the shampoos and the tampons, right in the middle, and the things we don't use all the time, like the vaporizer, on the top shelf." *Am I getting through to you, Louise? I know who sticks everything on the middle shelf.*

"Good job, Molly. And while we're on jobs, I'd like to talk to you about planning for the gala, and for our Christmas campaign. It's already the first week in October."

"Can it wait 'til I'm finished here? I've almost got last month wrapped up."

"I meant later. Could you possibly stay tonight, Molly? The board is meeting here, fruit and cheese, and I'd like to talk to you right after that."

"Tonight? Actually, I was hoping I could leave early tonight…"

"Is something wrong?" Louise seated herself in the chair next to Molly's desk. She was wearing her social worker's face again.

"No, well, yes. I'm a little upset. Tammy left today." Molly wanted, no, she needed, comfort. She had invited Kevin to dinner that night. Not that she could talk to him about Tammy, that would violate confidentiality, but just to be with someone who cared about her. Someone who would recognize that she was distressed, and after the inevitable lecture about changing jobs, would try to cheer her up, talk about other things, fun things.

"Tammy's apartment came through? That's great. That's what we're working toward, isn't it?"

Molly shook her head. "She went home. Took her kids out of daycare and moved back with her husband. And it's not the first time. I checked her file. She's left him twice before, and every time she went back."

"Unfortunately, it's common, Molly. We've all had to get used to it. Many of the women who come here go back to their abusers repeatedly." She sat up straighter. "See what you've done to me now? I'm up on my soapbox." Her voice became deeper, slower. "Recent statistics show that women in shelters return to their abusers an average of five times before they make the final decision to leave them."

"But I was so sure Tammy was different," Molly objected. "We talked a lot yesterday, about making an appointment to get her hair cut and looking for a job. I know she wouldn't have left if she had let us trim her hair." She thought back to her first day at SCAWF, Tammy's shorn head burrowed into her shoulder.

"It's not your fault, Molly." Louise leaned forward in her chair. "It was her choice. That's what we're here for, to help the residents make their own decisions."

Easy for you to say, Louise, she thought. You haven't been working with Tammy every day, trying to build up her self-esteem.

"Molly? Did she tell how her husband got to her?"

"She called her mother, and he was there. He said it would be different this time. He'd gone to see a counselor. One visit."

Louise nodded. "Did you talk to her about a safety plan?"

"Oh, yes. We went over all the steps, so she's prepared to come back if she needs to." Molly straightened the Telephone Screening sheet on her desk.

"Contact a neighbor every few days, so someone knows she's all right. Hide some money. Keep a bundle of clothes ready." Molly looked across at Louise. "But she said she'd heard the sermon before. And she doesn't need a plan because she'll try harder this time."

Louise nodded again. "That's a sad thing about some of the women here. They won't get angry and blame their abusers. They feel ashamed of what's been done to them, as if the whole thing is their fault. And that makes it almost impossible for them to change their situations." She paused for a moment, and then frowned. "But it's still their choice, Molly. You have to maintain a distance. Don't let yourself get caught up in the clients' problems."

Louise went into her office and Molly turned back to the computer. Maybe if Louise had ever had children… She couldn't stop caring about Tammy, or any of the others.

The phone rang again. Who was Patty talking to? At this rate, she'd never balance September. "Hello, SCAWF?"

The voice came harsh and loud in her ear. "I need a bed. You people got a bed?"

"Y-yes, we may be able to help you," Molly answered. "I'll need to ask you some questions." She pulled the screening sheet close again.

"No questions! Just tell me if you got a bed or not."

"I'm sorry, but we don't work that way. Are you safe now? Can you talk?"

The voice drowned her out. "I'll talk when I get there, soon as you give me the address."

"Wait a minute, that's not how we work." Molly found herself shouting to be louder than the caller. "We don't give the address. We do a screening first. I have to ask you some questions to see if you're appropriate for our shelter." Appropriate! Was that part of this caller's vocabulary? "What is your situation? Are you in danger?"

"Look, I need a bed tonight. I'll tell you my situation later."

That wasn't enough. "Where are you now?"

"At a friend's house, but I can't stay here no more. You tell me where you're at."

Molly tried another tack. "Can you tell me a little more? About the abuse you've been subjected to and the person who has been abusing you?"

"Honey, you don't need to hear about that. Just tell me you have a place for me."

Molly looked toward Patty. No help. She took a deep breath. "I know it seems to you that we are asking too many questions, but this is a shelter for women who are in danger of being followed by their abusers. Is that your situation?"

"My boyfriend comes home every day and puts his fingers in my pussy to see if I've been with another man! That's my situation."

The phone slammed down in her ear.

"What's the matter? You look stricken." Patty was finally off the phone.

"I didn't handle that well." She couldn't repeat the conversation. "I didn't get through to that woman." What should she have done? She tried to think of the techniques she had learned in the volunteer training: active listening, paraphrase, affirming the caller's worth. Could she have done any of that?

Patty shook her head. "Don't feel bad about it, Molly, sometimes we just can't help the people who call. The woman I was talking to phones about once a week, but she can't bring herself to leave. We all try to listen to her, build her up. I should have cut her off, or put her on hold." Patty frowned at the pile of papers in front of her. "I'll take the rest of the calls. You've had enough for today."

"No. No, I'll be okay. I can take calls."

Another phone call. She hoped it was the woman who had hung up. As she punched the numbers onto the screen, Molly heard Patty asking the screening questions: Where are you now? Are you safe? If you leave, would your abuser try to follow you? What part of the city does your abuser live in? Where does he work? She knew Patty was trying to determine whether the caller really needed a confidential situation like SCAWF, or whether she would be safe in an open shelter.

Let Patty handle it. Don't think about them. Gas, electric, sewer, garbage. Where is the water bill? She pulled a folder closer.

"Molly! I have to talk to you! Now!" A woman plopped down in the chair next to her desk. Regina. She had been at SCAWF for three weeks, and with only one week left she knew the systems as well as Molly did. She also thought she knew what she was entitled to.

"Can it wait, Regina? I'm really kind of busy here."

"No. That's what you said to me this morning, and I'm still pissed."

"All right," Molly turned from the computer. "What is it?"

"That health nut has signed up for dinner again, two days in a row!"

"What?"

"Rosemary! She signed up to cook dinner again tonight, and that's what I wanted."

Molly shrugged. "You know the rules, Regina. Rosemary leaves for work at six-thirty, and signs up for her chore before she goes. If you want the job, you have to get here earlier."

"But you know what she cooked last night? Too foo. Bean crud. Too foo and broccoli on brown rice. In-edible! Nobody ate it. So I promised the girls I'd fry chicken tonight, with mashed potatoes and cream gravy. I took the chicken out of the freezer last night, but they wouldn't let me sign the chore sheet before I went to bed. It had to be after six a.m., that's what they said."

"That's right, that's the way it is. If you want to get up at six tomorrow, we'll let you have an alarm clock."

"You know what she's going to do to that chicken? Probably take the skin off and boil it. Some people going to be very disappointed."

The phone rang again. Molly glanced across at Patty, still on her call. She picked up the phone. A wispy little voice said, "I can't stay here anymore. I have to get away."

Molly looked up. Patty was writing on the board: "Margie—hold until 8 p.m."

"I'm very sorry," Molly said. "We're full now, but I can give you the names of some other shelters." As Molly dictated half a dozen phone numbers, she had the uneasy feeling that the woman wasn't writing any of them down. This was the hardest part of her job.

On the other phone, Patty was saying, "Go to the fish market on the corner of Fortieth and Stone. Call us from the phone booth in front. We'll give you directions from there." A short silence, and then Patty said, "What about a bus card? Do you have a bus card? Because you can call us collect."

———

Patty told her to go home early and Molly did, not even stopping to say good-night to Louise. Christmas could wait. Was it only last week that she had driven home in such a glow? Nothing had gone right today. Lots of volunteers had come in, willing, helpful women, but none of them had taken crisis call training. So in addition to taking the overflow calls and trying to close the books, Molly had had to find jobs for the volunteers. In the morning, she sent them to the day care room with Naomi. They were all moms, they could keep the kids occupied. After lunch, a new bunch arrived. Those she put to work cleaning storerooms and closets, sorting and discarding outdated handouts. There had to be a better system for utilizing volunteers! And the calls—listening to problems that had no solutions, turning women away. Then, Tammy! If only she had known the right things to say she could have convinced Tammy to stay.

A red sports car pulled out of the parking lot as Molly drove in. Leatrice Wood, the young architect she had met in Kevin's office. Leatrice honked and waved, but Molly didn't feel like returning the greeting. Kevin's other associate followed a few minutes later, nodding and smiling but keeping both hands on the wheel. Molly parked her car and shuffled through fallen leaves to her front door. Kevin was probably waiting for her. What plans had they made for tonight? Her place or his? She couldn't remember. Oh, right, she had invited him for dinner. She put the teakettle on to boil, kicked off her shoes and sprawled on the sofa, plumping the pillows to fit just right. The doorbell rang. She didn't bend to kiss his cheek, the way she had been greeting him ever since Faith's party.

"You're not glad to see me," he said, rolling past her into the living room.

"It's not you. Bad day." The kettle shrilled and he followed her into the kitchen.

"I can find you a different job…"

"Let's not go there today…"

As she measured loose tea into the pot and poured the boiling water over it, he moved around the kitchen, peering into her refrigerator and opening the oven. "It doesn't look like you're expecting company."

"I meant to stop at the fish place on the way home." She poured the tea through a strainer into a green glass cup, and pushed the cup across the table toward him. "Isn't that what we decided to do last night, do you remember?"

"I think we decided we're calling out for pizza. Or was it Chinese?"

"I've never in my life invited company for dinner, and then ordered take-out."

"I'll make the call."

ELEVEN

This will be for one night only, Molly promised herself, as she pulled into the garage. Past Kevin's blue van, toward the corner was Kevin's white convertible, up on blocks and wrapped in a dustcover, waiting through the winter like an automobile mummy. Well, why not? The ancient Egyptians mummified the objects they worshiped—cats and bulls and birds. Why shouldn't American men wrap their precious cars?

Just this once, she would park her car in the garage under Kevin's building. She'd told him that she couldn't afford to rent the space, but he had insisted that it was hers whenever she wanted to use it. Ordinarily Kevin kept the space next to his prize empty, so that no one would nick the side of his car with a wide-opened door, but he trusted her to leave and enter carefully.

Sometimes it was easier not to try to argue with Kevin, so she had put the opener in her glove box and continued to park in her usual place in the outdoor lot. But tonight, with the dress to carry and the rain coming down…. She didn't mind getting wet, but the dress, even in its plastic garment bag, was delicate, and it wasn't hers.

So she had convinced herself. The distance between Kevin's building and her own was much shorter than the run from the lot. Or she could leave the dress locked in the car, if she left the car in the garage, and take it out tomorrow.

Molly ran her fingers across the garment bag on the seat beside her, feeling the voluminous folds, making sure it had not slipped from its place. Did Cinderella have similar doubts about attending the ball? Maybe not about wearing a dress more magnificent than anything she had ever owned. And even though Cinderella had met her Prince Charming at the ball, she had left her pumpkin coach with no grand expectations, except to be there, while Molly had responsibilities, to make a good impression as a representative of SCAWF.

All the way home, she had mulled over the afternoon's events, trying to figure out what she might have done differently. The windshield wipers swished right, left, right, left, not fast enough. Raindrops had splattered across the glass, blurring the on-coming lights into deformed stars. Rain and darkness created strange new shapes along streets that had just begun to feel familiar. Shrubs and trees became looming figures, darkened buildings turned into abandoned castles. And here amidst the enchanted forest is Cinderella, Molly thought. Or maybe Red Riding Hood, setting out to face the big, bad wolf.

October in Seattle. The start of the formal social season. Who cared? She had never approved of grand balls, where wealthy people paid lots of money to spend the evening in elegant clothes and beautiful surroundings, all for the privilege of donating to good causes. Why couldn't they just give the money to charity without the party? The bill for the decorations alone would keep SCAWF alive for six months.

Molly had leaned forward against her seat belt to peer out at the darkness. Long-time residents had warned her about this, the first of the winter rains. Is that why the party season started now? Yesterday she had driven home from work into a beautiful sunset, crimson and gold streaked across the sky. Tonight the sky had turned gray at noon and continued to grow darker and darker, until the rain began to fall. Not a Nebraska kind of rain, a storm that pelted down, hard, for thirty minutes and then moved off, but a steady rain that had fallen continuously for five hours, and, according to the weather reports, would go on for at least six more.

She had driven slowly, hugging the side of the road, but the other drivers seemed to have no concerns about the slick surface, the limited vision. A truck passed, startling her with a shower of muddy droplets against the windshield. She had fumbled for the window washer switch, then remembered that it was located on the stem of the turn indicator, just like the rental truck. Suddenly she was back in that other vehicle. So much had happened in two months—her job, learning her way around Seattle, meeting Kevin. Kevin! He never missed an opportunity to try to push her into a better job. She knew exactly how he would scold her when he learned about today's episode. "Why did you let them do that to you? Why didn't you speak up for yourself? Let me find you another job."

Louise had called her into her office after lunch, and introduced her to one of the board members. It was typical Louise. "Oh, by the way, you didn't stay last night, and I meant to talk to you…" In front of a board member! How could she refuse the invitation—no, the command performance—for the New Century Gala, a charity ball that targeted five different causes for support, SCAWF among them? Apparently it had never occurred to Louise that Molly might not choose to attend.

Even Grace Hollings, the board member who had brought her a dress to wear, was startled to learn that Molly had not already consented to attend the ball in the borrowed gown. But what could Molly do? The SCAWF board was "making up tables," and they needed a dinner partner for Frank Alexander. So she was going to accompany the infamous Alexander, the powerful trustee of the foundation that gave so much money to SCAWF.

But first, she had to get out of her car.

Molly eased herself through a ten-inch opening, trying to keep from brushing up against the wet side of her own car as she held the door away from Kevin's convertible. At least it's dry in here, she noted, but with her headlights off, the corner wasn't a whole lot brighter than the parking lot. She walked around to the passenger side to remove the dress. Ducking her head into the car, she slid her arms under the plastic garment bag.

Something out there—was it a sound or a movement—grabbed her attention. She caught her breath. From the corner of her eye, she saw motion—a quick change of color—between the cars at the far end of the garage. She stiffened, bent into the car, heart pounding, mouth suddenly dry. Was someone crouching there? Maybe working at the shelter had made her overly suspicious. Cautiously she started backing out. She heard a rustle, coming closer. Someone was there, definitely, too low to be seen behind the parked cars. She licked her lips. What should she do?

"Molly! I'm glad you're home. I was watching for you." Kevin rolled out into the center of the garage.

Take a deep breath, she told herself. Relax. She stepped back out of the car and straightened up, the dress held out in front of her. A twinge of pain flicked across her back, her neck.

Kevin stopped his chair in front of her. "What's happened? Is something wrong?"

"You scared me," she said. "I didn't expect anybody down here." She worked her shoulders up and down, easing the stiffness in her neck. "I thought someone was sneaking around behind the cars."

"I didn't think I was sneaking," he said. "I'm just not very tall."

Oh, dear, not again. She thought she was past the stage of making dumb remarks about him.

"I was watching for you," he repeated. "I was beginning to worry, when I saw you pull into the lot and then change your mind."

"You shouldn't worry about me. I had to stay late at work." He was too much, sometimes. Watching for me. And yet, what if something—an accident, someone lurking in the garage—had happened? Who else would care? Who would notice if I didn't come home?

"I don't know if anyone's told you this, but the streets here are treacherous after the first rain," he said, turning his chair around. "All the oil dripped onto the streets over the summer comes up."

"Everyone's told me that," she replied. They were moving toward the elevator.

"Did you buy a dress?" Kevin asked.

"No." This was not a good time to tell him about the gala. Her heart was still pounding from the fright he had given her.

"I brought an umbrella. I'll walk you to your apartment."

"You don't have to do that. I won't melt."

"No, but the dress you're carrying might spot."

They came up to the first floor lobby without speaking. Kevin unfurled a huge, multi-colored umbrella and tried to hold it over Molly and the dress. "My arm's too short," he said. "Let me take the dress."

Molly folded the garment bag in half and laid it across his lap. Then she took the umbrella, leaning close to his chair so that the umbrella would protect him and Grace Hollings' gown. They hurried through the rain to her building, still not talking.

Why am I acting like this? she asked herself. I'm not angry with him. He is the closest friend I have in Seattle. Why not tell him what the dress is for? Then she answered her own questions. She didn't like to make him unhappy, or worse, angry. She wasn't ready for an argument, and she was angry enough, with herself, without Kevin's scolding.

———

After Molly had kicked off her shoes and started the water boiling for tea, they sat in her kitchen and she told him how Louise had drafted her to attend the charity gala. "It was the way she did it, Kevin, that upsets me. In front of the chairwoman of the ball committee. And they all think Frank Alexander is an impossibly difficult person, but he's so important to the shelter."

Kevin was furious. "That isn't part of your job, Molly. You should have compensatory time off if it is. Otherwise, you shouldn't have to go to an event like this if you don't want to, even if she asked you in front of the whole board. You shouldn't have to spend an evening with a Frank Alexander on your own time."

She poured the boiling water over the tea. "I think Louise thought I would welcome the opportunity. It's not the kind of event I would get to ordinarily. In college I loved to dress up, but since then—

"I could have taken you to one of the galas," he said, scowling at the tea she was straining into his cup. "If you had told me you liked that sort of thing. I support a lot of these causes, without going to the parties." Molly didn't tell him that she had just been thinking the same thing.

When they finished their tea, Kevin insisted that she take the borrowed dress out of its plastic wrapping and try it on. First she checked the label. "I don't know this name," she said.

"What is it?" he asked her.

"John Doyle Bishop. I've never heard of him."

"He was famous here in Seattle. He had a shop on Fifth Avenue and was well known for bringing fashion to Seattle. But he's not around any more. He died a few years ago."

She took the dress to her bedroom. Sheer silky ripples of iridescent color floated around her as she pulled it over her head. She twisted and twirled in front of her mirror, making the colors dance around her. Her eyes looked brighter, and her cheeks felt warm with pleasure. When she came out, she was Cinderella again, ready for the ball.

Kevin's eyes, too, were bright with admiration, and some deeper feelings that she read as a kind of regret, almost sadness. He reached out and seized her wrist. "I claim the first dance with you," he said, drawing her closer. He wrapped his arm around her waist, nearly lifting her off her feet.

"Kevin, no," she protested, but he had pulled her onto his lap. She pushed against his shoulders. "Kevin, let me go!" He was so strong! He held her with one arm, his other hand turning the chair back and forth in wide arcs. He began to sing, "Dancing in the dark..."

"Kevin, stop. Stop. You're hurting me."

He turned around a full circle and then stopped. She slid off his lap, shaking the bright folds of silk to straighten them. "What were you thinking?" she chided, rubbing her wrist. "You could have torn the dress."

With a forced smile he said quietly, "You will be the most beautiful woman at the ball."

TWELVE

Molly stood shivering at the bottom of a grand, sweeping staircase. She drew her shawl close around her shoulders. It wasn't warm enough, but the sheer wool wrap was the most appropriate thing she had to wear over Grace Hollings's gown.

At the top of the stairs, she could see a high-ceilinged room, all gold leaf and carvings, full of men and women in evening dress, the bright colors and glittering decorations of the women set off by the somber black and white of the tuxedoed men.

Every one of those men probably owns his own tuxedo, she thought. She tried to remember when she had last attended a formal event. It must have been a wedding. How the men in the family had grumbled when their nephews and nieces specified "black tie" on an invitation! Ted always claimed the rented jacket never felt quite right on him, and truth was, she always knew which men were wearing rented suits and which ones their own. If Ted were alive, she thought, I wouldn't be here, all alone. I wouldn't be about to spend an evening with a Frank Alexander, or anyone else who is useful but unpleasant.

Elegant couples came up behind her, waited, then stepped around her to climb the red-carpeted stairs. Grey-uniformed maids greeted them and carried away their coats and furs. She should go up too, and find the group from SCAWF. She shivered again. Was there no other woman at the party arriving by herself? In the portico, she had seen the glances from the car park valets as she emerged, alone, from her car.

Three couples came up behind Molly, the women comfortably linked on the arms of the men, all laughing and leaning forward to talk to each other. There wasn't room on the stairs for six people; there wasn't room for four. They bumped her as they passed, and the two on the end stared at Molly while they mumbled, "Excuse me."

Stop this self-pity, she scolded herself. This could turn out to be a wonderful evening, like nothing you've ever seen before. She licked her lips and stepped forward. Her knees were shaking. For a moment, she felt she might tumble down the stairs. She gripped the velvet rope, regained her balance and continued up. If I weren't all alone… What if Kevin had decided to attend this New Century Gala? He said he supported many causes, without attending the balls. There must be a way for wheelchairs to be brought up to the level of the party, an elevator tucked away somewhere, but he would miss the grand entrance, this moment of arriving at the top of the stairs. Possibly why he stayed away.

A maid approached and held out her hand for the shawl. Was that a scornful look or did Molly just imagine the sneer on her face? Molly shivered again. Without the shawl, she felt naked and unprotected. Where was the SCAWF group? There was not one familiar face among the dozens of flushed, animated faces. Their eyes looked right through her. She tried to slip sideways, cross the room, find Louise and the others, but no one would move out of her way.

A waiter came by with a tray of champagne glasses. She took one and a paper napkin. Her hand tightened around the glass stem, as if that little paper-wrapped rod was all that kept her afloat in this sea of strangers. The voices rose, shouting words in her ear that were not meant for her. The crowd pushed in and shoved her along. She felt sweat beading on her upper lip. More faces, close up, looking at her without seeing her. Just as she began to think she should turn and try to get back to the stairs, the crowd parted and tossed her out on the opposite side of the room, next to a tall, open window, the sheer curtains blowing inside. There was Grace Hollings, all in red, a champagne glass in one hand, a tiny, jeweled purse and a long red chiffon scarf in the other.

"My dear," she smiled at Molly, "we've been looking for you. How lovely you look." She came forward, put her cheek against Molly's and kissed the air next to her ear. "That dress is much more becoming to you than it ever was to me," she murmured, so no one else could hear. Then she stepped backwards and said, in her normal voice, "Frank Alexander was here just a minute ago. I will leave you under my husband's care while I go to find him."

Grace touched the arm of the tall man standing behind her and did the proper introductions, a first name that Molly didn't catch and, "Molly Bennet from SCAWF." He bent forward over a stiff white shirt and a protruding cummerbund to look down at Molly. For a moment, Molly had the impression that she was looking up at a giant penguin.

"So you're another of those hard-working board members that keep SCAWF going," he said. "Is my wife a terrible slave driver?"

"Well, actually, I'm a staff member," Molly corrected him. "I work under the director. I don't have a whole lot to do with the board."

"Oh, I see," he responded. His face became perfectly blank. "How very interesting."

Instantly Molly realized that she had said the wrong thing. She should have told him how wonderful and hard-working Grace was. How could she bring the conversation back to praise of Grace? She started to say, "But the few times I've come in contact with Mrs. Hollings…" when the expression on his face changed again.

Now he was looking at her in a puzzled way. "That is a lovely dress you are wearing," he said. "Do you know, my wife used to have a dress very much like yours, many colors like that, and it was always one of my favorites."

O sole mio. Should she tell him she was wearing Grace's dress? Had Grace not told him that she was lending a dress to Molly, or had he forgotten? She was saved from having to say anything by a man who came up on Hollings's other side. Hollings greeted him, introduced Molly—again, she didn't catch his name—and the two of them proceeded to have a conversation that ignored her completely.

What a relief! She was safe here, as Grace had said, in a husband's care—anyone's husband would do. What was important was having the black tuxedo by her side. Molly finished her champagne—it was warm now—and set the glass down on a table. In a moment, a waiter came by with a tray, whisked away the empty and left her with a new, cold glass. As she sipped it, she glanced around. The crowd was dividing into small groups, probably the ten persons who would make up each table at dinner. Was their group of ten assembled yet? Grace Hollings's husband was there, and two women, one a board member whom Molly had met in the shelter. Both wore elegant black dresses, one embellished with gold threads, the other with multi-colored beading. The two men behind them must be their escorts; they were too relaxed to be waiters. Louise stood in front of the window, talking to the one board member that Molly sometimes worked with, Hank Stevens, their accountant. Louise was wearing black, too, a long, straight gown with lots of pearls. Molly could see a white bra strap peeking out at the edge of her neckline.

So where is the tenth guest, Frank Alexander, my dinner partner? she thought. He must be the straight back she could see standing with Hank and Louise. His hands were tightly clasped behind his back, as if one hand feared the other might get away. While he stood there, he bounced up and down, rhythmically raising himself on the toes of his shiny black patent leather shoes. She wondered where Grace had gone, looking for him.

She must have been staring; the two women in black approached her, nodding and smiling. They both spoke at once.

"So good of you to come."

"Here is this year's sacrificial lamb."

"She means you will be Frank's dinner partner. We've all taken our turn, but never more than once."

A chime rang out, and the crowd began to stir. Tall doors at the far end of the room opened. Grace returned, the bouncing man turned around and Grace brought him up to Molly. She was right, he was the notorious Frank Alexander. "Mrs. Bennet." He ducked his head toward her in a stiff little bow, and looked her over, head to toe. He must have approved, because he offered her his arm, and they began to move toward the dining room.

All the beautifully dressed people were smiling and nodding to each other. Molly noticed some of the women look at her dress, up and down. She smiled, they smiled back, but their eyes went right through her. Only Frank Alexander was not smiling at anyone. The crowd swept them along to the open doors.

The orchestra played a loud fanfare. The lights dimmed. For a moment, the noise level dropped. The doors flew open, and the waiters paraded out, each carrying a silver tray ablaze with sparklers. They walked out onto the tiny dance floor in the center of the ballroom and stood in a circle, trays above their heads, until the sparklers had burned out and the room smelled of firecrackers. Then they fanned out through the dining room to remove the spent sparklers and serve the desserts, and the conversations at the tables resumed.

Molly had eaten too much, she knew, and Grace's dress already felt too tight, but she couldn't resist dessert. Each guest was served a little box whose sides and lid were made of solid bittersweet chocolate. The box was "tied" with ribbons and a bow of white chocolate, and it sat in a sea of raspberry sauce. When Molly lifted the lid—its handle was a candied violet—it was full of white chocolate mousse.

The whole dinner had proceeded in that way. Each course was announced with a dimming of lights, a dramatic orchestral flourish and a parade of waiters. Each dish from the composed salad to the salmon in lobster sauce to *maigret de canard*, which Frank told her was duck breast, lay on its plate in a complex and elegant presentation. None of the other guests at her table, or at any of the tables around them, seemed to be impressed with the food that the white-gloved waiters set down in front of them.

The coffee arrived, and with it a tray of accompaniments. Condiments for coffee! White sugar, brown sugar, chocolate chips, cloves, bits of candied orange peel, cinnamon sticks! Molly kept thinking, if only my friends in Omaha could see this! But she couldn't say that to the others at her table.

In fact, it was difficult to talk to anyone at her table, except for the two men on either side of her. The centerpieces—huge bouquets of multi-colored flowers—rested on tall glass pedestals, so that they did not interfere with seeing the guests across the table, but it was impossible to hear them amidst all the din of clinking silver, conversations and music. On the other side of the table, Grace and Louise were rising. Louise caught Molly's eye and said something, but Molly couldn't hear what it was.

The man on Molly's right muttered something, beginning with the words, "Oh, Lord." He glanced toward Molly, noticed that she had heard him, and shrugged. "I hate this kind of event, but you know, it brings a lot of money in to SCAWF."

"You're a good sport," she told him, "turning out for your wife tonight."

"My wife? My wife's causes are political." He studied her, amused. "I'm the SCAWF board member in the family."

"I'm sorry, I just assumed—"

"You assumed that only women would be interested in supporting a women's shelter?"

"No, no…well, yes, I guess I did."

On her left, Frank Alexander commented, "At this point the meter should commence running."

She turned toward him. "I beg your pardon?"

"The meter. The money meter. I'm speaking figuratively, of course," Frank said.

Pompous ass!

"If you could quantify the applause during the presentations," he continued, "you could calculate how much each agency generates…."

She watched Louise, mounting the stairs to the dais, step on the hem of her long skirt. Molly gasped and held her breath, but Frank went right on talking.

"…five social welfare groups, equitable beneficiaries, each agency expected to fill ten tables…"

The man behind Louise grabbed her elbow and steadied her. Molly exhaled, loudly. Frank frowned at her, but persisted, "…the less committed agency, not well run, a staff and board that doesn't work. It would be easy for them to slough off, so to speak, fill only eight tables. Then not withstanding their inadequate performance, when the money is parceled out, all five collect the same amount."

"Oh, of course," Molly murmured.

"We have to keep accounts," he went on. "Not join forces with that group again."

How petty! Molly thought. Maybe an agency was so busy helping needy people that there was no time left to go out selling places at a table for hundreds of dollars per person. What if, instead of spending a fortune for the flowers, the food, the lavish silvery draperies that transformed the room into the interior of a cloud, everyone in the room had stayed home and mailed a check to the charity of their choice? Then the agencies could collect even more of the money they needed so badly, and I wouldn't have had to spend an evening listening to Frank Alexander's monologues.

She sneaked a look at her watch. The food had been marvelous, but too much of the evening had been like the conversation that had just ended. Frank would make a derisive, judgmental statement that was outside of Molly's experience, and she would have to ask him to explain. Then he pontificated for five or ten minutes, tearing down anyone or any position he disagreed with. She had already learned, this evening, much more than she cared to know about the trust that Frank Alexander managed, the frivolous wishes of the clients who had set it up, and his own cleverness in keeping to their intentions while exercising his own stern authority toward the recipients of their generosity.

I wonder what Kevin is doing now, she thought. She couldn't help comparing this evening with the first dinner she had had with Kevin. He had been so interested in her. The had shared so much. When she and Frank parted tonight, they wouldn't know each other any better than they had before the party.

The orchestra played another flourish, the lights came up, and the master of ceremonies called for attention. Behind him, Molly saw a row of people, including Louise and Grace. As each agency was introduced, one or two persons stepped forward from the group and gave a short statement of their mission. Poor Louise! Even from where she sat, Molly thought she could see Louise quivering. She looked so thin and frail. Molly's table and the other nine from SCAWF applauded and cheered after Grace and Louise's comments, but Molly noticed that the tables from other agencies were scarcely paying attention. As soon as Grace and Louise stepped back from the microphone, the people at her own table turned their backs to the stage and resumed their conversations, all except Frank Alexander, who nodded with satisfaction or frowned at the response to each presentation.

"Very satisfactory. Very satisfactory showing." Frank surveyed the table with a smug expression. Then he turned to Molly. "You may take some pride, too, in this turn-out for your agency."

"No, I'm afraid I can't take credit," Molly said. "I had nothing to do with getting our supporters here."

Frank frowned. "No? Tell me, then, what is it you do at the center."

"Well, my title is program director. I keep things running—personnel, finance, house management—so the residents' needs can be taken care of."

"You don't do anything to drum up support?"

"Only if it's something like a big mailing to get out."

"A mailing," Frank repeated. He nodded his head several times. "Like that petition to pardon Rebecca Ryan you people put out. You have anything to do with that?"

"No." Molly was glad he couldn't blame that on her. "That was before I came to SCAWF."

Frank pursed his lips and nodded twice more. "A mistake for your SCAWF, I think. This Rebecca Ryan, killing her husband. You lose support when you undertake to justify an act like that."

"I'm sorry she couldn't get to us before she had to kill him," Molly said. "That's why we exist, to help people like Rebecca Ryan."

"No, you don't want to think like that," he objected. "She belongs in prison. That's not the kind of person you want associated with SCAWF."

"What was she supposed to do?" Molly asked. "She tried three times to leave him, and each time he found her and dragged her back."

"That's no justification for murder. We have laws, a legal system."

"She tried the legal system, and it failed her. The governor recognized that when he signed the pardon."

"I don't hold with people taking the law into their own hands," Frank snapped. He held his own hands up in front of him and turned slightly away from Molly.

End of conversation, he means. Last word. To her own surprise, Molly leaned forward, so that Frank would be sure to see her. "And I don't hold with a law that doesn't protect weak people."

Frank stared at her, open-mouthed. He started to say something. Molly was terrified at what she had done, at the prospect of SCAWF's losing the money from the trust because she had dared to contradict Frank Alexander.

Another fanfare, too loud to talk above. The stage lights brightened while the room lights dimmed. The orchestra began to play lively dance music, and a parade of models twirled across the stage.

Saved! For a while at least, she was saved by a show of the latest fashions from L'Aristocrat, the corporate sponsor of the gala. It makes sense for them, Molly thought. They put on an expensive event, but all the partygoers have to rush off to L'Aristocrat to buy the latest evening attire to wear to the gala. At least I don't have to make conversation with Frank Alexander for a while.

What had possessed her to argue with him? What could she say to him later, after the fashion show, to placate him? What had Louise called it, "putting out fires"? Is he angry enough at me to withdraw his support from SCAWF?

Maybe if I just pretend I didn't say anything. Comment on the clothes as if nothing happened.

Molly looked at Frank. He had turned his back to her and pushed back from the table to watch the stage, as if she didn't exist. Well, I might as well enjoy the show. Bright colors whirling around the stage. Models strutting. Sporty wear. Afternoon dresses.

Beyond Frank, the two women, leaning forward in their chairs, scrutinized the prancing models. "Look at her move that dress," one of them approved.

The second nodded. "She really has the walk."

"I could never get my hips out so far, or use my arms like that."

"Are you models?" It hadn't occurred to Molly that these beautifully dressed women held jobs.

"In my youth," the nearer woman answered dryly. "When I had the energy to work so hard."

"So what brought you to care about SCAWF?" Molly asked.

The woman shrugged her beautiful shoulders. "Allergies."

"Allergies?"

"Yes. I got tired of coming to work with my eyes all red from crying, and telling people that I had allergies."

Now the models were swirling around the stage in evening gowns, long slender gowns, with glittering embroidery. Deep rich reds, black, blue. Soft-draped fabrics. Trailing scarves. Like the dresses that Grace and the other women at the table were wearing. With a sinking feeling, Molly realized that her frothy layers of diaphanous multi-colors, the dress with the marvelous label, was not like anything on the stage. The cut, the shape, the fabric, the colors were all no longer in fashion. No wonder Grace had lent it to her!

———

As soon as she flicked on the lights in her apartment, the telephone rang. It was almost midnight. "I was watching for you, just to be sure you came home safely."

Kevin, of course. He had no business spying on her. She had a life of her own! And yet, after Frank Alexander's cool dismissal at the end of the evening—would he withdraw support from SCAWF?---when she had left the party alone to wait for her car, when she had driven across the bridge so late at night and then up their dark hill, she couldn't get the *what-ifs* out of her mind. What if she had a flat tire, or an accident, or ran out of gas? Who would care, or even know, if she didn't get home?

"Thank you, Kevin," Molly said. "I am safe at home. Now you can go to bed."

"That's it? No report?"

"Kevin, it's late and I'm very tired. You can read about the party in tomorrow's paper, and I'll give you further details after that, if you still want them."

"What I want to know is, what kind of jerk were you out with who didn't pick you up and bring you home? I saw you drive up in your own car and walk up to your door alone."

She sighed, and kicked off her shoes. "That's who it was, a jerk. I just spent five hours listening to the dullest, most self-centered…" she sputtered, trying to think of the right word—clod, lout, boor—and remembered her ride home in the taxi, after she had returned the rental truck, when she was assigning the same list of names to Kevin. Not anymore. Would she change her mind about Frank Alexander too? Not likely. "I don't want to discuss it. Good night, Kevin."

"Wait." The sound of breathing came from the phone. "That's not—there's something I want to say." Another pause. "I'm glad he turned out to be a jerk, but I'm sorry he spoiled your evening. I wanted it to be a wonderful night for you."

Could Kevin be jealous? He is, he's actually jealous! He was afraid I would be attracted to Frank Alexander! After an evening spent with people who viewed her as part of the furniture, she had come home to someone who cared whether or not she'd had a good time.

"Molly? Are you still there?"

"I'm here, Kevin."

"If you will go with me to the architects' dinner on the twenty-ninth, I promise not to be dull or self-centered, and when the party's over, I will deliver you to your front door."

THIRTEEN

The phone had been ringing all afternoon, no volunteers on hand, and with the counselors at a meeting in the dining room, there was no one to answer but Molly. Three rings, four. She felt tempted to ignore the call. Nothing important had come in, only messages for the staff. Louise wanted the final figures from the New Century Gala that afternoon, but at the rate of the interruptions, Molly thought she would never finish. Five rings, six. Someone not about to give up. Well, they could wait, but... what if the caller was a woman in trouble?

The voice was hardly audible. "Molly? Is that you?"

Who would call me here? Her own voice dropped to a whisper. "Yes?"

"Oh, thank heavens. I've been calling all week, and hanging up when it wasn't you."

"I'm sorry, who is this?"

"It's me, Tammy. Don't you remember me?"

"Tammy, of course. How are you?" Poor Tammy, of the shorn head. Tammy who had left the shelter last month. It hadn't taken long. Molly had expected her to regret leaving.

A long pause. "I'm back with my husband." More silence.

"And are you okay?"

Another silence. "It's much nicer here than at the shelter. All those women crowded together. It's really a dump, you know? And the kids have a room of their own now."

"But how are you, Tammy?"

"He's really trying hard, Molly. He says he's trying. He's buying me new clothes to replace what he sold in the garage sale."

"Who is choosing the clothes, Tammy? Do you decide what you like, or does he?"

"And all the kids' toys that he sold in the garage sale," Tammy went on in a rush, "he says he's going to replace them at Christmas with better toys."

"Tammy, are you okay? Has he hurt you?"

"I gotta go. I just wanted to talk to you, but I can't…" The line went dead.

Molly put the phone down and bent her head into her hands. She felt like crying, or screaming. A murmur of voices behind her. "Molly? Is something wrong?" It was Georgette.

"Tammy just called. She's not safe, she was reaching out for help, and there is nothing I can do for her."

"That's right, there *is* nothing you can do. Unless she asks to come back, there is nothing you can do," Georgette said. "It isn't easy for any of us. And you can't urge her to return, even though you want to. She made her decision, and she's the one to un-make it." Then, "Meeting's over, and it's Megan's birthday. Join us for the cake. You'll feel better." A paper plate holding a huge wedge of chocolate cake swept dangerously toward her computer keyboard.

"Oh, dear, thank you." Molly reached up, but the offering swirled out of range.

"Not here. We're leading you into temptation." Georgette held the cake over Molly's head. "In the dining room. Social hour."

Molly hesitated. She had the report on the Gala to finish, but she had refused so many times to go out with the staff after work, when she had plans with Kevin. Maybe she could eat quickly and return to her computer.

When Molly followed Georgette into the other room, Megan and the other counselors and relief counselors were already settled in with their cake, sitting around one of the blue and white tables. Pencils and papers lay scattered over the table. Dirty dishes in lopsided piles covered the other tables. That shouldn't be, Molly thought. "Didn't anyone sign up for after-lunch clean-up today?"

Georgette handed her the wedge of cake and a steaming Styrofoam cup. She called back over her shoulder, "Who has the chore list?"

"Rita," Marian answered. "One more warning, and she'll have to leave." The other women murmured in agreement. Molly heard, "lazy" and "taking responsibility."

Molly pushed the plastic fork down carefully, separating the thick chocolate frosting from the cake. She remembered a long, comfortable afternoon with Rita, sorting a load of used clothing sent in by a church. "She doesn't seem irresponsible to me," she said. "Maybe something happened, and she didn't get back in time."

Megan shook her head. "If she went anywhere today, she didn't sign out."

"But you'll talk to her first, won't you?" Molly persisted. "Remind her about doing her jobs."

"Remind her again and again. Would you like to tell her?"

Molly shook her head, but said, "If you want me to do it..."

"Just kidding. We wouldn't send you. It's a counselor's job," Marian said. As if that had made a difference in the past, Molly thought. "But Patty's having her first turn as bearer of bad news. She's upstairs now, telling Stephanie that she'll have to leave."

Patty, the relief counselor, the least experienced of the group.

As if she had read Molly's mind, Georgette looked up from her cake. "Patty volunteered to talk to Steph because she needs the experience," she explained. "We coached her on what to say. We had no choice, Molly. We gave Stephanie two extensions, but she still didn't make any effort to find other housing."

Molly looked around at the women, all busy eating. It wasn't her concern, her responsibility. The counselors determined these matters. But Rita and Stephanie..."I've spent a lot of time with Rita and Stephanie. I like them both. They're basically good people..."

The other women laughed. "You like all the women here, Molly," Georgette said. "You want to nurture them, to be their mother, but they have to learn to nurture themselves, and you have to learn to distance yourself."

"But to put Stephanie out—" she persisted, "where will she go? Out on the streets? Back with her abuser?"

Grunts and grumbles, through the chocolate cake. No one answered. Then Marian, the most senior of the counselors, put down her fork and plate. "The meeting's over, Molly. It's the social hour. These aren't easy decisions, but after the weekly review, we try to put the problems back into the files, and we close them."

In other words, Molly, stay out of it, she thought. Consider yourself reprimanded. When the counselors fell behind, or didn't show up, who had to step in and fill the gap? And who could be dragged away from her own work? But she wasn't invited to the counselors' meetings and no one could question their judgment! What will Kevin say when I tell him about this meeting? If I tell him…If I want to be scolded again.

Marian, ruffling through a sheaf of yellow papers, chose one and handed it to Molly. A scrawled combination of names and numbers, in many scripts and colors of ink. "Here's our schedule for next month, Molly. Can you type it and get copies in our boxes by tomorrow?"

Molly set the paper aside. "If I can read it." She pressed the plastic fork into the last crumbs of cake, then started on the frosting. The first bite melted slowly around her teeth and tongue, with the rough, grainy texture of homemade fudge.

Patty stepped into the room, and headed for the coffee urn.

"Did you talk to her?"

"How did she take it?"

Patty shook her head. "I talked to Stephanie and I found Rita. Stephanie's very angry. I had a hard time convincing her that we meant what we said. When I finally got through to her, she was furious. Screamed and swore at me."

The other women murmured, "Reality. She has to learn to face reality."

"Actions have consequences."

"Here, Patty, we saved you a piece of cake."

Patty took the paper plate from Megan. "Just remember this day when I apply for a job as a full time counselor…. But whoever is working tonight," Patty looked around the group, "should be prepared. Stephanie may come down and try to manipulate you into giving her extra time."

"I'm ready for her," Georgette said. "I tried to tell her last week this would happen."

"What about Rita?"

"She was asleep. She's coming down."

Rita appeared in the hallway, face puffy, eyes red. "I'm sorry," Rita mumbled. "I didn't think lunch clean-up had to be finished so early. It's still hours before dinner." She refused the plate of cake that Megan extended to her and turned to the table of dirty dishes.

Molly finished her cake and returned to her computer. Voices in the hallway, then Marian looked into the room. "We forgot to tell you. Some of us are going to dinner and a movie after work, and we'd like you to join us."

"Oh, I don't know," Molly said. She had been upset with them at the meeting, dismissing her concerns about Stephanie and Rita, yet it was kind of them to keep trying to include her in their after work plans. She really did like the women, and she had turned them down so often. She knew she should be finding friends beyond Kevin. She had not made plans with him for the evening, nothing definite, but how would he react?

"We're going to see 'Gandhi,'" Marian coaxed, "five o'clock."

"I'm not sure I can be ready in time."

"...and have Indian food after."

"I'd like to go, if I can get finished. Where shall we meet?"

"Right here."

"I'll have to make a phone call."

Back to the computer. The Gala figures looked good. Louise would be pleased, and so would Frank Alexander. Maybe that's why she hadn't heard any repercussions over the way she had argued with Frank that night. She knew the report could be finished before five, and the staff schedule for next month could wait until morning. It could be fun to go out with the women, to be with them in a more relaxed situation and get over her feeling that she had been scolded. Was she wrong to care about the women in the shelter? How did the counselors manage to stay so detached? She heard Georgette slip behind the other desk, then sensed someone standing beside her. Rita.

"It's not fair to give me a warning. I really did think I had time to clean the dining room."

"I know, Rita, but it's out of my hands."

"Could you come with me, please?"

"Rita, I'm so busy..."

"Please?"

Molly followed Rita back to the dining room.

"Look at this," Rita gestured toward the first table. "Not one of you girls took care of your dirty dishes."

"I'll do it." Molly began picking up the cups, plates and plastic forks that the women had left behind. And who is irresponsible? she thought.

"No, I'll finish," Rita said. "I just wanted you to know that I'm not the only one who lets things slide."

"I'll do it," Molly insisted. And maybe I won't get the Gala report typed before the movie.

She stacked the plates and napkins, combined leftover coffee in three cups, and carried them over to the big wastebasket. It was full. Damn! Who was supposed to empty the baskets today? It felt good to stomp her right foot down on the heap of trash, twice, three times, smashing the paper into a more compact mass.

"Molly? You're attacking the trash. Is something bothering you?" Rita was watching her. "I said I would clean up."

"No, no. I started it, I'll finish it." She piled the plates into the wastebasket, lifted the plastic folded around the rim and gathered the bag together into a bundle. "I'll take this out. Get some fresh air." And think about what's bothering me. It was more than a few paper plates left lying around. Was it the job? The way the counselors treated me at the meeting? Or am I over-reacting to that? Or was it Tammy? Stephanie and Rita? As she descended the stairs to the back door, she thought, could the counselors be right, that I am too nurturing? Am I wrong to care so much for the women who come through the shelter, or to worry about those who leave? Was Kevin right that I should leave SCAWF and find another job?

She kicked the brick against the back door to keep it from slamming shut, and carried the plastic bag out to the dumpster. What a stink! The lid clanged shut. She kicked the brick out of the way and let the door close behind her.

Back in the dining room, Rita was wiping one of the blue-checked tables. She moved like a dancer, bending and swaying to reach the far side. Her long dark hair hid her face. When she finished wiping, she adjusted the plastic tablecloth, arranging the blue squares to fall in precise lines along the edge. She straightened her back, squinting at the table, and noticed Molly watching.

"You don't have to stand over me. I'm doing my chore."

"I wasn't standing over you. I was admiring the graceful way you move, like a dancer."

"Yeah, sure." Rita turned to the second table. "Don't worry. I'll finish it."

"I'm sure you will, and do a good job, too."

"So you don't have to stand there watching."

"We don't ask you to do daily chores to annoy you, Rita. It's the only way a large group of people can live together."

"Yeah, yeah, I know. I've heard it all before. If I don't do my chore I get a warning, and if I get, what is it here, two warnings, three? I'll be asked to leave. I know what shelter rules are like. I've stayed in enough of them."

"Rita, is something bothering you, do you want to talk about it?" Molly asked, Rita's own words from a few minutes before echoing in her head.

Rita turned away. Molly debated. Should I leave, should I confront her? Suddenly, Rita whirled around, facing Molly. "Look at me," she demanded. "Look at my face. What do you see?"

"I...I see beautiful skin, what do they say, flawless complexion..." Molly stammered.

"Does it say anything on my face? Does it say, 'hit me'?" Rita pushed her hair back and thrust her face close to Molly's.

"Nothing like that."

"What is it about me then, that I attract men who want to beat me up? Why is it every time I meet some guy who seems to be sweet and kind, just when I think, this time will be good, I deserve some happiness, he turns on me with his fists, or a knife, or, I swear to God, his shoe when he stepped in dog shit."

"Oh, how awful, Rita, you don't deserve..."

"Don't give me that shit, 'nobody deserves to be treated like that,'" she mimicked. "I have heard it and heard it and heard it. Do you know how many times I have had to run and hide from a man? Men who said they loved me? What is it about me?"

"I don't know. Have you talked about it in group, with a therapist..." Molly struggled for the right words.

"That shit. You all preach the same things. I'm so tired of that shit. Sometimes I feel there's no use getting out of bed. Sometimes I think I should just kill myself. I am shit, you know? I am just a piece of shit."

"No, you're not, you're not shit," Molly declared. The words came to her from somewhere, maybe something she had read. When? Where? It didn't matter. "Listen, Rita, I know what shit is, and believe me, you're not shit." She tried to make her voice as authoritative as she could. "And you're not going to kill yourself, understand? You can't do that to me. I'll never forgive you if you do."

"What do you care?"

"I care about you." The words came tumbling out. It was the training sessions for volunteers, all the exercises they had done, positive reinforcement, self-esteem building. At the time, they had seemed hokey, psychobabble, but now she watched the words transform Rita. And she meant every one of them. Six weeks ago she would not have been able to speak to Rita in this way. Now she had her priorities straight. Let the board wait for their report. And the staff schedule. And Kevin. So what if he did scold her for staying overtime at the shelter.

They sat down at the blue-checked table and made a list, all the compliments that Rita could remember ever receiving, all the qualities that anyone had ever liked in her. Then a list of things she liked to do: "Dance."

"I knew that from watching you."

"Paint. Not pictures, rooms, walls. Swim. Bake."

"Bake what? We have stuff in the kitchen."

"Chocolate chip cookies are my specialty."

"How about that! Eating chocolate is my specialty."

"We're in business."

———

Rita was fast in the kitchen, but Molly had to leave her there to get back to work. She had just finished the Gala report when the women began to gather in the office.

"Ready, Molly?"

"Just a second." She hadn't called Kevin yet. Quickly she dialed his number. "Hi," she said, "it's me." It was difficult to speak to him with all the women in the room. She knew they weren't listening, not deliberately, but it was impossible to have a private conversation here. She couldn't say his name out loud. "I just want to give you a heads up, not to worry about me."

"Working late?"

"No, it's not that. I'm going to dinner and a movie with some of the people from work, and I know you might be worried when I don't come home right away."

"A movie? What are you going to see?"

"'Gandhi.' And have Indian food." She saw that Marian had turned around to look at her, and Georgette, at the other desk, was watching her too.

"I didn't know you wanted to see that, Molly," Kevin said in a hurt voice. "I could have taken you."

"Well, it just came up suddenly and I thought I'd like to spend time out of work with the people here."

There was a long pause. "Of course, if that's what you want," Kevin said. "When will you be home?"

"I don't know. I'll be okay. Don't worry about me." They finished the call, and Molly looked up to a sea of concerned faces. "It's my neighbor," she said. "I have a neighbor who kind of watches out for me." The women didn't say anything. "It's because I'm new in the city and I didn't know anyone when I first moved here."

No one spoke. Then Marian said, "Let's go. We don't want to be late for the movie."

FOURTEEN

The phone rang just as she finished fastening her earrings.

"Ready, Molly?" Kevin asked. "It's time."

She checked her image in the hall mirror, from her hair to her high-heeled pumps. "Yes, I'm ready. Shall I meet you at your car?"

"You should not!" he objected. "I will come to your door to fetch you like a proper gentleman."

Molly smiled as she hung up the phone. Kevin wouldn't come right out and say this, but she understood that he meant her to compare his own behavior with Frank Alexander's. She turned from side to side in front of the mirror. Not bad. Her own classic black dress, two years old, more comfortable than the borrowed designer gown she had worn to the New Century Gala. A new long chiffon scarf like the ones that Grace and the other fashionable women had carried, now draped around her shoulders. Heads would not turn after her, but she liked the way she looked.

The doorbell rang and Kevin rolled in, wearing a dark suit with a pale blue shirt and a lop-sided bow tie. "How lovely you look," he said, handing her a florist's box.

Bending, she brushed her lips across his cheek. "I was about to say the same thing about you." She opened the box on the table. "Thank you. A white orchid! I didn't expect a corsage."

"Prom night. Of course I brought flowers."

Words popped into her head, from the distant past. "Would you like to pin it on me?"

"You'd better do it yourself. I'm all thumbs when I get dressed up. Look at the mess I made of this tie."

Molly stood in front of the mirror, trying the orchid against her shoulder, first the left side, then the right. She was sixteen-years-old again. What had the rules been, so long ago? Something about Kevin, sometimes he made her feel flustered as any teenager. Which shoulder? The ribbon up or down? Did old rules matter anymore? Flowers on the left would be crushed when you danced, she remembered that. But that wasn't a concern with Kevin, was it?

"I can fix your tie," she told him, finally pinning the corsage, ribbon up, on her left shoulder. "I always did Ted's. Come here. I have to watch in the mirror."

Kevin rolled into position, and Molly bent down behind him, her arms around his neck, her head close to his. As she watched her hands in the mirror, turning the colorful silk, she was acutely aware of her own breath, leaving her nose, bouncing against Kevin's cheek and returning to spread warm across her face. She tried to breathe as shallowly as she possibly could, but still her own breath came back, scented with Kevin's after-shave, making her dizzy.

"There." At last she could stand up. She left her hand on Kevin's shoulder to steady herself. "Good job, if I may praise myself."

Kevin put his hand over hers. "Molly and Kevin, what an attractive couple."

"I was thinking the same thing," Molly agreed. "You do look very nice tonight. I've never seen you in a suit and a tie before."

"Yes, well, that's part of the reason why I gave up my downtown office," Kevin said, in a changed voice. "So I could go to work every day in a so-called jogging suit."

"The casual look. Well, that suits you too, excuse the pun."

"I'll ignore it."

"But you look very nice in your suit," she repeated.

"A suit is fine for 'a man who puts his pants on one leg at a time,' as the saying goes."

Something about Kevin's voice, the closed look on his face, stopped Molly. She wondered, as they left her apartment and set off for the garage, how does Kevin put his pants on? He is such a private person, and then suddenly he will reveal something about himself in a tiny, casual remark. Maybe when I know him better I can ask him.

The wind blew up from the Sound, bringing the scent of salt water. "Do you think it will get colder? Should I go back for a heavier coat?" she asked.

He shook his head. "Once we get to the car, we won't be outdoors again."

"Are you sure?" She remembered that other night, the wind whipping through the downtown streets as she waited for valet parking to deliver her car. "At the SCAWF gala, I had to stand out—"

"That was the jerk they gave you as your date!" Kevin interrupted. "I would never have allowed you to go to a party like that by yourself, or wait for your car alone."

"Frank wasn't exactly a date," Molly declared firmly. "I work at SCAWF. Going to the gala with Frank was more like an assignment." You don't make it easy, Kevin, she thought, when I'm trying to be independent, so late in my life, and it's very tempting to be coddled and taken care of by a protective man.

"Listen, when the architectural society gives a party, we do it right," Kevin assured her. "At the convention center, the garage and the party are all in the same building."

The elevator doors slid open to the rows of parked cars. "And you won't have to stand around in a cold garage, either, waiting to get into the car," he promised. "I have a surprise to show you."

"A surprise?" They were approaching Kevin's van.

"Watch this," he said. "You know how we always have to wait such a long time for the door to open and the lift to come down?"

"Not really." In fact she was amazed at the easy way he entered and left the van.

"But we had to come up close to the van and unlock it with a key. Now watch. We're thirty feet away." He held out a little black box, like a television remote control. A whirring noise from the van, then the door slid open and a platform emerged. "See that? By the time we get there, the lift is already down."

"That's wonderful, Kevin."

He was glowing. "My invention. Will you get in by yourself, or do you want to ride on the chair with me?"

"I'll get in," she said. She watched him back his chair onto the platform, touch the black box again and rise up into the van.

"That's quite a gizmo," she said.

131

"Gizmo?" He stared at her. "State of the art," he grinned, rolling up to the steering wheel. There was no driver's seat.

"Music?" He asked. He punched some buttons on the dashboard. Duke Ellington's sound came from the back of the van. He changed the tune, the direction from which it came. "What would you like to hear?"

"This whole car is probably state of the art, but I still prefer the white convertible."

His smile grew wider. "That's to impress women."

"So why aren't we taking it tonight?" she teased. "I'm an impressionable woman."

"It was my spinal cord that was injured, Molly, not my brain. The convertible is a fair weather car, and it's stored now until spring."

Kevin was right. It was just a few steps from the handicapped parking stalls to the inside of the convention center. They joined the throng of well-dressed couples on the short ramp into the building. Molly's hand rested on Kevin's shoulder, the way she had seen the women at Faith's party claiming their men. A number of people greeted Kevin and smiled at her in a warm, friendly way. Did she think she wouldn't turn heads? Obviously people were watching her, as Kevin's date, not because of the black dress. Curious looks but not the cold measuring glances she had sensed at the gala. Or was it her own response to the two crowds?

The doors opened into a long, tall gallery. Ahead of them, a series of escalators rose two stories, maybe three, toward the brightly lit glass ceiling of an indoor garden, shiny green leaves reflecting the artificial light.

Molly glanced around. "There must be an elevator somewhere," she said, but Kevin was looking up toward the greenery.

"Look at that thing move," he said. "I love escalators."

There was something about the way he said it, not wistful at all. He wouldn't, Molly thought. He's not that crazy. "I'm sure there's an elevator," she repeated.

Kevin sat in his wheelchair at one side of the lobby, watching the people step on to the escalator. When the crowd thinned out, no one waiting to ride up, he started rolling forward. "Come on, Molly, let's go."

"Kevin, no, you can't..."

He rolled forward to the bottom of the escalator, reaching both arms out to let the moving rails run beneath his hands. Then he grabbed hold, pulling his chair forward onto a moving stair.

"Oh no, Kevin, no!"

"Come on, Molly," he called back to her over his shoulder.

"Kevin! You can't do that!" He's going to fall! she thought. She rushed onto the escalator, her heart pounding. She had to catch up with him! Could she stop his fall, or he would he knock her down and send them both to the bottom?

"Wait for me!" She started to climb toward Kevin. She would hold on to him, no matter how much he protested, and keep him from falling. Damn high heels. She couldn't move fast enough. He had already reached the first floor above them, rolled across the open space between the two escalators, and hopped onto the higher one. When Molly reached the top of the first escalator, Kevin was halfway up the next one. Above them, leaning over the railing at the top level, she saw a man in a blue blazer, walkie-talkie in his hand. Security. He called to Kevin, "Hey, you!" then started talking into his handset as he hurried toward the top of the moving stair.

Two security guards were towering over Kevin when Molly caught up with him. They stood in front of him, their backs to her, and they sounded very angry. From his wheelchair, Kevin peered under their elbows, grinning at her. The angry voices didn't seem to intimidate him; in fact, he appeared to be quite pleased with himself.

"Molly, I must leave you for a few minutes to go off with these gentlemen," he told her. "If you will wait for me here, I won't be long."

The crowd of people moved around them toward a wall of glass doors, but Kevin and the guards went off in the opposite direction. Great, thought Molly. What a juvenile trick. I am abandoned here because of his childish show-off behavior. He must have broken a law. She found a bench in the garden area and sat down. The lights, the trees, were beautiful, peaceful, she noticed, but how long could she stay here? The center would close after the party, and she didn't have a cent for a cab. She didn't know anyone. Without Kevin at her side, no one gave her a second glance. Besides, she was hungry. How could he do this to me?

"Mrs. Bennet?" The young man who had spoken to her looked vaguely familiar. "Mrs. Bennet, I'm John Jeffries, one of the associates who works with Kevin Corwin. I met you in his office a few weeks ago."

"Yes. I remember you." It was the day she had seen Kevin standing.

"I just passed Kevin, Mrs. Bennet, and he asked me to find you and bring you inside to our table. He said he'd be delayed a few minutes."

"That would be wonderful, John," she said with much relief. "Thank you." She rose to follow the young man through the glass doors. She smiled to herself at the deferential way he opened the door for her and held her chair. Either he equates me with an elderly aunt, she thought, or he is awestruck by Kevin.

Leatrice Wood was seated next to Molly, her breasts compressed into such a tight, low-cut dress that Molly feared they would pop out onto the table. She introduced the other guests, who turned out to be Kevin's associates or former associates. Molly insisted that they call her by her first name. They wanted to know why Kevin was delayed, and she gave them all the details. They were delighted. Obviously, they respected Kevin, but tonight's recklessness seemed to increase their admiration. At the same time, their curiosity about her relationship to Kevin was clear. The sidelong glances, their questions. Leatrice asked, in her breathless little girl's voice, "How do you feel when a grown man does such a wonderfully daring feat to show off for you?"

"For me? You can't mean that," Molly objected.

"Oh, yes, for you," Leatrice persisted. "I mean, in junior high there were creeps who did all kinds of dumb things to show off for the girls, but that was all they ever did, dumb things. For someone like Kevin, who has so much dignity and a position in the community—when he does something so public like this—I mean, how does that make you feel?"

"You must be a very inventive and creative architect," Molly told Leatrice. Leatrice beamed.

"But I think," Molly went on, "you're being overly imaginative in this case. Maybe Kevin felt very festive tonight and just impulsively acted out a wish that he had been suppressing for a long time."

"Yes!" The young woman leaned closer to Molly, her breasts rising dangerously high in her neckline. "Yes, that is exactly what I mean. How does it feel to know that you had that effect on Kevin?"

Molly laughed and shook her head. It was amazing how her mood had changed from gaiety to dejection and back again. These young people were fun. Kevin was missing it all. Where was he? Maybe he had been arrested and taken to jail. Should she be worried about him? Whatever was happening, it was his own fault. Had he really been showing off for her? But if Leatrice was right… better to change the subject. Say something flattering.

"There are so many women here tonight," she told Leatrice. "In my day they would all have been spouses, but I'll bet lots of them are architects themselves, like you."

Leatrice raised her eyebrows. "I suppose you are looking for Lily. Well, she's here."

"Lily?"

"Yes, Kevin's ex-wife. Aren't you looking for her?"

"No, no. I'm not."

Leatrice looked skeptic. "Shall I point her out?"

"No, no. Don't do that. I don't want to see her," Molly protested. "I didn't even know her name."

Leatrice ignored her objection, lifting up in her seat to scan the crowd. "There, there she is, her firm has a table near the front. She's the woman in blue."

Molly didn't want to look, but she couldn't help herself. A very ordinary-looking woman, her own age, perhaps, dressed very nicely. "Yes, I see her."

Leatrice was studying Molly expectantly, and she felt she had to come up with a comment. She remembered Faith's description. "She doesn't really look like a terribly competitive person, does she?"

"Competitive?"

"Well, yes." Molly hesitated. Maybe she had already said too much. But Leatrice was waiting. "Isn't that what happened? That Kevin's wife couldn't compete with him?"

Leatrice laughed. "Is that what he told you?"

"No, I've never discussed her with Kevin," she lied. Leatrice needn't know about their conversation after Faith's party.

"Well, the way I heard it," Leatrice said, with a look of smug satisfaction, "Lily was very happy in a small firm, doing remodels and adaptive re-use." She stopped for a moment. "Do you know what that is? Re-modeling old buildings with historic value instead of tearing them down?"

"I know about adaptive re-use," Molly assured her.

"But Kevin thought that Lily should be in a bigger firm, doing big projects. And he kept nagging and nagging at her to change jobs, until she couldn't stand it anymore, so she left."

"It isn't my business in either case, is it?" Molly wanted to end this dangerous conversation quickly. "Oh, look, they're serving the salads, and Kevin still isn't here."

She turned her attention to the plate in front of her, and tried to ignore Leatrice.

Their empty salad plates were being removed when Kevin finally returned. The young people at the table pelted him with questions. "Nothing happened," was all he would say, with a sly smile. "Let me catch up with the rest of you. I'm starved." While the waiters circled the table, serving the broiled salmon with asparagus and ladling Hollandaise over all, he attacked his salad.

The conversations turned to Molly's impressions of the city, and then to their first years in Seattle. None of them, except for Kevin, had been born there. "Are you sick of salmon yet?" Leatrice demanded. "That's all they feed newcomers for their first year in town."

"No, I love salmon, I'll never get tired of it." Molly glanced at Kevin. Ben had served salmon at their first dinner together.

John Jeffries, looking uneasy, leaned across the table toward Kevin. "I delivered the drawings this afternoon as you asked," he said, "but…the client isn't happy."

"Not happy?" The conversation around them ceased.

"Yes, he says the daycare center on the site will create too much noise."

Everyone looked at Kevin and waited. Molly began to feel uncomfortable in the silence. "Couldn't you plant some trees or shrubs around it, to absorb the noise?" she suggested.

"Trees are acoustically transparent," Leatrice scoffed.

"Yes, well, let's just say that trees don't stop noise," Kevin frowned at Leatrice. "But thank you, Molly, for at least trying to come up with a solution. I think the rest of us can bring in our ideas on Monday morning."

The waiters returned, replacing the salmon plates first with strawberry parfaits and then with coffee. The lights dimmed. The room filled with the scuffling sound of chairs being turned toward a huge screen. As Molly moved her chair around, Kevin backed away to make room for her, then rolled close beside her, his hand warm on her shoulder.

Bright images crossed the screen, houses, buildings, details of roofs and doors, the projects under consideration for awards that evening: a shopping mall, then a close-up of a shop front, then an interior of the store. A long escalator. She glanced at Kevin. A look of great satisfaction on his face.

After the award-winners had been announced and the statuettes accepted, the guests began to drift away from the tables. Two security guards waited for Kevin at the glass doors. "We hope you had a pleasant evening, Mr. Corwin," the taller man said, in a respectful voice.

"Most enjoyable," Kevin answered.

"The elevator is this way," the guard continued in the same even tone. "We will escort you to your car."

"Thank you, that isn't necessary," Kevin said, but it was clear that the guards intended to stay with them until they left the building. Molly walked beside Kevin, knowing her cheeks were bright red, terribly aware of the two guards following them and the stares of the other people, but Kevin seemed unconcerned with all the attention. He still wore the same self-satisfied expression.

"No more excuses!" Molly ordered, when they were finally alone in the van. "What happened?"

"There's nothing to tell," Kevin insisted. "They were not about to arrest a well-dressed, sober, successful, paraplegic architect on the night of the architects' annual dinner. Think of the adverse publicity!"

"What took so long if it was nothing?"

"Well, it took them a while to figure it out," Kevin admitted. "They had to make a few phone calls first."

Molly shook her head. "And that's it? They just let you go?"

"I had to promise that I won't ever do it again."

"Good. I hope you learned your lesson. What ever possessed you to do such a reckless trick?"

He paused for a moment, watching to ease the van into the moving traffic. "Well, it's your fault, actually. Or your inspiration."

"Me? Don't blame me," Molly said. "I was so frightened for you. I had visions of you falling, killing yourself. What did I have to do with it?"

"There was just something about coming in with the crowd, a beautiful woman on my arm," he mused. "Next to my arm," he corrected. "I felt so...so normal, as if there wasn't anything I couldn't do."

So Leatrice was right! "You won't try it again, will you? You promised."

"I'll keep my promise," he assured her. "I won't try it again." Then, after a moment, he added, "Not in that building."

FIFTEEN

They were laughing over nothing, some silliness, when they reached her front door. "It was fun, Kevin," Molly said. "Architects do give better parties than shelters."

"I told you," he agreed.

She unlocked the door. It was too early to end the evening. He felt so too, she could tell. Molly paused in the open doorway. "Would you like to come in for a cup of tea?"

"Tea. Yes. That would be fine."

She checked the hall mirror quickly as she passed, pushing her hair back behind her ears. Her corsage was still in place, but beginning to look tired. She kicked off her shoes, then unpinned the orchid and put it in the refrigerator.

Kevin rolled through the hall into the kitchen. "Oh, good idea. Can I make myself comfortable too?"

"Of course."

He untied his necktie and unbuttoned his shirt collar, then folded the tie into his coat pocket. As she waited for the kettle to fill, she watched him tug his coat tails out from under his seat and pull the coat over his head. She set the full kettle on the range. "I'll hang up your coat," she said.

"No, I'll take care of it." He rolled away into the living room.

She took the tray from the low cupboard. Cups, saucers, spoons, sugar. She heard sounds of the wheelchair moving around. What was he doing in there? She found a lemon in the refrigerator, sliced it, arranged the slices on a blue plate. Lemon smell on her fingers. Music. She followed the sound into the hall.

Her little radio had been moved from the coffee table to the hall table, next to the empty corsage box. The rug was pushed back into the corner, exposing the bare wood floor. She started into the living room.

"Not yet! Don't come in." He was rolling around the room, moving her lamps and tilting their shades, so they shone into corners and up to the ceiling. "The atmosphere must be perfect."

"Kevin, what's going on?" she laughed.

"We're going to dance," he announced. "But the rug in here is too soft, so we have to dance in the hall. There." He rolled out of the living room and turned off the hall light. The little radio glowed green in the near darkness. A man was singing, not a voice she recognized, and soft light seeped in from the other room. "Now, Mrs. Bennet, may I have the honor of the first dance?"

"Kevin, this is impossible," she protested.

"Yes, this is the night for impossibilities. Come, sit on my lap and we'll dance." He pulled the left armrest from his wheelchair and set it next to the radio.

"But I'm too heavy for you."

"Nonsense. I keep telling you, I'm very strong." He reached out for her arm and pulled her close. "See?" For a moment, she thought of that other night, when he had pulled her onto his lap. He drew her forward, more gently this time, and caught her, one arm under her knees, the other behind her back. He scooped her up and held her against his chest. In the dim light, she saw his eyes shining. "I won't put you down until you say you'll dance with me."

"Yes, yes, all right," she laughed. "Before you drop me, I will dance with you."

"That's more like it." He lowered her onto his lap.

At first she sat stiffly, upright, afraid she might hurt him, but he pulled her close against his chest. Her nose brushed his ear. "Kevin? Am I sitting in the right place?" Oh, no, she thought, I didn't say that right. "I meant, did I sit in a wrong place?" She felt her face grow warm. I'm glad it's dark in here, she thought.

"Perfect. You are in a perfect place. Hold on." His right arm tightened around her, and his left arm moved to the wheel. Music poured out of the little radio as he turned the chair slowly round on the smooth floor. The chair swung from side to side, gently, smoothly, but even so, she had the feeling that she might go flying off into the air. She had to hold on to his upper arms to stay in place. He was so muscular! She curled against his chest so that her face rested in the hollow under his chin, breathing in the faint remaining scent of his aftershave. Kevin began to sing along with the radio.

"There's a certain somebody I'm longing to see,

I hope that she turns out to be,

Someone to watch over me."

Of all people, she thought, Kevin was the last person she knew who needed someone to watch over him. How wrong she had been about him, on the day they met. There was so much more to him than to most men. There wasn't anything he couldn't do, if he wanted to. Like tonight. Here they were, the lights turned low, dancing. Later, she knew, they would end up in her bed or his. She was glad that she had changed the sheets on her bed that morning, the rosy pink colored set, like the dress she had worn to their first dinner, a color that made her skin glow. He had said, this was the night for impossibilities. He would know what to do, just the way he had found a way to dance with her.

The music changed. Now it was louder, faster. A woman singing in a throaty voice:

"It don't mean a thing if it ain't got that swing."

Kevin turned the chair more quickly, side to side, round and round, singing along, "Do-wah do-wah do-wah do-wah."

She laughed, "Kevin, slow down, you're going to throw me off the chair!"

Kevin's arm tightened around her. "Just snuggle up and hold on!" Molly pulled closer to Kevin, wrapping her arms around his neck to keep from spinning away. Round and round they twirled, faster and faster.

"Kevin, I'm going into orbit if you don't slow down."

He slowed and stopped. She pushed away from his chest and sat up on his lap, laughing, both hands flat against the front of his shirt. She felt his heart beating under her hand, the heat of their bodies rising around them. His right arm still held her tightly, and when the motion stopped, he moved his left arm to embrace her, too. His face was so near. It seemed the most natural thing in the world for Molly to lean toward him, to rest her forehead against his, press her nose to his. No need for words. The dim light, the music, their bodies warm from the dance. Breathing the same air. Then gradually something else. A scent, no, an odor, something reeking, fetid, like—like feces, but it couldn't be. And suddenly, Kevin was lifting her up and setting her on her feet, his face pained. He wouldn't look at her, but mumbled, "Sorry, Molly, I have to leave." The door opened and he was gone, not stopping even to take the armrest from the table or close the door behind him.

"Kevin!" she called, but the wheel sounds were moving away. She heard the outer door swing shut. As she reached the open doorway, a breath of cold outside air washed around her, drying the tears that had started to run down her cheeks.

SIXTEEN

It was hard to concentrate on the support group. The speaker was listing signs of a potential batterer, but Molly wanted to think about Kevin.

Poor Kevin. The distress on his face when he came down that morning to pick up his armrest. He'd said, "I have to explain what happened…"

Molly had rushed to stop him. "No, you don't, Kevin. It's okay. Forget it."

"You need to know—" he'd tried to continue, but she wouldn't let him.

"As far as I'm concerned, Kevin, nothing happened. I had a wonderful time at the party. I'm still planning to cook dinner tonight. Now let me get to work on time." Molly bent down and brushed her lips across his cheek. She had learned enough about incontinence in Ted's final illness. She didn't need Kevin's explanations. It was hard to read the look on his face as he wheeled around in the doorway. Chagrin and uncertainty, but also relief, she thought.

Tonight she wanted to make an extra effort to be upbeat, to prove to Kevin that last night's accident didn't matter. Special dinner, with flowers and candles. She half-heard the speaker ask if the batterer himself been abused as a child. Would a woman know that? Did people speak about that, even to their intimate partners?

I'm wasting my time here, she thought. She had planned to leave work early to shop. Then Louise had appeared next to her computer, just after lunch. "Am I interrupting you, Molly?"

Yes, Molly had thought, you are always interrupting me, but she said, "I have a minute, Louise, just a minute." She was trying to be firmer with Louise these days, after she had listened to a training session on setting boundaries. It was ironic; Louise had asked her to fill in for an absent counselor at a support group on boundaries, and it was there she had learned how to protect herself, to draw a line at unreasonable requests.

In the office, Louise had continued. "There's going to be a support group meeting this afternoon, and I'm short one counselor. I was hoping you wouldn't mind filling in again."

Molly shrugged. "You asked to have the volunteer hours done this afternoon," she said, "and I told you I needed to leave early."

"Oh, the volunteer hours. That can wait," Louise assured her. "I really need a counselor at the support group. We have a visiting speaker, Jayne Brooker. It wouldn't be appropriate not to have some one of us in the room. All you have to do is just sit and listen."

Why did that sound so familiar to Molly? "All you have to do…" from Louise, always meant that there would be extra work. And today was just like that. After Molly had introduced Jayne Brooker and started the women introducing themselves round the table—first name, brief statement of what brought them to SCAWF—she had rushed back to the office to duplicate Jayne's hand-outs: "How to Recognize a Potential Abuser," "Early Warning Signs," "It's All About Control." Jayne liked the meeting room to be dim, no bright lights overhead, so Molly had to dig some candles out of the emergency locker and set them around the table. At least she wouldn't have to shop for a dessert for Kevin. Rita had left a pan of chocolate brownies on her desk that morning.

Molly was still only half-listening to the speaker when she heard her say, "Rage. Did your partner get excessively angry over situations that were really minor?" But that was ridiculous. Kevin could get unreasonably angry—she thought of his reaction when she first parked in his parking space, when she blurted out the location of the shelter, and when a non-disabled driver had taken the disabled space, but that didn't make him an abuser.

Now she forced herself to listen as Jayne drew the women out, asking them to look back at their relationships. "It isn't a lack of love. Your partner loved you, as best as he or she was able, as that person conceived of love. It's about control. It's about fear of losing control, so they hold on more and more tightly. That's why it's so hard to get away. You know that. But I want you to look back at the times you spent together, way back, maybe to the first days that you knew each other, and think about the warning signs you didn't see then. How was your partner first trying to control you?"

The women murmured among themselves. A voice. Whose? Molly couldn't see in the dim room. "We were high school sweethearts. He said he loved me so much. I always had to phone him as soon as I came home from school. And if I was late, if I stopped to shop or have a cup of coffee with a friend, he was... he was..."

"Angry?" someone prompted.

"No. No, he was hurt. He was so hurt that I liked my friend better than I liked him. And I had to promise I wouldn't see that friend anymore."

"You were young. I was older and should have known better," another voice commented. "When we first met, we both lived in the same apartment building. He would watch for me every day, and come round to my apartment to see if I was all right. If I was late, he'd say he was worried about me. And I thought it meant he really cared about me."

Molly listened more intently. Kevin watches for me most days, she thought, and he worries about me, but he's not controlling, he's not abusive. He cares about me.

"I gave up so many friends." That was Rita. Molly recognized her voice. Had she finished cleaning the dining room already? It was her chore again today. "Every time I met a new man, I had to give up all my girl friends. Not that I had so many. The guys I knew said they were enough for me. I shouldn't have to need anybody else."

"Not even family," another woman chimed in. "I had to stop seeing my family. My husband said they didn't like him. He said I had to choose between him and them."

"You gave them up?"

"I had to sneak around. I saw them while I was at work, but never on a weekend. Never at Thanksgiving or Christmas."

A new voice. "At least you could go out to work. I had to give up my job. My husband said I didn't need to work. He said he could support his wife. But I liked my job, and I liked having my own money. The people I worked with were my friends. He said they were taking advantage of me. He said I should quit and get a better job. So I did. But none of the jobs I could take pleased him. So I just stopped working."

No one said anything more. Kevin tells me I should get a better job, Molly thought. He says he doesn't like Louise even though he's never met her. Is that controlling? I don't think so. Kevin wants to protect me. There's a difference.

"Go back to an earlier time," Jayne prompted. "Before you were married, or living together. What should you have seen then?"

Someone laughed. "When we first started dating, I got a phone call from his old girlfriend. She said she wanted to warn me. She didn't want anyone else to go through what she…" A laugh, or a sob, Molly couldn't tell which.

"What did you do?" the others prodded.

"Nothing. I figured she was just a sore loser. I told him about the call, and he said he had dumped her and that was her way of getting back at him."

A new voice spoke up. "He grabbed me once. I was about to leave the room at a party, and he picked me up. Not for very long. He just held me off the floor. He was that strong, and he said, 'I don't want you to leave.' "

"What did you do?"

"I said, I have to pee, and he held me a while longer, and then he put me down and said, 'Don't be gone long.' And the next day, I had bruises up and down my arms."

Kevin picked me up too, Molly thought. Last night when we danced, it was fun, but that other time, when he picked me up and wouldn't put me down, I was frightened. Just for a minute. He was hurting me. But Kevin didn't mean to control me. I just didn't know him well at that time.

"Even before we were married," someone said, the woman who had given up her job, "he was always finding fault with me. The way I did my hair, the way I dressed, my voice. But he said it was because he cared about me so much." Murmurs of assent. "And if we had a disagreement, it was always my fault. He could never accept the blame for anything."

"I shouldn't have rushed into that relationship. I moved in with him when I knew him less than a month, but he said it was so obvious that we were crazy about each other, why wait? Crazy, that's the word. But I was crazy to listen to him."

Molly felt a light tap on her shoulder. Louise. "I can sit in now," she whispered. "I know you were in a hurry to get home today."

"Thank you," Molly whispered back. She closed the door behind her, softly. That Louise. She was hard to read sometimes. Molly went back to her desk, turned the computer off. It was early, much earlier than she had intended to shop, and she had Rita's brownies. She stuck her head into the dining room, just to check on its condition. The wastebasket was full to overflowing. Well, Rita had baked the brownies; she could do this for her, she thought, gathering up the plastic bag.

She kicked the brick against the back door and carried the bag out to the dumpster. Same old stink. She walked a few feet out into the alley. Just a few steps away, the air smelled new, washed clean by the rain that had stopped only moments ago. A mountain ash tree, loaded with orange berries but still radiantly green, hung over an old fence. Below the tree, the weathered fence was faded to the same even gray color as the sky. Gray above, gray below, and the dazzling tree between. From low in the west, under the gray clouds, the last rays of the sun were shining through, igniting the tree. Such a dark, almost November day, but still there was this moment that she had been lucky enough to catch, when the setting sun shone under the clouds.

She leaned back against the fence, turning her face up to the tree. Some of those things the women had said about their abusers, she could say about Kevin. She hadn't known him long, just since August. He had a temper. He watched for her. He was always urging her to change her job. He thought her friend Louise was taking advantage of her, and he didn't want her to go out with the women she worked with. He had picked her up and held her, twice, but the second time she hadn't minded it at all. Just last week, when she told him that her son Joey had called, urging her to come back to Omaha for Thanksgiving, he had pulled a long face and said, "What! Leave me all alone?" And the things that Leatrice had said about Kevin's wife, that he nagged at her to change jobs. That sounded controlling, too. But was it? Kevin had been so kind to her, so good, bringing her food, listening to her. He cared about her, that's why he wanted what was best for her. There was a difference, wasn't there, between controlling and nurturing?

A little breeze shook the rain from the tree above her. It was time to go home. Maybe those other men were abusive, but not Kevin. She kicked the brick out of the way and let the door slam shut behind her.

SEVENTEEN

NOVEMBER

No matter how Molly scrunched the collar of her sweatshirt up around her neck, the cold gusts still managed to creep inside. She turned her back to the wind, hurrying to get her bulbs into the ground before the storm hit. She had worked out a routine, crawling beside the bare new beds, dragging her trowels, bulbs, and bulb food on a plastic garbage bag behind her. First she scooped a hole in the turned-up soil and sprinkled bulb food in it. Then she dropped a bulb, pointed side up, into the hole and covered it, patting the soil down firmly. She could plant ten or twelve bulbs, creeping alongside the bed, before she had to scramble to her feet to ease her aching knees.

During these pauses, stretching and stamping to relieve the pain, she could admire the neat plot the maintenance men had prepared for her. There were six wide beds, with three-foot swaths of lawn separating them. The soil was rich, with the steer manure and composted leaves the men had added when they turned the soil over and broke up the big lumps. My garden. Soon all the seed catalogues she had ordered would arrive, and she could fantasize over flower and vegetable choices all winter long. But today, these bulbs had to be planted.

She sighed and lowered herself to the ground again. Why did I buy these tulips? Gardening isn't fun on a day like today, with the fierce wind and the dark sky. In Nebraska she would have been listening for tornado warnings. People here said this weather was normal, November storms blowing in from the Pacific. Even so, she wished she had a radio. Or better still, she wished she were at Kevin's place, curled up on the big leather sofa in front of a fire. What am I doing out here? My nose is running, my legs ache, my hands are freezing.

And why did I tie my bandanna around my head? Now I can't wipe my nose, and my ears are still cold.

She pulled the sweatshirt closer around her neck, wiped her nose against her sleeve, looked up and saw Kevin watching her. How long had he been sitting there? Long enough to see her wipe her nose? Oh, shit. *O sole mio.* He called to her, but the wind carried his words away. "Look at me," she shouted at him. "I'm planting bulbs today. Do you think I'm crazy?"

He shook his head. He couldn't hear her either. He unlocked the brakes and rolled his wheelchair onto the lawn. The ground was wet and uneven, but he seemed to have no trouble pushing steadily across the grass toward her.

"Hi," he said. "I hoped I'd find you here."

The hood of his blue jacket had fallen back from his head and the wind was blowing through his hair, mussing it in a great, casual way. Her own hair was probably a mess, she thought, and why didn't I wear lipstick this morning?

"I'm planting," she said, gesturing at her boxes and bags. "Tulips and daffodils." She tried to sit back on her heels, but it hurt her knees too much. She stood up, brushing the dirt from her pants, then bent over and kissed his cheek, her cold nose against his warm face.

"I thought you were going to wait until spring to start your garden," he said, smiling up at her.

"I thought so too," she agreed, "but the stores are selling bulbs at half price now, and I figured just a few, for early color. I'll have my own flowers to cut in April."

He looked at the emptied bags lying on the lawn, held down by a large rock. "That's quite a few."

"About three hundred." She sniffed loudly and thought about wiping her nose on her sleeve again. Not in front of him. "This is almost the end of the planting season, but it's not too late. And next spring I'll cover them with annuals or vegetables."

"Let me help you," he said, releasing one arm of his chair and tossing it on to the ground near the bags. "I used to garden."

"Kevin, no, you…" she began, but he had picked up the boxes and the bulbs, and started off down the row. She bit her lip. She must learn never to say, "don't" or "can't" to this man. Not when he made up his mind. He was leaning way out over the side of his chair to drop a bulb into the hole she had left. "At

150

least do it right," she laughed. "Fertilizer first, then the bulb. And put the bulbs in right side up, so they grow toward the sun."

They worked together fast and efficiently. Molly crawled along the ground digging the holes, and Kevin rolled after her, bending sideways from his chair. "Bulb food, bulb, bulb food, bulb," he repeated, taking them from his lap and dropping them into the hole. "Bulbs gotta eat too." Then she filled in the soil over the bulb. Sometimes as he dropped the bulb and she scooped up the dirt, their hands met, tangling in the damp soil.

"Hey," he said, "don't go so fast. You're trying to fill the holes before I get the bulbs inside."

He started to imitate Tiny Tim singing "Tiptoe Through the Tulips," but he had forgotten most of the words. Together, they tried to recall the lines. They had the song almost complete when the rain started falling.

Cold drops hit her neck and ran down inside her sweatshirt. "Oh, no," she wailed. "We were almost finished." The cardboard boxes showed big damp marks from the first drops. She scrambled to her feet, rushing to collect the boxes and tools, shoving them into the plastic garbage bag. She gathered the empty bags from the bulbs and stuffed them into the bag too.

Kevin continued down the row, leaning far over to scoop holes in the dirt with one bare hand while he held on to the chair with the other.

"Run," she called to him, "run inside before you're soaked," but Kevin stayed where he was, finishing the row she had left. He had pulled the hood of his jacket up over his head, but his pants showed darkened spots from the rain. At the end of the row, he tried to turn the wheelchair. His hands slipped on the hand rims, and the chair skittered on the grass. He wiped his hands on his pants and gripped the hand rims again. The chair moved backwards slowly. He leaned over the side of the chair, filling the holes by pushing the dampened soil into each one and patting it down with his knuckles. The wind blew his hood back, and the rain pelted down on his hair. Lightning flashed in the western sky. A few seconds later, thunder rolled across Puget Sound.

"Leave them," she called, as she weighted the plastic bag with the big rock. "Let's run inside."

Kevin had reached the end of the row. He turned the chair towards her and pushed on the hand rims. His hands slipped down the wet rims. The chair jerked, moved forward, and stopped. The right wheel was caught in the corner of the planting bed. Kevin pushed hard on the hand rims again. The chair moved, stopped, and moved again. The big wheel slid down the raw edge of the bed. Kevin tried to lean in the opposite direction. The chair wavered, hung up on the edge. Then slowly, slowly, the wheel sank into the soggy ground. The angle changed and the chair toppled sideways. Kevin pitched out into the turned-up soil. A wheel spun slowly through the air, scattering the raindrops.

"Oh, God, Kevin, are you hurt?" Molly rushed over. She knelt in the mud at his side.

"It's okay. I'm okay." He was leaning on one elbow, a brown stain growing on his sleeve. "I'm okay, Molly."

"Let me help you." She knew he wouldn't like it, but she didn't care. She couldn't just leave him lying in the mud. She grabbed his elbow and helped him sit up.

"Chair," he said.

She righted the wheelchair on the grass and pulled the kerchief from her head to wipe away the dirt. Mud was smeared on the back and the seat. She pushed the chair closer to him. He gripped the front and tried to pull himself up into the chair. His hands slid down the bars. She remembered the way he had flipped himself into the chair at the pool, almost effortlessly. Now he sat in the mud, shivering, his wet pants plastered against his wasted legs.

Molly came around the chair and, with stiff fingers, held out her muddy bandanna. Lightning flashed again. The wind cut through her wet shirt. He wiped his hands and grasped the chair again. She took hold of his arm with both hands and pulled as hard as she could. Together, they dragged his body up against the chair high enough so that he could flip sideways and fall into it.

"Good," he panted. "Thanks." He sat in the chair, unmoving, breathing hard. Then he pulled his body up straighter and pushed against the hand rims. Nothing happened. The right wheel was stuck deep in the saturated lawn. He strained again to push the hand rims, but the chair would not move. Molly got behind the chair, her feet sliding on the turf, and shoved against him until the chair began to move. Then she ran behind him, pushing the chair across the slippery grass.

When they reached the sidewalk, hail was coming down along with the rain. Side by side, they dashed for her building. Under the entry roof, out of the wind, they stopped and looked at each other. She leaned against the wall, panting. His face was flushed and his hair flat against his head.

"Are you okay?" Kevin asked.

"I'm all warmed up now," Molly said, pushing her own wet hair back from her face. "How about you?"

"I'm fine," he said. "I'm just fine." He took her hand and pulled her away from the wall. She knelt by the side of his chair. A sharp twinge in her knees; she ignored it.

He leaned toward her and hugged her. It was awkward with the armrest between them, but she didn't care. He sat back, keeping his arms around her. "I had no idea you were so strong."

"I was afraid you were hurt."

He shook his head. "The ground was all turned up and softened. But you! I thought you would pitch me over the top of the chair."

They stayed where they were for a few minutes, smiling at each other. You idiot, she told herself. You're acting like a heroine in a supermarket romance, but she knew something was different. They had crossed some kind of boundary. Then her knees hurt too much to stay down any longer.

"I don't suppose you want to come in for a hot drink," she said, digging into her pocket for her key.

"What if we meet for lunch in an hour?" he said. "Ben's day off. I'll cook."

She nodded, still feeling in her pocket. Then she frowned and dug into the pocket on the other side. He waited while she tested all the pockets in her pants and her shirt.

"Oh, shit, I must have dropped my key in the mud."

She started back toward her garden, but he caught hold of her hand and stopped her. His hand was cold. "You can look for it later. Why don't you ring one of your neighbors? Then you can call the manager to unlock your door."

She began at the top of the panel, pushing every one of the buzzers for the eight apartments in her building. No one answered.

"I can't believe no one is home on such a crummy afternoon." Molly was starting to shiver again. She stamped her feet on the ground to warm them. "You go on home," she said. "You're getting chilled and you're all muddy." She bent over and kissed his cold cheek. "I'll go look in my garden."

She ran back through the rain to the turned-up beds and paced up and down between them. No key. She picked up the second armrest from Kevin's wheelchair, where they had left it. When she returned to her apartment building, he was still there. Each of them burst out at the other:

"You waited for me? You shouldn't have."

"You shouldn't have gone back there. You're all wet."

"Look at you. You're soaked."

"Me? Look at the way you're shivering."

When they had enough scolding, Kevin said, "Come up to my place. It's warm and dry. I'll give you a hot drink, and we can call the manager."

He rolled his chair into the rain again and moved swiftly toward his building. After a moment, Molly ran after him.

A few minutes later, Molly stood in the elevator hall while Kevin unlocked his front door. "What about all this mud?" she asked, watching the puddle at her feet grow bigger.

"Ben will take care of it when he comes tomorrow," Kevin answered, swinging the door open. "It's not important. Not as important as getting warm."

She stepped out of her shoes before she followed him inside. He disappeared down the hallway. Molly stood in the living room, trying not to drip. Rain drummed against the windows. The sky lit up, and then a few seconds later thunder rolled around the building.

Kevin came back with a bundle of cloth on his lap. "Here, put these on. These should fit you." He handed her one of his own velour sweat suits and a big white towel. "Get out of all your wet clothes. That door. Go on, it's okay. Take everything off. And dry your hair."

He rolled away down the hall again.

Molly looked at the soft gray pants and jacket. They were only cloth, she told herself, but she knew they were his clothes.

Her own clothes felt awful, wet and cold. Molly wanted to take them off, but…his clothes against her skin would be almost like…his skin next to her skin. She set the bundle down on the coffee table, picked up the phone, and dialed the manager's number. As the phone rang again and again, she followed the paths of single raindrops running down the window, merging with other drops on the glass. No answer.

"Now," she heard Kevin say from the hallway, "you can call the manager while I fix something to warm our insides."

He came into the living room wrapped in a long kimono, blue, the color of his eyes. "Molly? Why are you still in your wet things?"

She shook her head. "The manager doesn't answer. Everyone should be home on such a rotten day."

He rolled into the kitchen. "Try again in a little while. Meanwhile, you'll feel much better if you take off your wet clothes."

Molly pinched a bit of her sodden jeans in two fingers and tried to pull the cloth away from her skin. When she lifted the cloth in one place, it stuck in another. No use. She took the bundle into the guest bathroom near the front door. She looked awful! Hair all stringy and mud on her face. She turned her back to the mirror, pulled off her wet tops. The big towel felt good. So did Kevin's shirt, big and soft and loose. She dropped her jeans and her panties, and pulled on his dry pants, rolling the elastic up around her waist to shorten them. She rubbed her head with the towel, then finger-combed her hair into shape. Wiped the mud off her face. He was right; she felt much better. She draped the towel over her shoulders and opened the door.

Kevin was pushing a cart into the room. "Here, drink this," he said, handing her a mug. She held it in both hands, warming them. It held some kind of herbal tea, hot and strong, tasting of honey and rum. She tried to sip it slowly, but it felt so nice and warm going down. She finished the drink quickly.

"Let's both try again," he said, taking her mug and turning back toward the cart.

Molly dialed and waited, eleven, twelve, thirteen rings, but still no answer. When she turned away from the phone, he handed her the refilled mug. She drank this one more slowly. Still, it felt warm and soothing.

"This is so annoying," she said. "Look, I don't want to keep you. You go ahead with whatever you need to do. Shower and change. I will curl up on your sofa with my nice warm drink and call the manager again in a few minutes."

A crackle of lightning and thunder crashed across the sky. The lights flickered.

"You know, this isn't typical Seattle weather," Kevin said.

"It isn't?"

"No. Thunder and lightning. That's not usual. We get lots of rain, but hardly ever thunder and lightning." He rolled up closer to her, so their knees were almost touching. "Maybe this is all a sign," he said. "A portent."

"A what?"

"An omen. For you and me. Like in the movies. Lightning and thunder for the great love scenes. It's telling us that you should not go home. Stay here, Molly. Stay with me."

She drew the towel up from her shoulders and wrapped it around her head, shielding her face from him. Surely he could hear her heart pounding. From the shadows of the white folds, she watched him. He was sitting directly opposite her, his eyes almost piercing the towel to stare into hers. She pretended to dry her hair, rubbing her head with the towel, so he couldn't see her face.

"It's time, Molly. You know we've been moving toward this. Take off that silly towel and look at me." He reached out and pulled the towel away. "What's wrong?"

"I'm terrified."

"Of what? Of me?"

Molly shook her head. "What it will be like. That I won't know what to do."

"I'm scared too." He took her hand. His hand was rough and warm; hers was icy. "I don't know what it will be like, but I know I want you and I think you feel the same about me."

"I don't know what you will want...what you'll want me to do."

"I'll tell you. And you'll tell me. Will you stay with me?" A flicker in his eyes. He was scared too.

She nodded.

He backed the chair away from her. "Wait a few minutes. I need to disconnect in private. I'll call you. Will you come in when I call?"

She nodded again. There was a big lump in her throat.

He left her alone in the living room. This is what you hoped for, she told herself, starting with that familiar lurch deep inside, the first time you saw him with the sun on his hair and his angry blue eyes. She clutched her stomach and bent over. You wanted Kevin, the night when you danced. She hadn't thought she would feel like this. She had been waiting for him, up until this moment, but now she wasn't so sure. And yet she couldn't deny the attraction they both felt. That's why Kevin was in his bedroom, disconnecting.

Didn't it mean something, his telling her that? Letting her know he trusted her? He was so private most of the time.

Her stomach growled. The first time, with Ted, how had she felt? Scared. Relieved when it was over. Those other men, her misguided attempts to join the sexual revolution didn't count. Kevin was different. She cared for him, and he for her. But, what could Kevin do sexually? That was the question she had been asking herself since August. Now she was about to find out. What if she didn't like it? What if he was disappointed in her?

She felt a wrenching in her gut. Maybe she was getting sick. Oh, dear, what if she farted when she was with Kevin? Maybe today was not their day. Maybe the portents were wrong. She jumped up from the sofa and headed for the door. The rain might let up soon, or the manager might be home. She flung the door open. Above her, thunder crashed. The building shook, and white light spilled into the hall from behind her. The lights flickered and went out. There was blackness all around. Only the lights above the elevator remained, and she knew not to use the elevator in an emergency. She felt her way along the wall, back toward Kevin's door. It hadn't locked. She stepped inside and let it shut behind her. Beyond the windows, the lightning flashed again. She heard Kevin call her name. No excuses. It was definitely their omen. She felt her way through the living room toward the bedroom door.

EIGHTEEN

Molly paused in the bedroom doorway. She tried to identify the dim shapes in the room. She saw a double bed, a table with a lamp, his chair next to it. Kevin was sitting up in bed, watching for her.

"Come over here, Molly," he said, patting the mattress beside him.

She walked around the foot of the bed and sat on the edge of the mattress. He was propped up against several pillows.

"There's a lantern in the bottom of this table," he said, waving his hand. "Will you get it out?"

She opened a door and rummaged around, feeling the square shape of the big battery. "Is this it?" she asked, bringing it up to the tabletop.

Kevin reached over and clicked the switch. A sudden brightness blinded her. She covered her eyes, then peered at Kevin from between her fingers.

"That's too bright, isn't it," he said. "Wait a minute." He pulled the blue kimono from the bedpost and draped it over the battery lantern. "Is that better?"

"Kevin, why do you keep a lantern in your bedside table?"

He shrugged. "For power failures. It's safer than a candle. It's less romantic, but safer. Is that better?"

"No," she shook her head. She could see the pale stripes on the pillows behind him, the golden hair on his chest. "It's still too bright. Wait."

She took the lantern from the table and set it on the floor in the corner of the room. Then she doubled the kimono and spread it over the lantern. "How's that?"

"No, that's too dark. I can hardly see you."

She removed the kimono and turned the lantern so the beam was focused into the corner. This time she draped the lantern with only one thickness of cloth. "That's enough light," she said. "I really like it better dark. Okay?" There was so much she didn't know about Kevin. It was silly to fuss about the light.

She came back to the bed and sat on the edge again. He reached out and ran his hand along the edge of her cheek and behind her ear. She closed her eyes. His hand was so gentle and warm. Her skin tingled when he touched her.

"I need to see you," he said, taking her hand. He kissed the inside of her wrist and pulled her forward. Her fingers tangled in the hair on his chest. He kissed her, then kissed her again. He unzipped the velour jacket, slipped it from her shoulders and dropped it on the floor. His fingers traced a line from her ear under her chin and down between her breasts. "You are so beautiful," he said.

"And do you have enough light?" she teased.

"You glow in the dark, did you know that? You glow, you shine, you smell so good," he said, pulling her close and nuzzling her neck.

She sprawled across his chest, her skin growing warm, his skin hot beneath her palms. The familiar scent of his face rose, warm against her own. His hands and his mouth moved all over her body. He lifted her up onto the bed, pulling her trousers off. She kicked the tangle of cloth to the floor and stretched her toes toward the end of the bed. He pulled the sheet over her. She lay alongside him, skin against skin, basking in the sensations he aroused in her. When he pulled her up onto his body, she was ready. Her legs slid down to straddle him. She lay on top of him, kissing him, his hands cupped around her breasts. She felt his erection against her abdomen. He moved his hands down her body, lifted her pelvis, and directed her into place. She had risen to a kneeling position astride him, ready to absorb him, bending her knees to sink onto him. His hands on her buttocks pulled her down. She felt his hard maleness entering her body as she lowered herself. Hard, yes, pain, yes, but good, good pain. Then another pain, sharp, hurtful, shot up from her knees through her thighs.

"Oh, God, oh, ahh, no, no, I can't do it." She wrenched herself up and off of him.

"What's the matter?"

"Oh, my God, my knees…my knees are killing me," she moaned, rolling off Kevin. "Oh, those damn tulips."

"What?"

"My legs. My knees. I can't…I can't bend my knees like that." She started to cry. "My knees hurt."

"Hey, it's all right," Kevin said, putting his arm around her and pulling her close. "It's okay. We'll find another way. Molly, don't cry."

She snuggled into his embrace and buried her face in his shoulder. How could she disappoint him like this? And herself? Damn those tulips. She knew it was a mistake to buy them!

Kevin was holding her against his side, soothing her, stroking her with his free arm. Molly felt like such an idiot. What must he be thinking? He was too nice to say.

It was so comfortable here, lying up against him. Rain still tapped against the windows, not so hard anymore. The hall lights flickered, then came on. A whirring sound, the fans and motors starting up again, told them that the electric power had been restored.

"Come on," Kevin said, pushing her up. He kissed the tip of her nose. "Let's take a shower and then have lunch." He transferred into his waiting chair and rolled out of the room.

Molly's towel lay on the floor, tangled with the velour running suit. She wrapped it under her arms and followed him into a room like none she had ever seen before. It was not at all like the guest bath out in the hall. The floor, ceiling, and the walls were completely covered with white tile. At the far end, two showerheads on the wall, one high and one low. There was no curtain, no door, not even a rim to keep the water in. The whole room was the shower stall.

Another wheelchair waited just inside the room. This one was armless, shiny and not as big as the one he sat in.

"You get the water hot," he said, taking the towel from her.

She turned the knob to a midway point and pulled it out slowly. When the temperature was just right she stepped under the high spray. She closed her eyes and let the hot water run through her hair and down her body. "Um-m-m-m, this is nice."

Through the falling water, like looking through a gauze curtain, she saw that he had moved to the other chair. He rolled into the spray next to her and set the brakes.

She turned her back to him and took the shampoo from the shelf. She was running her fingers through her sudsy hair when she realized that he was sponging her back with long, gentle strokes. When her hair was soap-free, she opened her eyes and turned around. He rubbed the soapy sponge over her breasts and stomach. She took the sponge from him and began to scrub his shoulders, his neck and his chest. He continued to rub her breasts with gentle, soapy fingers. She looked down and saw that he was erect and ready. She touched him with one finger.

He put both hands on her buttocks and pulled her forward. She straddled the chair and leaning down, kissed him on the mouth. He pulled her closer. She lowered her body carefully, trying to bend from the hips. Her knee twitched… oh, no, not again…then relaxed. This time it would work. She lowered herself on his waiting erection. This was what she had wanted, this sensation, ever since the first time she had seen him in his white convertible. She planted her feet firmly on the floor and raised her body just a bit, not far enough to break the connection, and then plunged down again. His hands held firmly onto her buttocks and his mouth was busy doing wonderful things to her breasts. Again and again, she rose and plunged, rose and plunged, until she felt an inner explosion and was finally spent. She collapsed against him. Her body was stuck to his and her head rested on his wet hair. With gentle hands, he was soothing her back in long calming strokes. "So," she said to herself, "now I know."

NINETEEN

Molly stretched her toes toward the foot of the bed, her hands to the headboard above, then relaxed. She raised her body for a moment to pull the nightgown crumpled around her waist down toward her knees. Her arm brushed the space next to her. Still warm. She could hear water running in the bathroom. Kevin took forever in the bathroom every morning, but he tried to be out before she woke up. He must have slept late this morning. The window opposite was bright with blue sky. If she sat up, she could probably see the Olympic Mountains on the western horizon, snowy peaks sharp in the cold, clear air. But she didn't have to sit up if she didn't want to. She could stay like this forever.

She stretched again, rolled over on her back. It was hard to believe how familiar this room had become, the big bed with its soft percale sheets, the window that Kevin kept uncurtained, the lamp he insisted on lighting when they made love. His pajama top was still draped over the shade. She had spent more nights in the past two weeks in this bed than she had in her own, had developed the habit after work of coming straight up to his apartment from the parking garage without stopping at her place first.

This morning they could look forward to the whole day together. She had to decide whether she should get up now and go to the kitchen for a cup of the coffee she could already smell, brewing in the automatically-timed coffee maker, or wait for Kevin. They could bundle up and go out for a walk in the weak autumn sun. Later they could have lunch, picking the meat off the carcass of yesterday's turkey. Or they could not get dressed, bring the coffee and some food to the bedroom, and spend the day in bed.

It should please Kevin, later in this unusually bright November day, to make love with the afternoon sun streaming in the window. What else could she do to make him happy? Because the last two weeks had been, for her, the most extraordinarily pleasurable time of her life. Her body grew warm and curled with delight when she thought of the sex—that was such a cold, clinical word for the bliss, the ecstasy, she felt with Kevin. After they had worked out an arrangement with pillows under his body, so that she wouldn't have to bend her knees so sharply, she could be on top all the time. But it was not just the posture of their bodies that made the difference. In her marriage, crushed beneath Ted in the missionary position that he preferred, she could never move as freely as she wished to. When she lay or sat astride Kevin, it was almost as if his inability to move at all freed her from constraint, gave her the opportunity, the permission, for ecstatic movement. And even beyond what she was enabled to do for herself, Kevin was the most attentive, most sensitive lover that she could imagine. She could hardly believe how much he seemed to be aware of her responses, how closely he was attuned to her feelings. And, he said, it was because of *her*. He'd said, "When your body gets warm, you grow fragrant, shining, I can see that, smell it, feel it with my hands. I love your movements in my arms, against my chest." She thought of her pleasure as her gift to him, to share with him the tension of her spine, the way her whole body shuddered, even though he had no climax of his own.

Thinking of him, she pulled the sheet over her head and kicked her legs toward Kevin's side of the bed, breathing deeply of the smell of him coming from the churning linens.

"What is all this activity in the sheets? Can I be part of it?" Kevin pulled the sheet away from her face.

He must have come into the room while she had been fantasizing over their lovemaking. Now he was sitting next to the bed, bare chested, clean-shaven, smiling at her. "And what do I see here? Rapture? To what do I ascribe this rapturous face?"

He was unbearably attractive. She couldn't look at him. How long had he been watching her? Could he read her mind? He must know what she had been thinking, the power he held over her. She turned away from him. Every cell of her body sensed his presence, his warmth, the smell of his after-shave. She could never have any secrets from him.

She heard the brake lever moving, felt his weight on the mattress as he transferred to the bed. He grabbed the headboard—it squeaked and shook—and pulled
his body close to hers. He nuzzled her neck, his breath warm on her back, minty
smell mingling with the after-shave. She closed her eyes to shut out any unnecessary
distractions. His fingers caressed her bare arm. "What were you thinking about?"

"Nothing," she lied. "Just…savoring the moment."

He was silent for a while, his hand kneading her shoulder. It didn't matter.
They had all the time in the world. He must feel that way too. He said, "We can
prolong the moment."

She was caught up in enjoying the rhythm of his moving hand. "A moment
is a moment is a moment."

He pulled her nightgown out from under her hips and pushed it up to
her shoulders. His fingers pressed into her back, walking up and down along
her spine. Sex before breakfast, she thought. Why not? And after, too. "That's
nice," she murmured. "I like it here."

"Then stay here, Molly. Move in with me." His fingers continued their
march up and down her back. She lay perfectly still. Maybe she had misunder-
stood. It was too soon. Or was it?

The thought had already crossed her mind, more than once, that if they
continued this way, Kevin would ask her to live with him. But not yet. She had
pushed the idea away. There was too much to think about first. Did she want to
give up her own apartment, her independence? Not her job, certainly, never that,
but the freedom to come and go? And there was Joey. How should she present
this new arrangement to her son? She had already roused his curiosity when
she told him she would not be coming back to Nebraska for Thanksgiving. He
knew nothing about her relationship with Kevin.

"I mean it, Molly. You like it here. I like having you here. Move in with me."

"I—I can't," she stammered. "I'm not ready. I—we—don't know each
other well enough."

"I know you," he said. "You have freckles on your back. You moan when
you come. You snore. What more should I know?" Fingers moving. "What do
you want to know about me?"

"Not true. That wasn't me." Her mind went blank. She didn't moan. She
didn't snore. She tried to think. There must be something. So much she didn't
know. She needed time. "I have a year's lease on my apartment."

"I know your landlord. I can fix it. Come on," he insisted. "Give me one good reason. Anything you don't like here, we'll change. What is it? The color scheme? The food? The sex? What can I do to convince you to move?"

Her mind raced. Think, think. She rolled on to her stomach, burying her head in the pillow. His hand moved to her neck, kneading. "One reason," he said, "give me one good reason." His hand ran up and down her arm.

"I think I'd better leave," she murmured into the pillow. "I need to go home and think about this."

"I won't let you go," he said. His hand moved down her arm, his hand on her wrist, his body across her body, pinning her down.

"Kevin, I need to think about this." She pushed against him. He was heavy, heavier than Ted had ever been. "Let me go."

"You can think here, with me." He was unmoving.

"You're hurting me, Kevin. Let me go." She tried to lift herself up, to scoot away from under his arm, but his grip tightened.

"Tell me you'll move in with me, or I won't let you go." His voice was teasing, but his hold did not relax. She tried to kick away from him, gently at first, then with greater strength. He didn't move. Of course, he couldn't feel her kicks, even if she might be hurting him.

"Kevin, let me go, let go!" Her voice sounded strained and desperate, but he didn't respond. A voice came into her head, from a darkened room, someone, one of the women at the support group, *"He held me off the floor. He was that strong. And he said, I don't want you to leave."*

A horror of knowledge crept up her spine, her neck, the hairs on her head. She felt as if her brain would burst from the mass of insights racing through it, stories she had heard from women coming through SCAWF, lectures she had heard in training sessions.

She pushed against him one more time. He didn't budge. The voice came back. *"I told him I had to pee."* "I have to pee," she said.

He rolled away from her. Cool air rushed in to touch her back, then seemed to grow more and more voluminous, the space between them at first only inches wide becoming broader and broader, until it seemed they were miles apart, separated by a vast, un-crossable emptiness. She pulled herself to the edge of the bed and stood up, her back to him. She couldn't look at him. "You hurt me," she said.

From across the void, she heard him say, "I didn't intend to hurt you. I would never hurt you. I just want you here so badly. There's so much we could give each other. Talk to me, Molly."

"I can't. I need time." She stood unmoving, her hands covering her face.

After a few moments, she heard the mattress shift as he left the bed. She heard his chair moving, then the sound of a door closing, and then nothing at all.

TWENTY

DECEMBER

Molly dropped the mail and her mittens on the desk so she could fish around in her purse for Ted's handkerchief. Where was it? She found a tissue packet with one new tissue left, but that wasn't as good, not nearly as comforting as the old fabric made soft by many washings. What was wrong with her? She was so absent-minded these days, losing the last of Ted's old handkerchiefs, forgetting to buy more tissues, leaving her good driving gloves at home. It must be this cold that she couldn't shake, in spite of the Vitamin C and the herbal teas. And, she hadn't slept well for so many nights, or eaten a decent dinner. Not since she wasn't spending her evenings with Kevin.

She dropped the empty packet into her nearly full wastebasket, blotting her nose carefully with the last tissue. Kevin. No. She had too much to do this afternoon. She would not allow herself to think about him. She stood beside the wastebasket and sorted through the used tissues from her coat pockets, inspecting them before letting them fall. Her nose was always running these days, her eyes weepy. With all the Christmas music on the radio, sometimes she couldn't stop crying.

From the other office, Louise called to her. "Molly, I'm glad you're back. We need to get all the holiday donation requests out to last year's donor list before we leave tonight."

"Tonight? I don't see how I can."

"Get the volunteers to help you."

"Right," Molly answered, still inspecting tissues. "The volunteers." The volunteers were showing up late and leaving early in these weeks before Christmas, or not coming in at all. And those who did come to work were needed to collect the Christmas gifts from stations around the city, clothing and food that would keep the shelter going all year long.

There, this tissue had an un-used corner. Which would hurt her poor nose less, blowing or sniffing? She blew carefully, then sniffed and blotted. She wiped her eyes and added the tissue to the over-flowing basket. Tonight for sure she would take the plastic bag out and dump it at home, she thought. Faster than carting it out to the dumpster in the alley. She stomped her foot into the basket, crushing the contents into a more compact mass. There, that made room for the junk mail that would be discarded as soon as she took her coat off.

"Did you bring the mail?" The young woman stood in the doorway, a hopeful expression on her face. An infant in a blue corduroy carrier on her chest whimpered, while another child, whining and clinging to her hand, tried to pull her back toward the hall.

Molly nodded. Poor Jeanine. Poor kids. They were always fussing. Without removing her coat, Molly turned to the stack of envelopes and began sorting through them. Four piles: junk mail, mail for the shelter, for current residents, and for those who had moved on. Lots of donations these days, as the year drew to a close and the holiday spirit moved people to send checks to SCAWF. She would have to keep track of every envelope, to be sure that each donor received a thank-you letter, but the junk mail could go straight to the round file. Her nose dripped on the desk when she bent over. She took the last used tissue from her coat pocket and held it against her upper lip. "Sorry, Jeanine, there's nothing here for you."

"Are you sure?" Jeanine asked, patting the baby with one hand while the other was tugged behind her.

"Maybe tomorrow."

"Not later today?" Jeanine's hopeful expression faded. "They keep filling the boxes all day long. Maybe later this afternoon my check will come in."

Molly shook her head. She raised her voice so Jeanine could hear her over the noise of her children. "I don't have time to go to the post office more than once a day."

"I really need my check," Jeanine called over her shoulder, as she was pulled away.

"Don't we all," Molly muttered as she placed the mail for the residents in a basket near the door and dropped the mail for former residents into a box on top of the filing cabinet.

She tossed the last tissue into the wastebasket. Maybe in the closet, she thought, opening her desk drawer. Now, where are the keys?

Two volunteers bounced into the room. She recognized tall, red-haired Helen, but the other woman, an older woman in jeans, sweatshirt and diamond rings, was not someone she knew.

"Oh, Molly, you're back, good, we need you to tell us where to put the Christmas gifts," Helen said.

The keys were not at the front of her drawer. Damn!

"My friend Elaine came along to help carry. We've made two trips, and hit all six drop-off churches," Helen went on.

"We left the gifts piled in the hall, but they're blocking the exit if there's a fire," her companion added.

"Give me a minute, will you?" Molly snapped. "I haven't even had a chance to take my coat off yet."

The women looked at each other. "We just want to get started," the older one said, "so we can finish before we have to leave."

"Fine," Molly flared. "For starters, you can take all the gifts down to the basement."

"That's what we needed to know," Helen declared, as the two left the room.

"Talk about PMS!" Molly heard from the hallway.

"Umm. I thought she was too old for that."

Why did I talk to them that way? Molly asked herself. We need volunteers with enthusiasm. I've been so miserable lately, and I'm taking it out on everyone around me. It's this cold. No, it's not. It's Kevin, absence of Kevin. She lifted the black notebook of names of women not to be readmitted—drinkers, drug users, and violators of confidentiality—at the back of the drawer. The big key ring lay underneath. Good. She would hang up her coat, then go apologize to the volunteers.

Molly unfastened the padlock on the closet behind her. "What's this?" she said out loud. Three big new cartons occupied the most convenient spot on the center shelf. The smaller boxes that had been displaced were piled one into the other on the upper shelves. Not one of the labels Molly had carefully marked on the boxes—dental care, baby care, cosmetics, personal hygiene—was show-ing. "What's in these boxes?" she called. Her throat hurt when she spoke so loudly. "Who put this stuff in here?"

"Oh, that," Louise said behind her. She had come into Molly's office. "When yesterday's volunteers came in from picking up gifts at the churches, some of the church women had made these little bags to give to each new resident as she came in."

Molly sighed. "I thought we agreed that we couldn't accept any other dona-tions, except Christmas gifts, until after the holidays. We don't have storage space."

"The volunteers didn't know. They went straight to the first church from home. It's not that much," Louise shrugged, "only three boxes."

"Well, they can't stay here." Molly pulled one carton forward and lifted it off the shelf. She set it on the floor outside the closet and opened it. Inside were dozens of little drawstring bags sewn from brightly colored fabric. She picked up a bag made of red bandanna material. She had a bandanna like that. She had tied it around her head the day of the big storm in November, when she and Kevin planted the tulips. Her eyes filled with tears.

Louise was watching her. Molly pulled the bag open and looked inside. Toothpaste, toothbrush, comb, two tampons. A package of tissues. "We'll have to put these downstairs," she sniffed, "along with the Christmas gifts." She dug into the bandanna bag and transferred the packet of tissues to her pocket. "I guess we could keep a few bags up here," she said.

"Molly, is something wrong?" Louise asked.

"No, nothing," Molly answered. "Just this cold has affected my nose, my eyes. It may look like I'm crying, but it's the cold." A voice in her head said, *"When I came to work with my eyes all red from crying, I told people I had allergies."*

"If you feel like talking," Louise continued, "I know this is a stressful time here right now, with all the stuff coming in that has to be acknowledged and put away, but if you need to talk to someone, I can always make time for you. You have been so efficient here, and learned our ways so quickly, that I didn't think to schedule an evaluation meeting. I haven't told you how well you are doing. We could have tea, if you'd like, in my office. I have an electric pot, all steamed up."

As she talked, Louise seemed to change again, the way she had changed on Molly's first day at SCAWF when she talked to Molly about women in transitional stages of life. Her voice evened out, her back grew straighter, the expression on her face became reasonable, impartial, open. She seemed to Molly to be neater looking, too, crisper, if that were possible. Molly let herself be drawn by this professional Louise into the inner office.

Seated in the worn chair, still in her coat, a cup of tea in one hand and a tissue in the other, Molly hesitated before she began. Maybe she should not talk to Louise, but Louise was waiting, in her social worker's manner. "Where should I begin?"

"Wherever you'd like," Louise encouraged.

Molly took a deep breath. Louise already knew that she had met someone. "The man I told you about, the one who helped me move in. That is, the man who has a houseman who helped me move."

Louise nodded.

Once she had started, it was easier. "I've been seeing him. I've been seeing a lot of him." Molly sipped her tea. How much more should she tell Louise?

Louise waited.

"He was so helpful to me, so kind." Molly thought of the great sex. "And so—loving." She didn't have to be specific. "There's a lot I don't know about him. People told me things, but I didn't believe them. And I'm not sure if they're true. He hurt me…I think. I'm not sure if he hurt me. He says he didn't mean to hurt me."

Louise had a way of nodding her head once or twice just before she started speaking. "Some of the women who come to us, as you know, aren't sure of what is happening to them," she commented. Molly noticed that she didn't ask for details. "So you have talked to him about what happened."

Molly shook her head. "He said he was teasing. He said I had spent too much time talking to abused women. We haven't talked much since. He's tried to call, but I didn't want to talk to him. And he sent a note. With Ben. That's his houseman. And a roasted chicken." Her nose was running again. "But I sent the chicken back." Louise handed her another tissue. "And there's something I haven't told you yet. He's paraplegic, in a wheelchair."

"Does that make a difference to you?"

"Not any more. At first, I was curious." Molly thought of that day long ago, lying in her bath, wondering about sex with Kevin. She couldn't tell Louise, who had never been married. "Now it's just who he is."

"Maybe you shouldn't see each other for a while. Cool down. Think things over. Spend time with other people."

"I don't know any other people. I spend all my spare time with Kevin."

Louise smiled. "In high school, you were always surrounded by a crowd of people. You were always organizing trips to movies or tennis parties. Don't you go to church, to a gym?"

Molly shook her head. "He is... he was so much fun to be with. I didn't want to be with anyone else."

"What about his friends? Did you meet people through him? And the people here at SCAWF? They do lots of things together. Or me. We haven't spent any time together, outside of work." Molly couldn't tell her what Kevin had said about her job at SCAWF, and about Louise herself. "But now you're unhappy, and you don't want to continue this way. What would you like to have happen now?"

"I don't know," Molly answered, sniffing into the tissue. "There's something else. I didn't tell you everything. It wasn't anything hurtful that he said. He may have been... have been... abusive. Physically abusive."

If Louise was surprised or shocked, she didn't show it. Molly waited for a lecture on signs of an abusive personality. There was nothing that she hadn't already thought of herself. Louise would try to point out that Kevin had been controlling, that he had isolated her from other people, and that they had rushed into an involvement much too quickly. But she didn't. She said, "It isn't easy to talk about this, but of course you already know that, from working with our clients."

Molly took a deep breath. She knew that women had difficulty talking about their abuse, but she hadn't realized how difficult it was. Now that she had said the words, it was easier. She said them again: "Physically abusive. Maybe. I'm not sure."

"Many of our clients are not sure they have been abused when they first call us." Louise crossed her arms in front of her chest and looked up at the ceiling. "You know, social workers are not encouraged to play therapist for their friends."

"I don't need a therapist," Molly protested. "I need a friend."

"As your friend, then, let me say that you know a lot about domestic violence from your time working here these last four months. You know more than most women do when they call us for the first time. But one thing that our clients learn quickly is that it's much easier to deal with their situation if they don't try to face it alone. I think you should talk to Jayne Brooker."

"No!" Molly protested. "No, I can't talk to anyone else. I'll figure it out myself."

"Jayne Brooker is the expert on recognizing the abusive personality. You heard her in group. I'm surprised that you haven't called her already. When we were in school together, I always knew I wouldn't have to work very hard when we did projects together. The Molly I knew then would have exhausted every resource to learn everything there is to know about batterers."

"He's not. He's not a batterer. It was just one time. He didn't mean to hurt me. He was teasing."

"Yoo-hoo, hello," the volunteers called from the outer office. "We're back."

Molly dried her eyes and stood up.

"If he was only teasing, Molly, ask yourself why you aren't speaking to him. It doesn't have to be Jayne Brooker. We have a list of therapists who work with some of our residents. I'd be happy to go over the names with you, to help you choose someone who would be compatible."

I knew I shouldn't have talked to Louise, Molly thought. A therapist! I don't need help from a stranger.

In the outer office, Helen announced with satisfaction, "All the gifts are put away, in the back store room. And we have to be on our way."

"Oh, no," Molly burst out. "I need you."

Helen looked at her with raised eyebrows.

"There is so much paper work that has to be done today," Molly begged. "I was counting on you to stay a little longer and help."

"Sorry," Helen said, but she didn't sound sorry. "I have plans for the rest of the day. I have someone waiting for me."

"What will you do?" Elaine asked.

"I guess I'll get the letters out myself. I'll stay this evening and work as long as it takes."

Elaine pursed her lips. "If I can get a ride home later, I can stay a little longer. My husband is working late tonight. No one will miss me if I don't come straight home."

No one will miss me, either, if I don't come straight home, Molly thought, and felt the tears beginning to gather again. "That would be wonderful, Elaine," she said.

TWENTY ONE

The phone was ringing when Molly entered her office the next morning, but by the time she put down the grocery bags, settled them solidly so that they wouldn't topple over, the caller was gone. She picked up her keys and mitten from the floor, caught the drip from her nose with a tissue. Where was the other mitten? And where was the counselor? The other desk was empty. Who was going to answer the phone? Not me, not again, not today. She found the big key ring in the desk drawer and opened the closet. Boxes of ditty bags still there from yesterday, filling the most accessible shelves. Shit!

After she'd draped her coat on a hook, she turned to the grocery bags. The volunteers would be here soon. Her cold was no better. Worse, if anything. She shouldn't have stayed up so late last night. Start the coffee first, then arrange everything else, she thought, but her nose came before anything. She pulled the big box of tissues out from under the mail, broke the seal and tugged at the top tissue. A handful of torn pieces. Nothing was going right today.

"Molly," Louise came in from the hallway, "bad news again. Marian called in sick, and didn't get a relief counselor."

Molly shook her head. "I can't do it. I have volunteers coming in to work on Christmas gifts. There's no way I can cover the phone."

"It's a busy time for all of us, and I know you're not feeling well. I have some calls out. Someone will turn up soon."

Someone always turned up to rescue Louise, Molly thought.

"But until then, we'll just have to muddle along as best we can," Louise went on. "I'll handle the calls, but we had a new woman come in last night. Daphne. I'll need you to do the intake."

Molly turned away from Louise, thinking, I should have called in sick myself. Stayed in bed all day, made a decision about Kevin. If only I had time to think about him, without all these other problems. Was he really only teasing, as he said? But he had held her down, and it had hurt. She had been so frightened! Still, she didn't have any bruises. So was he abusive?

Behind her, Louise was still talking. "Molly? Molly, are you all right?"

"Yes, I'm sorry, Louise, I was just thinking," Molly stammered. She would have to put Kevin out of her mind. "About the volunteers, what we need for them. I had the feeling I'd forgotten something."

"That's what I just asked," Louise said, with a touch of annoyance. "Do you have everything you need?"

"Yes, I think so." Molly rummaged through the grocery bags. "Coffee, tea, cookies, sweet rolls, bread, cheese, lunchmeat. I think I have everything."

The doorbell buzzed behind them. Louise raised her eyebrows. "No one should be coming this early."

Molly picked up the intercom phone. "Hello?"

"It's Tammy."

"Who?" She looked at Louise. Did they have a volunteer named Tammy? Not on her list.

"Me. Tammy. I've come back."

Tammy? Molly's mind raced. There had been so many women in the three months. "Tammy?" The shorn hair! On her first day, when that angry man had tried to force his way into the shelter. Then Tammy had left the shelter, convinced by her husband that he would change.

Molly opened the front door. The frightened face looked up at her. "Tammy, how are you?" Her hair was trimmed now, to a short length. The patches of clipped hair weren't obvious until Molly looked closely. Tammy's children clung to her, one on each side. They all followed Molly down the hallway and huddled in the chair next to the desk, both little girls scrambling onto Tammy's lap.

"I had to come here," Tammy said. "I didn't have no place else to go."

Molly perched on the edge of her desk. "It didn't work out when you went back." It was a statement, not a question.

"At first, he was so sweet. No one ever treated me so sweet. Then, I don't know what I did, but he changed. He was just like before."

"The honeymoon stage. Tammy, didn't you go over that in group? How, at first, a guy will be so sweet, promise you the moon, and then gradually he begins to be abusive, first a little bit, and then more and more? Didn't you hear about the cycle of violence?"

"People were always preaching at me like that. The honeymoon stage, then the abuse begins again. I got so tired of hearing that. And I thought if I tried harder…"

"Oh, Tammy, you poor dear. It isn't anything you did or didn't do, it's him. He's the one with the problem." Molly sighed. If only they could convince the women who came here of that, they could close the shelter, she thought. "Did you have any trouble getting here? Did your abuser follow you?"

"Do you mean Ricky? My husband?" Molly nodded. Tammy shook her head. "He doesn't know. He's at work. He works until late tonight." She swallowed, then went on. "He told me I had to clean the house, that it better be clean when he got home or I'd be sorry. I was vacuuming the sofa, poking behind the pillows, and I heard some money rattling in the pipe, you know? He never lets me have money. So I opened the bag to look, and it was enough for bus fare. I walked up to the school to get the girls and came here."

And here you are, Molly thought. No clothes, no money. Do we have three beds? She looked at the chart. Yes, there was space. Still, something bothered Molly. She picked up the Do Not Admit notebook lying on her desk and leafed through it. "What's your last name, Tammy?"

"Ferguson."

"Of course. I'm sorry. There's so much going on here now, I can't think…" She found the *F*s, then *FE*. There it was. Yellow sticker. Possible violation of confidentiality. Yes, that was it. The flicker of fear that had crossed Tammy's face when the man tried to break in. She had told someone the location of the shelter.

"Tammy, you must be very honest with me." Molly sat down at her desk so her eyes would be level with Tammy's. "If there is any possibility that your husband can find you here, this isn't a safe place for you."

Tammy pulled her daughters closer and bent her head over them, hiding her face against the younger girl's neck. From that angle, the patches of new hair showed soft and fine.

"Tammy? When you last stayed here, did anyone learn where the shelter is located? Could Ricky follow you here?"

"My mom. My mom dropped us off at the corner, a couple of times, when it was raining real hard. She saw where we turned in."

"Do you think your mom might tell your husband where you are?"

Tammy nodded. "She says a wife has a duty to her husband and children, to stay together. That's what God intends."

Molly shook her head. "You can't stay here, Tammy." Tammy looked up, panic on her face. "It's okay, we're not going to abandon you. We'll help you find another shelter. You'll be all right."

"But I like it here."

"I'm sorry, Tammy." How easy it is to say these words now, Molly thought. Three months ago I would have had difficulty saying them. "You just can't stay."

———

"Does everyone have tea or coffee?"

The eight women in the dining room did not look up or stop chattering. It's my cold, Molly thought, they can't hear me and I can't yell. She looked around for something that would make noise. Paper cups. Plastic spoons. Steam rising from the electric coffee maker. She lifted the lid of the coffee maker and tapped it against the side a few times. The conversations stopped.

"Good morning, everybody. Do you all have tea or coffee?"

Murmurs of assent. Molly recognized Elaine and Helen, from yesterday. Good for them. Elaine had stayed, helped with the mailing until Molly drove her home at seven, and now she was back for more. Different designer sweatshirt, same diamond rings. And Helen. Molly had been afraid that Helen would not come back, after her own nastiness toward the volunteers. She would have to make a special effort to be charming to Helen today. Tiny, of course. One of their most faithful volunteers, she came in at least once a week. Tiny still went back to exaggerated street slang occasionally, the way she had spoken on Molly's first day at SCAWF, but now it was addressed to all, not an attack on Molly. They weren't friends, exactly, but they had developed a style of working together. She did not know the other women.

"My name is Molly Bennet. I am the staff person in charge of Christmas gifts here at SCAWF, the Seattle Center for Abused Women and Their Families. I want to thank all of you for giving up your precious time at this very busy season to come here and help us out." She had to stop to cough. Sympathetic noises from the group.

"Before we begin to work, I want to emphasize one more time the great importance of confidentiality in the shelter. You must never tell anyone—not anyone—where the shelter is located. It could jeopardize the lives of the women who are staying here."

The volunteers looked at each other, absorbing the seriousness of Molly's words.

"But that said, we want you to be comfortable while you are here. There will be coffee and tea in the dining room all day, with cookies and sweet rolls, and we'll put out sandwich makings around noon. Please take breaks often." More murmurs. Approval. Good. That was right out of the volunteer manager's manual: feed the volunteers.

"And be sure to pick up a name tag, so we can get to know one another." She patted the paper stuck to her shoulder: Hello, I'm MOLLY. "This is what needs to be done." Molly took a list out of her pocket. "We have six stations around the city, mostly in churches, where people have been leaving gifts for the shelter. Two of you have agreed to do pick-up. The rest of us will be downstairs unwrapping and sorting the gifts we already have, and then later rewrapping them. So get yourselves supplied with cookies, and we'll get started. Who is going to do pick-up today?"

Two women detached themselves from the group, and Molly gave them the list, with driving directions and the names of their contact person at each stop. By the time she was finished, the other volunteers were dropping their paper cups in the wastebasket and brushing crumbs from their fingers. Chatting, the women trailed behind Molly through the dim basement hallway to the big storeroom. They gasped when she unlocked the door to an enormous pile of gift-wrapped boxes, rich in color and texture, the metallic papers and ribbon shining in the light of the single bulb on the ceiling.

"Wow!"

"Santa's workshop!"

"Lord have mercy." This from Tiny.

Molly moved around the big tables in the center of the room. "We brought some lamps down so we could see," she explained, turning on floor lamps. "Be careful of the cords, they're all over the floor." She waited a few minutes while the volunteers moved into the room and recovered from their initial surprise. "Our work is in front of us," she announced. "We have to open each one of these packages and sort the contents. Then later we'll have to re-wrap. So if you have any hostile energy to get rid of," she said, lifting a beautifully wrapped blue and silver box, large enough to hold a coat or a robe, "this is your chance." She ripped the blue and silver paper and dropped it on the floor.

"No!"

"Oh, no."

"I'm sorry, ladies," Molly explained. "There's just no other way to find out what's inside."

"But we can try to save the paper," one of the women protested, a gray-haired woman who reminded Molly of her grandmother. No name tag. "Slit the tape with a knife and take the paper off carefully."

Molly shook her head. "We'll be here all winter if we try to do that. I know it seems harsh. We ask people not to wrap their gifts, to send the paper and ribbon alongside, but they just don't."

"I remember when I was a kid," Crystal said slowly, running her fingers across a red and gold wrapped box. "We always spent one evening, a week before Christmas, wrapping presents for poor people, talking about how much it would mean to those folks to get something nice on Christmas morning. I hate to think someone rewrapped everything we put together with such love."

Whoops, wrong track, Molly thought. "Maybe, in that situation, you knew something about the people that would receive your gifts," she suggested. "A designated family."

Crystal's face brightened.

"We can't tell our donors about the people who will receive their gifts," Molly went on, "partly because we can't reveal anything about the people staying here, and partly because we don't give everything away at Christmas."

The women muttered. They didn't like that. Molly took a deep breath. "We have so much coming in at this season. It wouldn't be fair to give everything to the families who happen to be here now, and have nothing for the ones who arrive in a month or even next summer. So we store most of what we get, and distribute it throughout the year."

"Sounds fair," Elaine commented.

"If you put it that way," came from Tiny.

"I guess so."

When she felt sure that the volunteers had accepted the situation, Molly continued. "All the gifts on the tables have to be opened and taken out of the boxes. Put the paper in these garbage cans, the boxes under the tables. Then sort the gifts. Women's clothing in this corner, children's in that corner. Toys over here. Other gifts—you'll find jewelry, cosmetics, purses—here near the door. Got that?"

"But this box is marked," the grandmotherly volunteer insisted. "See? 'Women's robe, size 12.' Can't we just set it aside?"

"It's wasteful, I know," Molly told her. Her own grandmother would have reacted exactly the same way. "But we don't know, do we, what kind of size 12 robe it is. What if it's a wool plaid, and we give it to someone who likes frills and lace? Even in a place like SCAWF—especially in a place like SCAWF—a woman is entitled to something suited to her own taste."

"If it has to be done," Elaine said, "let's get started." With great gusto, she tore the paper from a big, odd-shaped package with an enormous red bow.

Bless you, Elaine, Molly thought. Many happy years in your designer sweatshirts and your diamond rings.

"Can't we at least save the bow?" Grandmother asked.

"Yes, I think that would work," Molly agreed. "Any fancy trim that can be saved and re-used easily," she emphasized the last word, "let's put over here, with the new gift wrap."

"Oh, my," Elaine exclaimed, looking at the assortment of toys she had uncovered. "This could outfit a whole nursery school." She moved the toys to the right area. "Let's separate the dolls from the other toys," she suggested, "so every little girl will be sure to get a doll."

"Every little girl who wants a doll should be sure to get one," Tiny corrected.

"Of course," Elaine was unperturbed. "If a little girl wants a truck, we'll give her a truck."

"If you're all sure of what to do, I'm going to leave you for just a minute," Molly told them. There was still Tammy, and the new woman.

"Are the girls all settled in daycare?" she asked, coming in to the office. Without waiting for an answer, she continued, "How are you doing?"

"Not good." Tammy held up the list of phone numbers. "No one has room."

"Maybe you'll have to go outside of Seattle, Tammy. Do you have family or friends in some other city who would take you in?"

"I always lived here."

"We may have to change that for awhile. You're going to try another list of out-of-town shelters. These will be long distance calls, Tammy. Have you ever made long distance calls?"

The girl shook her head.

"Well, for a long distance call, you always punch the one first, even though it isn't written down. That way you can call Tacoma or Bremerton or Everett."

"But I don't want to go to any of those places." Tammy's eyes filled with tears. "Why can't I stay in Seattle?"

"You called all the numbers on that paper. Those are the shelters in Seattle."

"Maybe if you called. Maybe they have spaces they wouldn't tell me about."

"No, Tammy. You have to call for yourself. You have to learn to make your own decisions. Then a person like Ricky won't be able to take over your life."

Tammy sighed. "Gimme the list," she said, snatching it from Molly's hand.

Downstairs again, Molly heard the women exclaiming as they tore open the packages. "Look Molly, mittens!" Helen held up a box for Molly to see as she came through the door. "Can you believe it? Someone gift-wrapped this big box of mittens all together. I wonder what they were thinking. All sizes, all colors in one box."

"I used to knit mittens all the time," Grandmother said, fingering a baby's tiny thumb-less mitten, "until my grandchildren wanted gloves with TV characters."

The women worked quickly, ripping the paper and opening the boxes, all except for Grandmother. Molly watched her sorting through the pile. What was she looking for? She found a short, narrow package and felt it carefully. "Ah," she announced, and looked up. She blushed when her eyes met Molly's. "This is an umbrella. I'm sure of it. No need to unwrap it, is there?"

"Not if you're sure."

"Then I'll put it over here," she said, with great satisfaction, and then went back to inspecting the pile for other gifts that didn't need unwrapping.

The other women continued to tear open the packages.

"Look at this!"

"Oh, my!"

"How about this!"

In the midst of the noise, Louise came down. "Phone call for you, Molly, line one." Who could be calling her? She didn't know anyone, except Kevin and Ben. Would Kevin call? What if something had happened to him?

Tammy had taken Molly's desk, so Molly picked up the counselor's phone. "This is Molly."

"It's Nancy. Jane and I are picking up Christmas gifts."

"Yes, Nancy. Is there a problem?"

"I don't know. Something funny. We're at our last stop, but before we got here, they say a call came in. Someone left a message that they're bringing in a lot of gifts and we should be sure to wait for them."

"Who left the message?"

"They didn't say, and what we want to know is, should we wait for them or should we come in?"

"No, Nancy, don't wait. We'll be making one more pick-up before Christmas. Come on in."

Louise was standing in the door of the inner office watching her when Molly hung up. "Problem?"

"I hope not," Molly sighed. "Someone called one of the drop-off points and said we should wait for a lot of gifts. Was that some kind of mischief, or just some well-meaning person who didn't want to be late?"

Louise turned back into her office. "We'll know soon enough."

"Molly!" Tammy brought her back from all the hurtful possibilities that had filled her head. "Molly, I've made all these calls and they're all full! Now what do I do?"

"Keep trying. You'll just have to go a little further away." Molly left an unhappy Tammy with another list of long distance numbers and went down to check on the gifts again. The women's voices sounded angry as she approached the room.

185

"Molly," Tiny was indignant. "Look at this!" She held up a heavy knit sweater, re-embroidered with lavish leaves and flowers.

"It's gorgeous. I wish it were mine." Molly took it from Tiny and held it up against her body.

"Oh, yeah?" Tiny grumbled. "Take a good look."

Molly turned the sweater from front to back. A wisp of yarn caught her eye. At the waistline in the back, there was a large round hole. "What in the world?" The hole was almost three inches across, a perfect circle. "What is this?"

"You tell us," Elaine fumed.

"And look at this," Helen chimed in. She held up a long quilted satin robe, deep blue. "Look here." A straight slit extended about ten inches from the hem up the side of the robe. The slit was not in a seam but parallel to it, about two inches away.

"What's going on? Where did these come from?"

"They all came in these gold foil boxes," Tiny complained.

"But that can't be. These are McGuire's boxes. The store sent us a load of gifts."

"Every one of them is deliberately damaged. It's unconscionable!" Elaine proclaimed.

"Huh? Talk English, girl! It's just wrong!" That was Tiny.

Molly was thinking out loud. "They're taking a tax deduction. I signed a receipt for a thousand dollars worth of wrapped gifts."

"It's not fair! It's not right," Elaine continued. "They shouldn't be sending damaged merchandise just because the recipients live in a shelter. The women here are just as entitled to nice new gifts at Christmas as anyone else."

"That's not it. They don't trust the women here," Tiny explained. "They're thinking, if a poor woman gets a nice expensive sweater for a Christmas gift, the day after Christmas she will take it back to McGuire's and ask for the money back. But a sweater with a hole can't be exchanged!"

"I don't believe this. Either way. I can't..." Molly mumbled to herself as the women around her grew angrier. Not now. Take control. "All right, everyone, let's settle down," she exclaimed. "This is a good time for a coffee break. Everyone upstairs!"

The women grumbled as they left the room. Molly stayed behind, gathering all the gold foil boxes. Hide them. Where? She opened the door of the food storage room across the hall and locked the gold boxes in with the cases of canned fruit.

Cookies and coffee helped. The shared anger at McGuire's brought them closer. Tiny practiced saying "unconscionable" for Elaine, who told her, approvingly, "You've got it."

As they left the dining room, a woman stepped out of the counselor's office, then retreated. "Daphne? Daphne Redinger?" Elaine greeted her warmly. "Have you come to help too?"

The woman came out slowly. Bright pink spots on her cheeks. "Hello, Elaine."

"I wish I'd known you were working here today," Elaine told her. "We could have driven together."

"I'm not here to work," the woman murmured. Was this the new resident? Molly studied her. Probably her own age. Elegantly dressed. Just slacks and a sweater, but of gray cashmere, and the pink blouse must be silk. Silver-blonde hair, a little messy, but that color, that style, had to be done by a professional salon. And Elaine knew her! Best get her inside.

"You ladies all know what to do without me," Molly said quickly. "Daphne? Come in. We'll make this as easy as possible."

Tammy looked up from Molly's desk and quickly scooted her chair closer to the wall, pulling the telephone with her. The little girls followed her, leaning in toward their mother.

"I guess we can go to the dining room for privacy," Molly suggested.

Daphne shrugged. "It doesn't matter." She seated herself next to the counselor's desk, and Molly joined her.

Molly tried to speak softly, so Tammy couldn't hear. "Are you settled in your room? Anything you need?"

"Toothpaste. I left in such a hurry, and I…I have no money. It's embarrassing…"

"No, don't feel that way. We try to have everything here a woman could need." Molly rose and unlocked the closet. Which box in the messy pile held the dental stuff? "Here. We have these little bags that a group of church women make for us…" She offered Daphne a bright calico bag.

Daphne turned away. "Oh, no, please…I'm not quite that…"

Molly opened the bag, removed the sample-sized tube of toothpaste and brought it back to the desk. "I'm sorry about Elaine. I'll talk to her. I'm sure she won't tell anyone she saw you here."

Daphne shrugged, "I will be their topic of gossip soon enough."

"I'll make this as easy as possible." Molly drew an intake form from the box on the counselor's desk. "I'd like you to tell me what happened to bring you here today, how you heard about SCAWF…"

"How I heard." Daphne tucked a loose strand of hair behind her ear. Molly noticed a broken nail on an otherwise perfectly manicured hand. "I have known about SCAWF since it was first started. I have supported it…written checks, attended the galas…"

"Oh," Molly blurted out, "I went to the New Century Gala this year. Maybe I saw you there."

"It's quite possible." Daphne pushed the hair back again. "Don't look so startled. We're not that different, those of us writing the checks, from the women who come here."

"But, why?" Women like Daphne shouldn't need to come here, she thought. "You could have gone to a hotel…"

Daphne shook her head. "My dear husband emptied our bank accounts, cancelled all my credit cards."

"He can't do that," Molly protested.

"He reported them stolen. Same thing. Then he threatened me and began throwing things, so I left."

"Would he follow you?"

"Oh, yes. He doesn't care about me, but he cares about his reputation."

"Had your husband ever been abusive before?"

"Always. I just wasn't smart enough to see it." She turned her face from Molly and stared at the wall for a long time.

"Daphne? Are you all right?"

She nodded, took a deep breath and turned back toward Molly. "It took me a long time to wake up. The name-calling, the way he humiliated me in front of our friends. I thought that was just his way. And he always provided for me. Nice home, nice car. Then when he started to…to slap me, to hit me with his fist…I thought, stay, for the sake of the children…" She laughed. "As soon as our children could, they left. And they said I had been stupid and spineless to stay."

Molly thought of her own son, objecting to her move to Seattle. "Our kids get a little bit of independence, and they think they know everything."

"No, they were right." Daphne took another deep breath. "And when they said they weren't coming home for Christmas, I looked around at my beautiful, empty house and asked myself, 'What are you doing here?' But I made the mistake of telling Donald that I was leaving."

Molly glanced across to the other desk. Tammy sat open-mouthed, her eyes full of tears.

"Tammy! You have calls to make!"

———

Molly had become so proficient at settling new clients that it didn't take long to write Daphne's intake report. A short history, and her plans: to find a lawyer, get a protection order, and obtain financial support.

Back in the hallway outside the sorting room, Molly stopped to take a deep breath. Deep breathing relieves stress, she'd read that somewhere. In in in, out out out. She pressed her hands against her face. Her hands were cold, so nice and cool over her eyes. She leaned against the wall, her whole body absorbing cold from the bare plaster, and then turned her face to cool the other cheek. In a minute, she would go in, look at the piles of gifts, explain the next step, hand out the request lists from the clients, start them rewrapping. For now it was enough to be cool, almost calm, to wait in the dim light listening to the women talking.

"Christmas day is one party after another," Elaine was saying. "Christmas Eve used to be our family time, but now none of the kids will be home. Maybe I'll go to church."

"When my family was home, they went to church, while I stayed home cooking." It was Grandmother's voice. "Now I go to church Christmas eve and Christmas morning, both. Anyone wants to see me, they can fit their visit in with my schedule."

"Do you open presents at night or in the morning?" Tiny asked. Chorus of voices, sounding evenly divided. She and Ted had opened their special presents to each other late at night, when they were alone. Molly remembered a string of pearls once when she had expected a blender, a lace and satin peignoir the year she was pregnant. And their last Christmas, the year he was so sick, diamond earrings. She never had learned how he had managed that.

"Our family never did get straight on Christmas," she heard Helen say. "My family did our big celebration on Christmas eve. Warren's family did it in the morning. Somehow we never ever worked out an arrangement that was right for us."

Tammy rushed into the hallway. "I found a place, Molly. It's in Portland."

"That's great, Tammy." Molly hugged the exultant young woman. "Do you know how you're going to get to Portland?"

"It's three hours by bus. I asked them did they have a place, and they're saving it for us. I'll call them from the bus station."

"That's good. Do you have bus money?"

"Louise found me some. And she's going to get us some clothes." Tammy wrapped her arms around herself and squeezed. "You know, you counselors keep saying, make your own plans, help yourself, but I didn't think I could do it. But I did."

"How long can you stay there?"

"Four weeks!"

"Good, that's good, Tammy, but four weeks can go by very quickly. Now that you know that you can plan for yourself, you have to work with the counselors in Portland to get yourself a new life."

"Don't preach at me, Molly! I have four weeks."

Sending Tammy off to care for her children, Molly pushed herself away from the wall and joined the women ripping and tearing in the storeroom.

"Whoo-ee!" Tiny squealed. "Now what do you think of this for an abused woman?" She lifted the skinny straps of a peach-colored nightgown and held it high above her head. Molly could see the whites of Tiny's eyes, her white teeth, through the gossamer fabric. "This is a gown for a woman whose man keeps the lights on when they make love."

Molly's eyes filled with tears. Kevin kept the lights on so he could see her, his pajama top over the lampshade to soften the light. Damn! She had tried so hard not think of him. If she could keep herself busy, concentrate on tearing up giftwrap and jamming it into the wastebasket, then he shouldn't creep into her head that way. Tissue, she must have a tissue, her nose was running, her eyes. She bent over, hiding her face from the others, and pretended to pick up torn giftwrap from the floor. "Try to keep the floor clear," she sniffed, stuffing paper into the garbage cans.

The volunteers ignored her. All of them, even Grandmother, were absorbed in their task, discussing the gifts, reminiscing about their own Christmas pasts. The pile of wrapped gifts diminished, the piles in the corners grew bigger.

Three hours later, Molly drove through the December rain to the bus station. On the seat beside her, Tammy clutched a paper shopping bag containing a nightgown, underwear, a sweater, jeans, and a shirt. She had one of the church women's ditty bags full of toiletries and one of the new pairs of mittens. Tammy had been so excited when they gave her the little bag. Not like Daphne, but Tammy wasn't Daphne. In the back seat, the girls had another shopping bag between them. They would be safe for a short time, at least, unless Tammy violated confidentiality again. "Now Tammy," Molly lectured, "you're a grown woman. You must not tell anyone, even your own mother, where you are. Can you do that?"

Tammy nodded and started to cry.

"Tammy, I'm sorry, I didn't mean to upset you." They had stopped for a red light. She reached into her coat pocket and found a tissue, a new one, for Tammy. "It's just that I don't want you to be hurt anymore. I want you to learn to take care of yourself."

"I know. I'll be all right, don't worry about me."

Molly waited in the station until the bus pulled out. As she drove back to SCAWF, her own words echoed in her head. *"I want you to learn to take care of yourself."* All well and good, but even better would be two people who took care of each other.

TWENTY TWO

Molly stood outside the entrance to her building, shaking her umbrella and folding it up before she went inside. For the past two weeks she had gone back to parking in the lot, a short run through the rain to her door, instead of parking in Kevin's nearer garage. It didn't seem right any more.

He was sitting in front of her door when she came inside. "Molly, you have to let me explain. We have to talk."

"You shouldn't be here, Kevin." She unlocked her door and pushed it open. "I told you I needed time to think."

He rolled through the doorway after her.

"Don't take your coat off," she warned.

"I'm not planning to stay very long."

"It's very cold in here," she continued, crossing to the thermostat on the far wall. "And it takes a while to warm up."

"I guess I forgot what it's like to leave home every day. The heat is always on in my house..." His voice trailed off, then continued hopefully, "We could go up to my place..." He didn't finish the sentence.

Molly didn't answer, but turned to the kitchen, still in her damp coat, and busied herself with the teakettle.

He followed her. "Molly, you must understand that I would never willingly hurt you. I can't help that I am so strong." He lifted his hands from the armrests and dropped them again. "I have a lot of upper body strength. You must know that. I push myself and my chair around. I lift myself out of my chair every twenty minutes. You've seen me do that."

She remembered that he had told her how he had to lift up, to prevent his skin from breaking down. *"Because I sit all the time there's pressure on my skin, on my butt and my thighs,"* he had said.

"So I'm strong." As he spoke, he pushed himself up off the chair and held himself there. Molly remembered the first time she had seen him, sitting in his open car, his arms and shoulders bulging inside the bright, white shirt. "It's because I'm disabled, isn't it? It's hard for you to accept."

"No, not at all, it was never that." That was a lie, she acknowledged to herself. It had been a problem at first, but not any longer. "Kevin, I can't think right now. We are so busy with Christmas presents, and year-end donations, and new clients coming, and strange things happening. Give me some time."

"Of course, Molly. But what kind of strange things?"

It was none of his business, but she had developed the habit of telling him about her day. "I don't know," she said. "Strange things. Yesterday someone called one of our pick-up spots and asked us to wait for him to deliver some gifts. Then he didn't show up. Today at the post office box there was a man watching me, I think. Maybe not. Maybe he was just standing out of the rain." The words tumbled out. "And one of our clients had to leave town because she broke confidentiality."

She paused, then went on, "December is so dark and gray. And I have a cold." Why am I telling him all these things, she asked herself, and answered, because I don't have any other friends. I really am isolated. But did Kevin do this to me? He is so easy to talk to.

Kevin was speaking. "…It doesn't look as if you have any dinner started. I know that Ben was making soup today, and my apartment is already warm. If you came up, just for a little while…"

"You'd better leave," she said.

All the next day she went through the motions of her job automatically—picked up the mail at the post office box while peering carefully over her shoulder to see if anyone was watching her; supervised the volunteers rewrapping the last of the gifts; inspected the stacked and checked-off gifts to make sure each resident received most of the items on her wish list, plus a few luxuries besides; gathered the beautifully wrapped packages into big, clean trash bags, one for each resident and one for each child; and stowed the remaining gifts in the basement storeroom so that in-coming residents in the spring and summer would all have new slippers and nightgowns and robes and even bath oil and body lotion.

All day long, she tried not to think about Kevin. All day she thought about nothing else. It was so confusing. All of the warning signs of the batterer that Jayne Brooker had talked about might have been Kevin. He might be isolating, controlling. Maybe his wife had found him controlling. But maybe he is just a nurturing person. Where is the line? She knew he cared for her, she was sure of it. Had he been isolating? Maybe she enjoyed his company so much that she didn't look for other friends. Maybe he didn't mean to hurt her when he held her down. He could have been teasing. His voice had been teasing. Was the great fear that she had felt over-reacting? She didn't have any bruises the next day. And he had been so good to her. Like Tammy said, *no one ever treated me so sweet.*

At the end of the day, sitting in front of her computer, she still didn't know what to think. Someone was speaking to her.

"I'll make it up to you," Patty repeated, wrapping her scarf around her head. "Some time when you want to leave early."

"It's okay, Patty. I don't mind staying on."

"Well, good-bye then."

Molly turned back to her computer. November was closed. There were new bills to pay, the payroll, but those could wait. She didn't feel like starting any new projects.

Outside her window, the same dark gray. The lights in the shelter burned all day at this time of year, but it was never bright enough. A gust of wind, rain spattering against the window. She remembered that day in November, watching the raindrops run together on Kevin's window.

She swung the chair around to her desk. Daphne's folder lay there, waiting to be moved to the inactive file. Daphne had left this morning, taking charge of her own life, as the counselors advised, just as Molly had done a few months ago. Or had she? If I'm really in charge of my own life, she asked herself, why am I feeling so rotten?

A door slammed behind her. Lorraine, the night-shift counselor, closing the closet.

"Oh, Lorraine, I didn't hear you come in." She glanced at the window. Completely dark!

"Really." Lorraine looked at her quizzically. "I've been talking to you. I said, are you going home now, or do you want me to lock up this closet?"

"Oh, sorry, I'm leaving." She waited for Lorraine to step aside, took her coat off its peg, and tied her scarf around her head. A blast of cold air hit her when she opened the front door. She put her head down and stepped off the porch into the rain. Even with all the leaves gone, the big old trees diverted most of the light from the street lamps. Her car was parked almost at the end of the block. As she hurried along, an engine started up. Now why couldn't that person have left this morning, when she needed the parking space close to the house? The wind blew icy cold drops against her legs. It took both hands to keep her coat closed.

Inside the car, she turned the windshield wipers to their fastest setting, and leaned forward to peer through the wet glass. It wasn't easy to drive in this weather. Was that red light reflected in the wet pavement a traffic signal, or just a Christmas decoration? The car behind her was following too close. It was hard enough to see without those bright lights reflected in her mirror.

Up onto the freeway, the bridge to West Seattle. Must be an accident up ahead. Cars were crawling along. She turned on her radio, switched from station to station, seeking a traffic report. The rain was coming down even harder, drumming on the metal roof. She inched along with the others, bumper to bumper, until finally she could turn up her own road. She hated this kind of driving, with the car behind right on top of her!

What a relief it would be to get home, even if home would be empty and cold. No friendly phone call from Kevin, no welcome tapping at her door. She started to turn into the parking lot, then changed her mind. It would be so much easier to park in the garage. Last night she had parked in the lot and run through the rain. She'd thought she shouldn't be using the space he had given her anymore. But he wouldn't mind…. She was sure he wouldn't mind if she parked in the garage on a night like this.

The lights behind her were following her into the apartment driveway, into the garage. She didn't want to meet any of the other tenants tonight! She drove to her space at the far end of the garage, near Kevin's two cars and waited. I'll just sit in the car for a few minutes, she thought, and let that other driver leave.

After giving him enough time, Molly opened her door and slid out. Careful. Kevin's convertible, under its white cover, was not to be banged into. She sensed a sound, a movement, at the other side of the garage.

"Hello? Is someone there?" Once before, Kevin had frightened her here, watching for her, and last night he had been at her door. It wasn't right. He shouldn't be watching for her. "Kevin?" No, it must have been the wind or her imagination. Or was it wishful thinking? She started toward the elevator when she heard it again. No mistaking this time, someone was there. "Kevin?"

"Bitch!" He jumped out from between two parked cars. "I know you. You're one of those bitch dykes from that shelter."

She heard roaring in her ears, her heart pounding. This isn't happening. She opened her mouth but no sound came out.

"Surprised you, didn't I, bitch?" His face was ugly, twisted with hate. "Didn't I?" he repeated, louder.

Her dry throat wouldn't speak. She licked her lips. Yes, she nodded. You surprised me. What will I do? Help me!

"You know where my wife is," he stepped closer to Molly, and she stepped back, "and I wanna find her."

Molly shook her head.

He moved even closer. "Tammy Ferguson. Tell me where Tammy is."

She didn't know, she really didn't know. Tammy had never told her the name of the shelter in Portland. She stepped back again, up against Kevin's van. He came after her. Tammy's words ran through her head. How Ricky had clipped away her beautiful hair, beating her with his fists. She said he didn't use a gun or a knife, as if that made a difference. Molly thought, maybe I could run from him. She looked from side to side.

"Don't even think about it," he snarled, grabbing her wrist with one hand. He pulled her up against his body. She noted the snaps straining to keep the faded Sonics jacket closed over his fat stomach. Smell of stale fried fish. She turned her face away and saw his misshapen ear, the lobe torn. Memorize, memorize details. She turned back. The whiskers on his face stood up, black against pale sickly skin. Black hair, torn ear. God, if you let me live through this, she prayed, I will be able to identify this ugly man.

Now he had both her wrists, her purse fallen to the ground, coins and keys scattered all over. He pushed her back against the van, her arms against her breasts. "Tell me where she is!"

A movement behind him. "Take your hands off Molly!"

Kevin! Ricky's grip relaxed, then retightened. He looked back over his shoulder, just long enough for Molly to think, he's here, everything will be all right. Not enough time to break away.

"Stay out of this, gimp!"

Kevin came up fast, close, and grabbed the arm holding her wrist. Molly felt her own arm pulled away from her chest. She was falling forward, drawn by her wrists. Then one wrist was free and in a moment, the other. She leaned back against the van. Kevin was struggling with the ugly man, their arms locked, the chair rolling back and forth.

Ricky broke away, panting, legs wide apart. "Hey! I don't fight with fucking cripples! Just tell me what I want to know and I'm outa here."

He started back toward Molly. Before he could touch her, Kevin rolled forward again. The man turned, arms lowered, and knocked Kevin's arms up and outward. He grabbed the wheelchair by the armrests and pushed it back. Kevin leaned forward and seized Ricky's jacket front, pulling the collar tight around his neck. The two men were balanced, one holding the armrests, the other the coat. How long could they stay that way? If she had a weapon, she could hit Ricky, make him let go. Molly looked around. There was nothing, no tools on the floor, no abandoned parts. Kevin didn't allow the tenants to trash up the garage. Her fists tightened. Suddenly Ricky jerked, the chair rolled backward and Ricky tossed the left armrest onto the concrete floor. Ricky lunged forward again, grabbing Kevin around the neck and pushing him toward the left side of his chair. Kevin's arms went up, straining to reach the other's neck, his face, but at the same time faltering, losing the equilibrium that kept him seated in the chair. As Kevin swayed to the left, he flung his right arm out, clutching the remaining armrest. If he fell out of the chair...

Molly had to save him. There must be something—the armrest! She picked it up. It wasn't very heavy. The men were still connected, grunting, struggling forward and back. She clutched the slender pillar in both hands, wound up, and swung the padded arm, hard as she could, against Ricky's head. He staggered forward against the wall and looked at her, wide-eyed. Perfect! She had caught him off-balance. She heard Kevin say her name, but she was watching Ricky. What next? He looked from Molly to Kevin, back at her again. "I'll get you later, bitch," he panted, and started toward Kevin.

This time Kevin was ready. As Ricky charged forward, hands reaching out for the attack, Kevin grabbed Ricky's wrists. The chair rolled backwards. Kevin pulled him close, low, face on his lap. Ricky turned and twisted, but Kevin was stronger. He held Ricky's arms immovable. Ricky began pumping his legs, pushing and pulling the chair. The two men and the chair ricocheted back and forward between the cars like some crazy beast. Molly studied the beast, watching for the right moment. Then with all her strength she swung the armrest at the back of Ricky's knees. He stumbled and fell. Kevin pushed Ricky's wrists down and flipped him on to his back. He lay on the floor, arms reaching up to the chair. He thrashed and flailed, scrambling to stand up. His feet flattened on the floor, his back arched off the ground. Kevin pushed him down again. Ricky screamed a string of profanities, writhing on the floor. Then he closed his eyes and stopped struggling.

"Are you all right?" Molly still held the armrest in her hand, ready to attack.

Kevin nodded, breathing hard. "How about you?"

Ricky flopped a few times but stopped when Kevin pulled on his wrists.

"A little scared, still." She rubbed her wrists. "You were fantastic."

"So were you. Coming after him with that armrest in your hands, and the face of the righteous avenger."

"I was so afraid he would hurt you."

"When I saw him coming after you…"

They stood in the dim light of the garage, smiling at each other, no sound except the scuffling and the heavy breathing of their prisoner, stretched out on the floor. For a moment, Molly was back three weeks, basking in the warm emotion in his eyes, the pleasure she had drawn from him, the familiar lurch of desire that rose unbidden within her. Treacherous body! She tried to focus on Jayne Brooker's list. Gratitude wasn't on it.

Ricky rolled to his side. "Hey, look, a woman and a fucking cripple," he whined. "If you were a real man, I would have hurt you. I never really tried. You turn me loose, I'll just go away."

Kevin forced his wrists down again.

"Okay, okay!" Ricky lay still.

"How long do you think you can hold him?" Molly asked.

"Until the police arrive. If you will just go out to the phone in the hall and make the call."

Waiting for the police to arrive, Molly sat in the open door of the van, watching Kevin hold Ricky down. There was so much Molly wanted to say, and yet the words wouldn't come out. "If you hadn't come down..." she began, shaking her head.

"You know I always watch for you," Kevin told her. "But tonight...I just had a feeling that something was wrong."

"You saved my life."

"I wasn't going to kill you," Ricky thrashed on the floor again.

Kevin pushed him down. "You, quiet!"

"Saved my life," she repeated. "He must have followed me from the shelter. I was fretting about that car right on my back bumper..." She was starting to shiver.

"You really must find a different job now, Molly. You aren't safe at your SCAWF. What's wrong?"

"A delayed reaction, I guess. I'm cold all over."

"We don't have to stay down here, once the police arrive. Come up to my house. It's warm up there. We can open a bottle of wine. Ben left something wonderful for dinner, I'm sure." His voice was soothing and kind.

She thought of her own apartment, dark and cold. The run through the rain to her door. Her refrigerator with nothing wonderful in it, nothing at all in it. What did she have to fear from Kevin? Would it hurt her to go with him this once, to observe him carefully, stop him when he became overly constraining? But now that she knew more about abuse—she remembered the way he had held her down, how strong he was. Even if he couldn't help...

The police arrived, and after a few questions, they left with Ricky.

"In some cultures, you know," Kevin said, "when you save a person's life you are responsible for that person for the rest of her life." He smiled at her. "Come up, Molly, just for dinner. Not for life."

Just for dinner, she thought, and the argument continued in her head. He was a potential abuser, she could see that now, he fit the images she had learned, but now that she knew him better, she could make him change, she could insist that he accept her wishes. Dinner, and afterwards she would go home. Not go to bed with him, not right away, although she would want to. First they had to talk about what had happened, and later, after they had worked out an arrangement.... He could change, she was sure of it. She could be friends with him and have other friends too. He would have to promise never again to tell her to change her job, never to hold her down. He wouldn't hurt her if he knew he was hurting her.

"Come with me, Molly." That wonderful smile. He turned his chair and began rolling toward the exit to the hallway. After a moment, she followed him.

AUTHOR'S NOTE

In the early 1980s I accompanied my husband, Don, to a meeting of the American Academy of Physical Medicine and Rehabilitation at the Baltimore Convention Center. Late one afternoon, after a day of touring by myself, I returned to the Center to look for my husband. The lobby was dim and empty. A tall escalator was running silently toward a destination near the ceiling.

As I waited there, wondering where to go next, a lone wheelchair rolled out of the shadows on the other side of the lobby and headed toward the escalator. If the man in the chair saw me, he gave no sign of acknowledgement. He rolled up to the foot of the escalator, put both arms out to grasp the handrails, and pulled himself onto the moving stair. I watched in amazement as he rode up and up, and then rolled out of sight.

What kind of man, I thought, would attempt such a daring feat? He must be some kind of superman, superior in every way except that he could not walk. In that moment, Kevin was born. I took quite a few years to think about him and the novel I would write, but I knew it must have an event where he rides up a tall escalator. That's why I took an author's liberty of setting a scene in the Washington State Convention Center in 1983, even though that convention center with its tall escalators was not completed until a few years later.

I had had some success as a writer of textbooks, cookbooks, *Backpacking with Babies and Small Children*, and *Camping with Kids*, but I always knew I would write fiction some day. For Kevin, I had in mind at first a conventional romance, where the disabled hero would prove himself by saving the life of a doubting woman. Needing to put the woman in a situation where she was in harm's way, I decided that she should work in a shelter for abused women. For years I had been sending donations to New Beginnings, an agency in Seattle committed to ending domestic violence, but I had never been inside their shelter. My request for a visit was denied, but the volunteer coordinator agreed that if I took the training course for volunteers and gave them a year of service, I would have access to the shelter.

Almost twenty years later, when I retired from volunteering at New Beginnings, the staff held a beautiful luncheon in my honor. I still count the agency as a favorite charity, and consider many of the staff there as dear friends. I'm no expert, but I know a lot about domestic violence, thanks to New Beginnings, a wonderful organization. I want to assure my readers that the Seattle Center for Abused Women and their Families, SCAWF, which I invented for *Show Me Your Face*, is nothing at all like New Beginnings, which is a well-organized, well run and caring organization. None of the characters in *Show Me Your Face* are based on women at New Beginnings, and the examples of abuse that I invented are not nearly as horrendous as some of the stories I heard there. The clients at New Beginnings are helped by "advocates" not "counselors" (there's a difference), and none of the executive directors that I knew were as disorganized or flaky as Louise Joiner.

I also know a lot about spinal cord injury and paraplegia, and again I am no expert, but I live with a man who is. Don likes to talk about his work, and I am a good listener. For many years on trips to his medical meetings combined with brief vacations, I sat through lectures and conversations on medical topics. I couldn't help overhearing Don's half of the calls that disturbed our dinners at home, and I became acquainted with some of his patients. I also read some of his literature on disability and spinal cord injury; one magazine that I found particularly helpful is *NM NEW MOBILITY, life beyond wheels*, a publication for active-lifestyle wheelchair users.

Don told one of his patients, Bob Soper, that I was writing a book about a paraplegic and he asked to read my manuscript. Then he asked to meet me. When Don drove up to Bob's house in West Seattle, I was stunned to see a white convertible in the driveway. Bob told me he did not like Kevin, because he had erections. He turned to Don. "Is that possible?" he asked. When Don nodded yes, Bob shook his head and handed the manuscript back to me. Yes, Bob, there is a condition called incomplete paraplegia; the level of function depends upon where the injury occurs. I am grateful to Bob, who is no longer in our world, for reading and talking to me that morning.

I also wish to thank my critique group, who listened to the chapters, read the final manuscript, and offered guidance and encouragement: Diana Brement, Victoria Brown, Sandra Larkman Heindsmann, and Dobbie Norris. Those good friends were not happy with the ending of my novel. They wanted changes that just don't happen in the real world of domestic violence. Thanks also to other readers, my friend Mike Kennedy, my son John and his wife Marisa Pena, and my daughter Judy who followed her father into Rehabilitation Medicine.

Most of all, thank you to my husband Don, who brought his work home with him, so that both our lives were full of stories of successful rehabilitation;

To his patients, who openly shared their problems with me, so that I wrote down some telephone messages that had me blushing;

And thank you to the staff of New Beginnings, the wonderful shelter for abused women that is nothing at all like SCAWF. I am especially grateful to Susan Segall, current executive director, and to Sara Parker and Roberta Peterson, advocates with whom I worked closely.

And to the clients of New Beginnings who were incredibly strong and brave,

This book is humbly dedicated.

ABOUT THE AUTHOR

From a very early age, Goldie Gendler Silverman loved to write poems and stories. Her first paid published work was an advertising jingle in the *Omaha World-Herald* when she was still in grade school. For this she was paid one dollar.

Since then, Goldie has been one of the writers of the *Phoenix Reading Series* (remedial readers); co-author of four low-fat low-salt cookbooks; author of scripts for Seattle tour guides; and author of *Backpacking with Babies and Small Children* and *Camping with Kids*. Far from Omaha, she now writes from her home overlooking Lake Washington. Hiker, camper, high school and university teacher, world traveler, mother of three and grandmother of four, Goldie brings all of her skills and interests to everything she does..

Made in the USA
Charleston, SC
12 December 2015